"Why didn't y
she flashed.

"I don't know!"

"Why didn't you tell me thirteen years ago? Why didn't you tell me that first day in the cabin?"

"You didn't want to hear it any more than I wanted to tell you. You didn't want to talk any more than I did. You wanted one thing and one thing only."

"But why did you let me go on believing—"

"That I'm just a man? A man with a weak spot—"

"The man I love!"

For an instant, feeling so deep she could swim in it flooded Lucas's eyes. But then it was gone. As soon as he felt her surrender, he drew back. And smiled. A hard, distant, humorless smile. And then he let her go.

Dear Reader:

Romance readers have been enthusiastic about the Silhouette Special Editions for years. And that's not by accident: Special Editions were the first of their kind and continue to feature realistic stories with heightened romantic tension.

The longer stories, sophisticated style, greater sensual detail and variety that made Special Editions popular are the same elements that will make you want to read book after book.

We hope that you enjoy this Special Edition today, and will enjoy many more.

Please write to us:

Jane Nicholls
Silhouette Books
PO Box 236
Thornton Road
Croydon
Surrey
CR9 3RU

CAROLYN SEABAUGH
Cicada Summer

Silhouette Special Edition

Originally Published by Silhouette Books
a division of
Harlequin Enterprises Ltd.

First published in Great Britain in 1991 by Silhouette Books, Eton House, 18-24 Paradise Road, Richmond, Surrey TW9 1SR

© Carolyn Matthews 1990

Silhouette, Silhouette Special Edition and Colophon are Trade Marks of Harlequin Enterprises B.V.

ISBN 0 373 58106 8

23 – 9103

Made and printed in Great Britain

This book is respectfully dedicated
to the volunteer adult-literacy tutors
across the country and to their students.
Hold on!

CAROLYN SEABAUGH

was born in Seattle but has lived just about everywhere else since. Says the author, "The Colorado Rockies, the green hills of Texas, the smell of oregano growing wild on the Texas plateaus, the wildflowers of Alaska's spring . . . I miss them all!" Home is now Washington, D.C., and nearby Harpers Ferry, West Virginia, where she often goes to rest, write and reflect.

Carolyn's writing career began with "the usual high school poetry," she says, and her work was anthologized in youth collections. While her own two sons were growing up, she wrote short stories for children's magazines. She also contributed to local newspapers in several of the cities where she lived.

Another Silhouette Book by Carolyn Seabaugh

Silhouette Special Edition

Lean on Me

cicada (sĭ-kā'-dä) *n.* An insect belonging to the homopterous family with a stout body, wide, blunted head and two pairs of large transparent wings. Wingless cicada nymphs hatch from eggs laid near the ends of small tree branches, fall to the ground and dig down as much as two feet into the earth. Thirteen or, in some broods, seventeen years later, the cicada tunnels to the surface, latches on to the nearest vertical object to shed its outer skin and then unfolds its wings, flying off to find a mate. Only the males sing.

Prologue

White satin sheets. Or cotton? Cotton would cool the heat of their bodies. Yes, definitely cotton. And chilled Chablis in long-stemmed wineglasses... no, beer, Oklahoma champagne. They were drinking it straight from the cans. The phone would be unplugged, the window open to the afternoon breeze, and music, of course. Lucas had chosen it. What kind?

A fly buzzed by her ear on its way to the Senate conference table down below. She ought to be paying attention, Susanna Foster reminded herself. She leaned away from the hot vinyl back of her gallery chair. Her best silk blouse felt permanently glued to her shoulder blades.

That was the trouble with fantasizing about someone you'd never even kissed, she thought, someone you hadn't even *seen* for all of thirteen years. It was hard to get everything right.

Not that she had any choice, at least not in the matter of who played the starring role in her daydreams. It had always been Lucas. Broad-shouldered, sandy-haired, silent Lucas Grant. The boy she knew in seventh grade. The only man she'd ever known who could blush.

The senator's yellow legal pad came down with a smack on the conference table. In a puddle of sweat from the ice-water pitcher, the swatted fly lay belly-up.

"All right," the elderly senator said. He tossed the pad on the table. "All right."

Susanna snapped to attention. He *couldn't* be quitting. Not after all their work.

At the end of the table, a gavel banged. "Committee's adjourned till after the summer recess, gentlemen. Thank you, Senator Stout, for yielding."

"Come on, Suzy, I'll buy you lunch."

"You always call me Suzy when you know I'm going to get mad."

"I call you Suzy because that's what your father called you. Senator William Foster—I always admired the man. Fine person. A little too dedicated, maybe. Bit of a hard driver. A lot like his daughter, come to think of it."

She slowed her habitually hurried step. Being compared to her workaholic father had always made her feel proud. Lately it weighed her down.

She took the senator's arm and tucked it into hers. He clucked as usual at her too-thin wrist. Susanna fumbled for her sunglasses. In another minute, the white-hot Washington sun would spotlight the dark circles under her eyes for him, too.

The old man seemed to hold his breath as she steered him through the revolving door and down the steps of the Capitol building toward the limo waiting below.

"Damn humidity," he muttered. "Might as well be in Oklahoma."

A blast of cool air hit them when the chauffeur opened the door. "Georgetown for lunch, son," the senator said. "Make it the Arrowhead. I'm feeling a little homesick."

Susanna held her tongue while the senator insisted on directing the chauffeur through the tangle of noontime traffic. Then she waited as the maître d' saw to it that he got his favorite table. From it, he could see the *Trail of Tears* mural that showed the Cherokee Indians on their long, forced winter march through Kentucky to the Oklahoma territory.

When he'd tipped back his chair, she launched her attack. "We worked all winter on that bill. How can you let it go like that, without so much as a fight?"

"Now, Susanna..."

"Don't 'Now, Susanna,' me, senator. If you'd just held out a little longer, maybe offered some of those statistics we worked out late last night, or data from that state-by-state survey—"

The senator held up his hand to hush her. "If we'd done all that, we'd still be sitting in that hot committee room, arguing about a bunch of numbers. Now turn around and look at the beading on those moccasins. They're real enough to walk right down and join us, aren't they?"

Before she could retaliate, the waiter brought their usual order, steaming bowls of black-eyed pea soup with greens, and slabs of hot corn bread, dripping butter. Susanna's anger gave in to her empty stomach.

After a few hurried bites, she had intended to pick up the argument. But the senator was studying her, his bushy white eyebrows drawn up to meet the lock of white hair that fell down over his forehead. Crumbs of corn bread clung like tiny sunflowers in the crevices of his cheeks, and his chin was smudged with butter.

Susanna softened and handed him her napkin. His would already be on the floor. The senator dabbed at his mouth and leaned a little forward in his seat, the way he always did when he had something important to say.

"A lot of people think that when a bill gets hung up in committee, it's because of stubbornness or special-interest groups," he began. "But you know how I feel about that. I want to be damned sure that this is the route to go. Best way to do it is to listen up good, let your opponents have their say. The senator from Missouri's been making sense. Now I'm not as sure as when we started."

"But I thought you wanted to do something for the elderly."

"Not just *something* for the elderly, Susanna. I want to be sure the bill will really help them. All these studies, all these numbers...I just don't know. I can't see the *faces* anymore."

She pushed the slice of lemon off the lip of her glass and watched it blur as it fell through the water. The senator was right, of course. Like other big policies she'd researched for him, this one had grown increasingly distant from the people they'd hoped it would help. But that was just part of the price that they paid, wasn't it? Just another *personal sacrifice* in the name of making a *meaningful contribution*. Susanna picked up her spoon and plunged it into her glass, determined to capture and mash the slice of lemon.

"Had your hearing last week, did you?"

She looked up, surprised if only for an instant. Her father's old friend had always been able to read her moods. She dropped the spoon in the glass.

"It's finally over," she said. "After two years in limbo, I'm Susanna Foster again, and Daryl is back on the campaign trail, lobbying for a new Mrs. Daryl Dobson."

"Maybe you should say *officially* back on the campaign trail," the senator grumbled.

She glanced at her reflection in the mirror behind the senator's head. Two bright spots had pushed through her olive complexion to color her cheekbones, and her wide, dark eyes were misty. The hurt was gone over Daryl's infidelities, now that she'd finally been forced to face them. And romance was tucked safely back into her treasured fantasies. So why the sudden stab of defeat? *Because she'd been a fool, that's why.* But never again.

She sat up a little taller in her chair and took one last look in the mirror. Daryl had lavishly, too lavishly, praised her straight, dark hair, insisting that she keep it long. She'd hated it that way. Now she could cut some of it off. Go back to her shoulder-length braid.

She flipped her hair over her shoulder. "He'd better finish his courting soon," she said. "I hear the new PAC he joined has a busy year planned."

The senator shook his head. "That shouldn't make any difference. You can't postpone life for politics, even in an election year. These young lobbyists never learn."

Susanna touched the carnation in the vase between them. "I get carried away, too, when I'm working on a project."

"Especially when you think the public will benefit. But you don't switch sides for profit, Susanna, not in your personal nor in your public life. You don't go following the biggest money. It's not just a job to you, like it's always been to Daryl. But don't let that make you stick like glue to the Elder Care Bill, or any other project, for that matter. Once it stops talking sense to you about real people, let it go."

"But this bill is important. A summer's delay could finish it off."

"Maybe it's meant to be finished off, Suzy. And they're *all* important. You've claimed as much for every piece of work I've given you over the past six years. Hush up now, and finish your soup, and listen to what I have to say. We're going home."

"*Home?* You can't be serious. It's only the middle of July. We always stay till August. There's so much work to do—"

Once again the senator raised his hand. "You need the rest, and so do I. Don't try to tell me you don't. You've got to quit driving yourself, Susanna. First thing you know you're going to get where you're headed, and there won't be anything there. Go home. Get back in touch with that little kid I used to know, the one who cared more about some dadburn wounded crow she'd found than about the statistics on aging in the twentieth century."

"But—"

"*Damn it,* I think this corn bread's been reheated. Let's get on back to Capitol Hill."

Home, she thought. Home to the red brick streets, sole survivors of urban renewal. Home to the big silver water tower on the hill above town announcing Welcome to Wilamet in huge black block letters to anyone crazy enough to look up into the blinding Oklahoma summer sun. Home to the red dust that sifted into your shoes and the burned-up Bermuda grass that crackled beneath them when you crossed the baseball field. Home to the cool darkness of the Okla Theater, its feature a sleepy three months behind the Tulsa movies, but still the only show in town. Home to the rolling hills, the pin oak trees, the smell of sheets hung out to dry in the sun. Home to simple things, things you could trust, like her mother's orderly house and her sister Maggie's baking...*and men who could blush?* No. Home to predictability. Home to the cicadas.

Chapter One

Susanna pushed with one bare toe till the porch swing moved fast enough to make a breeze. Another buff-colored insect flashed copper bright in the early-morning sunlight, then dive-bombed into the shadow of the porch. It hit the front screen door, bounced once and careered off toward Little Willy's playpen.

The baby squealed and lunged. Susanna laughed as her sister, Maggie, shooed the bug away. Beating wings like the sound of crinkling cellophane carried the insect out to the yard. Little Willy howled.

Maggie scooped him up and sat down on the swing beside Susanna. She held the baby up before them. "Don't you go torturing those helpless creatures, William Grant. The Cicada Princess is home for a holiday."

"The *Cicada Princess*?" Susanna groaned. "Don't make me remember."

Maggie put Little Willy over her shoulder. He promptly reached for Susanna's braid.

"I don't want to forget, not ever," Maggie said. "It's my favorite memory from being seven. The other girls on the float all screamed, but my big sister just untangled that bug from her hair and sent him bumbling on his way."

Susanna sighed and carefully disengaged the baby's hand from her braid. It smelled of zwieback mixed with baby powder. The fragrance tugged at her heart.

"That was a long time ago, Maggie."

"Thirteen years, to be exact. Just think, those bugs have been sleeping two feet underground all this time. No wonder they haven't the faintest idea where they're going."

Susanna remembered the senator's warning. "Like me," she said softly.

Maggie shifted the baby and reached for her sister's hand. For a moment the only sound was the creak of the swing, Little Willy's thumb popping in and out of his mouth and the droning hum of the insects.

Susanna gave the swing another push to keep it going. "Maybe it fits that this is a cicada summer, Maggie. I've been underground, too. I never noticed what was going on around me, right under my nose, to be exact."

"You couldn't help it. You were always naturally trusting. And you worked so hard, first to get through college and then in your job."

"I should have made time for Daryl."

"Would he have been there if you had?"

Susanna flinched. It was the kind of pain you felt when you forgot and tried to use a pulled muscle too soon. She thought she'd been left just feeling foolish, ashamed that she'd buried herself in work and looked the other way. But maybe it was good that she still felt bruised. Maybe Daryl's dishonesty had made her wary enough that she'd be more careful who she trusted.

"You get right to the heart of things, Maggie. You always did. Anyway, Daryl *was* there in the beginning. Sometimes I think I married him because I was so darn homesick—"

"You love Oklahoma, so you up and married Daryl Dobson. Makes sense, I suppose. He was someone from home. Someone who spoke with the same easy accent."

"Even if he soon learned big-city words and big-city lies." Susanna squeezed her sister's hand and let it go, then reached for the copy of *Washington People* she'd bought at the airport. Impatiently she flipped through it. Every page pictured a cluster of smartly dressed men.

"I wonder how many of them are just like Daryl?" Susanna said. "Washington men now, no matter where they came from. Movers and shakers for sure, but so used to saying the things that they think the voters are dying to hear, and pretending to be someone, *anyone*, they think you want them to be—pretty soon they're believing they *are* those fake images. And you're believing it, too!"

She tossed the magazine aside. "I wonder if there's an honest man left?"

"There's Little Willy and Wayne, and there was Daddy, Susanna. And there's someone else out there for you. Someone you just haven't found yet."

Susanna shrugged. What did it matter, anyway? The heck with the candlelight dinners, the house in the country that Daryl had promised, the intimate lovemaking, the planning a family that never would happen. Not in real life, anyway.

But *something* had to matter. A short time ago she had thought the Elder Care Bill mattered, yet she was beginning to realize that if one piece of legislation went down the tubes, then there would be others to take its place.

"I'll get a good rest and get back to the city where I belong. I'll be okay, Maggie." I can always work harder, she thought. *That's* what I'm good at.

In the pine-paneled kitchen of Lucas Grant's cabin on Lake Eufaula, Little Willy arched his back and grabbed for his father's glasses. The computer keyboard teetered precariously on the edge of the kitchen table.

Lucas hung the clean shirt he'd grabbed after his shower on the back of his brother's chair and gave his damp, shaggy hair one last swipe with the towel. "Let me take him, Wayne."

"Thanks," Wayne said. He pushed his glasses back up along his nose. "I've almost got your monthly totals. Oh, hey, I think he's wet."

Lucas held his nephew at arm's length and grinned at him. "Time for a change, huh, big man? Where's his stuff?"

"Here." Wayne reached for the diaper bag under his chair. "I had to pack it myself. Maggie had her mind on taking her sister shopping. And her mother was in a rush to drop me here and make her Tulsa appointment. I hope I got everything."

"That's okay, you know I keep a supply of— Her sister?" Lucas shifted the baby to one arm and reached back to the kitchen counter to turn down his intercom stereo. The orchestra was coming to the thundering part of the overture.

"Her sister, Susanna, from Washington. She just got divorced. Didn't you meet her at the wedding?"

"I met her . . . a long time ago. That year before Dad got really sick," he said. "When I gave seventh grade a parting shot."

"Oh." Wayne bent back over his work. Lucas watched his brother's fingers fly over the computer keyboard. *So the*

Cicada Princess is back in town, he thought. He turned toward the bedroom, bouncing Little Willy.

"Maybe you ought to be glad you never learned to read that well," Wayne said without looking up. "You should see the pile of work she brought with her. Makes all the accounts I handle look like grade-school stuff."

Lucas stopped in the doorway but didn't turn back. *Glad* he was practically illiterate? He'd adjusted to it, that was all. Toby was retarded, Lonetree had one arm and he, Lucas Grant, couldn't read or write worth a damn. Some things you just had to accept.

The baby wiggled in his arms, grabbed at the mat of hair on his chest and held on tightly. Lucas laughed.

"This kid's got a grip, Wayne. He'll be one heck of a mate when we get him out on the boats. Someday he'll run this marina with his dad's brain and his uncle's muscle. It'll be a hell of a business then."

"It's turning a pretty penny now. When you're finished with Little Willy, come here and look at these figures. We're going to have to find you another tax break. You're making money hand over fist. You've got to think about the future."

"I've thought about the future, Wayne. I can't see how it'll be much different than it is now."

"That's ridiculous! The business is growing."

"Maybe we ought to slow it down, little brother, or sell out. You can't go on like this forever. You've got your own clients. Clients you don't have to hand-hold. Clients who can do their own head work, read their own daily copy of the *Wall Street Journal*."

"You pay me good money, for Pete's sake. It's not like I'm doing this for nothing."

Lucas shrugged.

Wayne pushed his glasses back up again and looked at his brother. "I thought you *liked* it out here on the lake. That flagstone fireplace you put in last year made winter down-right pleasant. The house, the garden, those cabins up on the hill. Maybe if you'd just come into town more often, and stay a while when you did, socialize a bit, get to know some women..."

Lucas laughed. "I've known some women."

Wayne scowled. "Somebody who'll stick around for longer than a fishing trip. Somebody warm and...somebody more like Maggie."

"Maggie's one of a kind."

"I know." Wayne chewed the end of his pencil.

"It's okay, little brother. You're right. I like it out here on the lake. There's no place on earth I'd rather be, even if things were different."

Lucas watched relief smooth Wayne's brow as he settled back to his keyboard. It was something he'd never under-stood—Wayne's need to act the caretaker. It was as though his younger brother had felt responsible when he, Lucas, had lost so much time in school and finally dropped out to manage the farm through their father's long illness. But couldn't he see? Wayne loved his books. He, like his father before him, loved the land. He always had. Lucas turned toward the bedroom with Little Willy.

He laid the baby on the quilt-covered bed and gave him Wayne's old silver rattle. He ought to let Wayne take it home, he thought. But the rattle had belonged to their mother. She'd played with it. Maybe others before her. There were lots of names in the family Bible.

He remembered watching her with a seven-year-old's keen perception as she unpacked the rattle the day before Wayne was born. *Save this for the baby,* she'd said, as though knowing that the other things in the trunk would be dis-posed of once she died. Had she known then that she wouldn't live to give the toy to Wayne? Or pick the first fruits of the cherry orchard? Or teach her oldest son to read?

Lucas shrugged. It wasn't her fault. And it wasn't his father's fault; the old man had been unable to read himself. It was a twist of fate, one of the many that had shaped their lives.

He had the soggy diaper off in a minute, but lingered over the clean one, getting the tabs just right. It seemed like yesterday that he was doing the same for his brother. Yesterday that he was the helper, instead of the one being helped.

The baby looked up with bright blue eyes, eyes like all the Grants from generations back. *The better to read with, big guy.* Wayne, he knew, would make damn sure Willy did learn how to read.

Back at the table, Willy on his knee, Lucas listened to his brother.

"First thing we need to talk about is wages."

"I've settled that already. Toby gets another dollar an hour, and Lonetree, seventy-five cents. The rest of the men go up, oh, say a hundred fifty a month."

"Lucas, you've got to be kidding. You can't raise your retarded bait-shop helper and the boat guides more than you raise your assistant. Besides, what does Toby want with more money? You cover all his needs as it is."

"It's time he had a fund, maybe one of those accounts you set up for me. I want to make sure there's something for him if anything ever happens to me."

Wayne did some quick calculations. "It looks okay. In fact, it's actually a very good idea, for both you and Toby. Now what about Lonetree?"

"He wants to keep his salary down. He's afraid if it climbs too high, he'll lose his disability."

"So why not give it up? He doesn't need the compensation."

"Not financially, no. But that arm he lost in Vietnam is what he's all about. He says he's a living symbol so people won't forget what a big mistake the war was."

"Still protesting? Won't he ever learn?"

"He's got a right to his opinions, Wayne, to live as he pleases," Lucas flashed.

"Okay, okay, I know how you feel—"

"He's also the best guide I've got on the team, and now he's managing those houseboats."

"And he can read?"

"Of course he can read. He's been doing the ordering for the store for months."

"I wondered why you hadn't asked me to do it. I mean, was I doing something you didn't like, or what?" Wayne fiddled with the computer keyboard, avoiding his brother's eyes. His glasses slipped to the end of his nose.

Lucas groaned in silence. He thought back to the time that Wayne had cut high-school football practice for an entire week, just to come home and cook their dinner. Lucas had been so angry when he had found out, he'd flat out refused to eat. Wayne had cried like a kid. That was the first time he'd realized how strong Wayne's need was to pay him back. But for what? And for how much longer? He'd done the same as any older brother left in charge when the parents died.

Lucas softened his tone. "You were doing a hell of a job on the ordering. I just thought Lonetree needed something more to do, that's all. He gets depressed when he's not busy. He already knows the place like the back of his hand."

Wayne looked up quickly. "I hope he *doesn't* know that you can't read."

"*Damn it,* Wayne. Why is it so all fired important to keep my problem a secret?"

"Nobody needs to know, that's all. It doesn't make any difference as long as I'm around. If word got out, it might hurt your business. That's why I haven't even told Maggie. We've been over this a million times, Lucas."

It doesn't make any difference? Lucas looked down at the baby who was falling asleep in his arms. He shifted to make him more comfortable. The press of the warm little body against his bare stomach, the feel of the baby's skin, soft as the fluff of a dandelion beneath his hand—nothing he did made him feel like this. Not seeing Wayne through college and helping him start his business, or providing a home and a job for Toby and Lonetree. Not pulling in the biggest catfish on record, or even landing the clients from Texas.

It was more like walking through the woods at nighttime, when all your senses were sharper than usual. How could he tell Wayne, who took it all for granted, that he'd give up almost anything for a son of his own like Willy? But not like this. Not the way he was. *Illiterate.* He wasn't totally unable to read as his father had been, but close enough. No son of his would ever have to answer for that.

"I'll put the kid down for a nap, Wayne. And I'll hang around the cabin. You can go down to the marina and pass out the checks."

"Lucas..."

He turned in the doorway and looked back at his brother.

"Lucas, the raises are fine. I'll put them through in the morning, along with a deposit to your retirement account. Then I'll open another CD. Think about finishing that new cabin before the end of the year. You could use the deduction."

"Sure, Wayne. Thanks."

Lucas carried Little Willy back to the bedroom and laid him in the cradle. Another month and his nephew would need a crib. He'd make this one out of cherry, from the wood he'd cut in his mother's orchard before the government had flooded it, along with most of the farm, to fill the lake. He'd been saving that wood for something special. Now he knew what. He rocked the cradle with the toe of one bare foot.

Out of the window, the noonday sunlight shimmered on the lake, pressed down by the darkening clouds. Thunder rolled in the distance. Lucas thought of the first few bars of Beethoven's Fifth. There would be no fishing this evening. Even the cicadas were quiet.

"Maggie, you don't have to take me shopping. It looks like it's going to rain. Besides, I can buy anything I need in Washington. They've got the biggest collection of shopping malls on the East Coast."

"Um-hmm. Then why weren't your suitcases filled with new clothes? That silver jumpsuit we saw in *Washington People* would look great on you."

"Oh, Maggie—"

"I know, I know. The malls are great, but you never get to them."

"I'm too busy."

Maggie smiled. "Too busy and too conservative. *And* too darn cheap."

Susanna laughed and smoothed the cool cotton skirt of her simple cinnamon-colored sundress. "I guess I never got the Emporium out of my system. Why pay all that money when really nice sportswear is made right here in Wilamet? That's not being cheap, it's just being sensibly frugal."

"Frugal? Maybe. Or maybe it's just your hometown loyalty. Call it what you will, you know you never could pass up a bargain, Susanna Foster. Now where do you want to go first?"

"How about Sweet Secrets Lingerie Outlet? Then that new craft shop on Main." Susanna hesitated just an instant, and then she went on. "We can save the Emporium for another trip."

Maggie eyed her curiously. "Why do that? It's right on the road to the lake."

Susanna rolled her window all the way down and held out her palm, buying time. The first drops of rain splashed over it. "I thought you might take me home first, before you go out to the lake to get Wayne and the baby."

Beside her, Maggie let out a satisfied little chuckle. "Susanna Foster, I don't believe it! You're still harboring a grudge against Lucas Grant."

"I'm not!" Susanna jerked her hand in and rolled up the window.

"Oh, yes, you are. I can hear it in your voice."

"Maggie, what makes you think I'd remember some embarrassing little incident that happened when I was barely a teenager?"

"That *little incident* cost us our usual Saturday afternoon movie at the Okla, that's why. You wouldn't go out for a week. And it was your own fault, Susanna. You're not even sure he ever got the note."

"He sat right behind me. I left it on his desk. Besides..."

"Besides, what?"

"He *blushed*. I'd drawn these hearts all over it. Little ones, big ones—can you *imagine*? Oh, Lord, Maggie, I'll never live that down."

"Come on," her sister said. "You were just a kid."

"I was thirteen," she said to Maggie.

She'd been thirteen and old enough to make her first mistake at confusing fantasy with love. Susanna smiled wryly, remembering. You had to be thirteen to get to be Cicada Princess. Lucas was sixteen going on seventeen. He'd missed all that school because of his mother's death and his father's illness, so they'd kept him back. "Sixteen seemed so grown up," she said out loud.

"For Lucas, it was. Did you know his father died the year after we left Wilamet for Daddy's term in Washington?

Lucas practically raised Wayne. He's a good man, Susanna. I think you ought to give him another chance."

"Another *chance*? Maggie, you can't be thinking... *Maggie!*" Her sister had that little smile she always wore when she thought she'd figured things out. Susanna was thinking that it would be useless to protest further when she saw Maggie stiffen slightly, her fingers tightening on the wheel. "Is your back still bothering you?" she asked, concerned.

"It's nothing, really," Maggie answered.

"At least let me take over the driving when we head out to the lake."

Maggie tried to ease back in her seat. "It's getting better. I'll do the driving. You can sightsee."

"*Sightsee?* I lived in this town for half of my life. And we're only six blocks from Main Street. We could have walked downtown if it weren't for your back."

Maggie nodded toward the big white house on the approaching corner. "The Petrie boy finally got out of the navy," she said.

Susanna gave her sister a penetrating look. Changing the subject was Maggie's way of forgetting discomfort. She thought of her brief trip home eight months ago for Willy's arrival. By the seventh hour of her sister's difficult labor, she'd heard all the gossip about everyone in Wilamet, from ten years back to the present.

Susanna watched as they rounded the corner and the house came into full view. "The cupola is peeling again. I thought the Petrie boy'd sworn he wouldn't come home till his mother bought aluminum siding."

"Guess he decided painting the house wasn't half as bad as submarine duty. Oh, look, they're putting the new windows in at the grade school. Doesn't it look modern? Maybe by the time Little Willy gets there, we won't even know the place. And they've finally finished that room in the basement for Mother's class."

"Is she still pushing for the adult literacy center?"

"Harder than ever now that she's retired from teaching."

"I'm not surprised," Susanna said. "I remember how shocked she was when she tried to get the parents of her first graders to read to them and discovered that many of the adults could hardly read themselves. I guess she'll try to straighten that out."

Maggie hesitated. "I think she's a little overwhelmed by the situation."

"No wonder. I've heard about some of the studies. It seems incredible. Thirty-five million American adults read below the level needed to function adequately in society. That's thirty-three percent of the adult population. Another 2.3 million join them annually. That brings it to—"

"You and your figures, Susanna. You're sounding more like Daddy every day."

Susanna flinched at the comment and wondered why. Hadn't she set out to do that very thing? Be as much like her father as she could be? Put brains before beauty, serve others before self, *do something* with her life? At least she'd succeeded at *that*, she thought grimly. "Tell me about the literacy center," she said to her sister.

"There's not that much to tell. Mother thinks they'll be lucky to get it off the ground. Something about competition for government funding."

"It's probably the issue of the guarantee. Government funding has to be reevaluated every year. Without guaranteed funds, programs have trouble making long-term plans or hiring permanent staff. But we're working on that. I read just last week that—"

"Susanna," Maggie interrupted impatiently, "you ought to *see* some of those people. There's a woman I'm tutoring who cries with frustration at the end of every lesson. She's afraid that her children will all grow up before she's had a chance to read them a fairy tale. And there's a man about sixty who's just lost his driver's license. Remember all those warnings they put up when they built the new bypass? He got four tickets because he couldn't read the new signs fast enough to respond. Now he's got no way to get to work. And they're not just poor people, either. Last week I met—''

Maggie went on with another story, but Susanna no longer listened. She thought about the senator, about his regrets that the Elder Care Bill was somehow missing the mark. Susanna turned and touched her sister's shoulder. "Oh, Maggie, you're so lucky. Maggie, you're seeing the *faces*.''

"The faces? Sure... Speaking of faces, I hope you're ready for *that* one.''

Susanna groaned as Maggie pulled her old blue Mustang into the Sweet Secrets parking lot next to a brand-new maroon Chevy station wagon with Dealer on the license plates. Maybell Richardson was trying to talk to her friend, Gladys, and maneuver herself out of the driver's seat at the same time.

"Susanna? Susanna Foster, is that *you*? I *do* declare!''

"It's me, Mrs. Richardson.'' She allowed herself to be pulled into a smothering hug. A puff of lily of the valley talc rose up and almost made her sneeze. Over Maybell Richardson's shoulder, Susanna rolled her eyes skyward at Maggie's grin.

As quickly as Maybell had grabbed her, she let her go. "Oh, I'm so sorry. It's Susanna something-or-other now, isn't it, dear?''

"No, Mrs. Richardson. I'm Susanna Foster again. I'm divorced.''

"Oh! Well, these things do happen. Does Bobby Joe know you're back in town? And *available*?" Maybell leaned close to Susanna in a conspiratorial sort of way.

"I just got in last night. And . . . I'm not really available."

"Oh, yes, she is," Maggie said. "Don't listen to Susanna. She thinks her life is over."

The older woman chuckled and turned back to her friend. "Did you hear that, Gladys? Susanna Foster is finished with men. We'll see what my Bobby Joe has to say about that." She turned back to Susanna. "I'd always hoped that you'd be *my* little girl someday, Susanna. Perhaps I'll get my second chance."

"Why on earth did you tell her that?" Susanna shrieked when they were finally alone in a Sweet Secrets dressing room.

"Shhh, she'll hear you. Maybell Richardson will be all over town by sundown with a story about you. We might as well make sure it's the one we want spread around. Though she'll probably add that you look like you've been through hell. Susanna, why don't you *eat*?"

"Daryl was never at home."

"What does that have to do with it?"

"When he wasn't home, I could work on reports all evening. Dinner was just an interruption. When he left, I couldn't break the habit."

"Well, I'm cooking tonight. Fried chicken with gravy and mashed potatoes."

"Maggie, haven't you heard of low-fat diets?"

"I'm going to make something I know you will eat."

Susanna watched her sister wriggle out of her dress and turn her back to hang it on the dressing-room hook. Her slip was snug across her hips with the aftereffects of Little Willy. Add another four months to the eight that had already passed, she thought, and Maggie would be slender again, though Susanna almost envied the roundness of her sister's healthy body. When Maggie turned, Susanna saw why the slip was tight.

"Maggie, your tummy..." Her sister's eyes grew soft and dewy. Maggie fiddled with the hangers. Only then did Susanna notice that the slips she'd picked to try on were all from the maternity rack.

"Maggie?" she said. "You're not—"

"I'm pregnant again, Susanna. Now please don't fuss."

Susanna pulled her sister into her arms and hugged her hard.

"Oh, Maggie, it's so soon after Willy, and you had such a difficult time. Dr. Gurley said—"

"Dr. Gurley's been wrong before. Remember how he said I'd never have kids? Besides, I didn't plan this. I was nursing Willy till a month ago. I guess I waited too long to go back on the pill."

"Does Wayne know yet?"

Maggie hesitated, then shook her head. "I wanted to wait till you were here for moral support. You know Wayne. He's such an old worrywart."

"Oh, Maggie, you should try to tell Wayne now, before you really begin to show. Give him the chance to be supportive."

"And Mother?"

"Well-l-l," Susanna hedged. "You know how I hate even little falsehoods, but you might put that off awhile, though Mother's been so busy trying to run my life, she hasn't had time for running yours."

"It's only because you're the oldest, Susanna. It could have been the other way around, if you'd been born second instead of first."

Susanna laughed. "Maggie Foster Grant, you'd have made a *terrific* congressional aide!"

"And you'll make a very good mother someday."

Susanna's laughter faded as she slowly shook her head. You couldn't have kids without a husband . . . at least, *she* couldn't, anyway. And the last thing she wanted was another chance to fail at something as unpredictable as marriage. She wasn't cut out for it, that's all. She'd stick to her work, her projects, and leave the babies up to her sister. She turned and grabbed the first of the hangers.

Maggie took off the slip she was wearing and wriggled into the one that her sister held. Susanna pulled it down and tried to smooth the gathers at her sister's belly. Beneath her fingers she almost thought she could feel the baby move.

"The slip's too small, Maggie. At this rate, as early as it is, you'd better go up a size."

The rain was falling in earnest by the time they crossed the dam. The lake stretched out on either side like acres of crumpled tinfoil. The catfish lines with their colored floats bobbed up and down in the choppy water.

"When we get there, I'll just pull up and honk," Susanna said. "No sense getting out in this rain."

"Don't you want to see the big stone fireplace Lucas built? It covers one whole wall of the living room."

"Maggie—"

"He's my brother-in-law, Susanna. He's not going to go away. You can't just ignore him forever. Turn right up there at the stop sign."

The winding road veered sharply toward the water, and Susanna had to slow down. She was glad she had when a deer loped out of the bushes and crossed in front of them. It disappeared into a grove of pin oak trees, leaves quivering as the raindrops pelted them. Susanna rolled down her window to smell the rain.

They passed the marina first. The small, low building of whitewashed clapboards sat on pilings sunk in the water.

Two long wooden piers stretched out from it on either side, and boats were tied up in most of the slips. Someone was getting gas from the big red pump at the farthest pier. He tipped his head but didn't wave. His long dark hair was banded at the back of his neck, and Susanna saw that he had just one arm.

"That's Dave Lonetree," Maggie said. "Vietnam."

Beyond the marina, a little farther down the shore, three square floating buildings plus one smaller one were tied up to another dock.

"They're houseboats," Maggie said. "Lucas bought them last year. Lonetree manages them. I keep begging Wayne to rent us one for a week. Just imagine—no telephone, no TV. You could float clear out to the middle of the lake and just sit there, or tie up in some quiet cove...Susanna! Why don't *you* do it? A week of rest out here would do you a world of good."

Susanna tightened her grip on the wheel. *Rest? Oh, sure. She'd get plenty of rest with the star performer in her fantasies bumping into her waking life.*

"Mother would kill me." Susanna picked the obvious excuse. "I can't avoid the grand inquisition for a week. You told me she was about to pop with curiosity last night when she got in. You should have let her wake me up. And then you sneaked me out this morning while she was still in the shower—"

"I wanted you all to myself, that's all, and she was in a rush to get off to her meeting in Tulsa. Mother and all her questions can wait. I think you should do it. Wayne can bring your bags out to the lake this evening. You've hardly unpacked them, anyway."

"But, Maggie..." Susanna slowed the car to a crawl. A long, low cabin of pine and stone and glass had come into view. She couldn't tear her eyes away from it. She braked and began to turn the car around.

"What are you doing?" Maggie asked.

Her answer came out in a rush. "You said that Lonetree manages the houseboats. A week alone is *just* what I need. No phones, no meetings. I might even get some work done."

Maggie was silent, waiting, Susanna knew, for the real reason behind her sudden change of mind.

But even if the words had formed in her mind to express what she was feeling, Susanna could never have spoken them. A man was standing at one of the windows. Someone tall and muscular, broad shouldered and bare chested. Someone out of a dream. The man was holding Little Willy. She knew it was Lucas Grant.

Chapter Two

"You've cut your hair."

"It's cooler this way."

"I like the braid."

"You *do*?"

He stood opposite her, barefoot as well as bare chested, his back to the rain-drenched glass wall in the living room, his thumbs hooked in the pockets of his faded jeans. The top snap, above the zipper, was undone. She could see the taut muscles of his stomach and the thin line of dark hair below it, disappearing into his pants. Susanna jerked her eyes up. He'd said something, but she'd missed it.

"I'm sorry?" she said.

His blond eyebrows lifted in momentary confusion, and ridges appeared in his suntanned forehead. Susanna labeled the look disarming. If anything, it made him even more attractive.

"No, *I'm* the one who's sorry," he said.

"Oh. *Oh.* You mean about the dance." Susanna breathed a sigh of relief. "I'm glad you finally mentioned it, Lucas."

She tried to look beyond him, out through the sheeting rain beyond the window to the lake at the bottom of the hill. But all she could see was the reflection of Lucas's suntanned shoulders, broader than she'd remembered, and his head of shaggy, dusty-blond hair. She cleared her throat and glanced at the floor at his feet.

"It was nothing, really," she said. "Except I couldn't understand why you didn't tell me in person, or call me, or even leave me a note."

"Leave you a note?"

"That you couldn't go. Or didn't want to. I mean, I would have understood. I was tall for my age, but I was still only thirteen. You were sixteen. You probably thought I was just a kid. Good grief, can you believe we're having this conversation after all this time?"

Susanna stopped for breath and looked up at Lucas, expecting a teasing grin. Instead a streak of red was traveling up from his throat. Suddenly time spun backward, and she was a girl again, turning around in her school desk, hoping against hope for an impossible answer from a boy too shy to deliver it.

"I . . . I never meant to embarrass you, Lucas. I can't believe you still . . . Lucas, you know how thirteen-year-old girls are . . . all those hearts . . . I guess I got carried away." Susanna gulped another breath and hurried on. "It was just that I'd never have let Mother push me into running for Cicada Princess at all, except . . . I wanted to ask you to the dance."

There, she'd said it. Her one Wilamet secret was finally out in the open where they could laugh about it and forget it. She'd had a schoolgirl crush on Lucas Grant, and he'd rejected her. What could be simpler?

"You were asking me to take you to the Cicada dance? That's what the note said? Susanna, I never read it. I can't—"

"You never *read* it?" She'd done it again. Made a dumb mistake by letting her fantasies get in the way of reality. "Lucas...forgive me. You must think...I *haven't* been thinking about it all these years...exactly. It's just that Maggie mentioned the Cicada Princess thing this morning and got me remembering...."

Susanna tried to calm the confusion in her thoughts. But suddenly all the years she'd spent working in Washington and coping with Daryl were rolling off of her. She was spinning, intoxicated, in unfamiliar air. Just like the crazy, bumbling, first awkward flight of the cicadas. She'd been ready enough to come out of the ground, but she hadn't counted on finding the self she'd buried thirteen years ago. Was this how all newly divorced women acted? No wonder the fantasies were back.

Susanna took a deep breath. "I can't believe I've been so silly," she said. "Let's just forget it and be friends, okay?"

The hand she held out to him was even more graceful than Lucas remembered. Her wrist was thin, her fingers tapered long and slender. He remembered those fingers. She'd had a way of running them down her braid whenever she was thinking. He'd watched her do it, countless times, when she'd sat in front of him at school. She'd done it again a moment ago. He wanted to bring those fingers up to his lips. Instead he pressed her hand and let it go.

Susanna smiled. "Now," she said, "what was it you *were* trying to apologize for?"

Lucas swallowed the unaccustomed dryness in his throat. "My appearance. I wasn't expecting company. I'll get my shirt."

"No!" The word jumped out before she could stop it. The flush she'd just managed to suppress flowed back with

fury. The same crushing heaviness she'd felt at thirteen seemed to envelop her chest.

Her words, when they came, poured out in a rush. "I mean, please don't change your clothes on my account. I'm only here for a minute with Maggie to pick up Little Willy. I just thought I'd stop in and say hello."

"How long are you staying?"

She lowered her eyes, then found them inches from his bare chest. The mat of curling blond hair would tickle... "Not long. I'm not staying long."

"Oh, yes, she is." Maggie came into the living room carrying Little Willy. "She's going to stay an extra month this year. And she wants to rent a houseboat. For *rest*, not work. She needs a good, long vacation. The lake is the perfect place to start it."

Little Willy held out his arms to his uncle, and Lucas reached for the baby.

Maggie had taken everything off of Willy but his diaper. Lucas lifted him and buried his face in the baby's stomach. Willy giggled and grabbed a handful of Lucas's shaggy hair. Susanna watched it curl around the baby's stubby fingers till a rush of unexpected feeling made her look away.

"Do you have a houseboat available, Lucas?" Maggie persisted.

"Maggie...really, maybe I shouldn't. You know Mother will—"

"Mother can wait, Susanna. She's all tied up in those Tulsa meetings, anyway. For once just think of yourself."

Lucas kissed the baby's hand and shifted him to his hip. "The three large boats are rented," he said to Maggie. "But Susanna can have the small one for as long as she'd like it. Lonetree hasn't quite finished the painting, but it's nothing critical. He's got plenty of other things to do down at the marina."

His blue eyes shifted back to Susanna, and she was sure she saw them brighten.

"There's room to cook," he went on, "a table, a couch, a comfortable bed, and it has a small deck off the back. There's a head, but no shower. You can use the one at the campground, or come up here. I'm down at the lake most mornings and evenings. The door is always open."

"She'll take it!" Maggie said. "Starting right this minute."

"Take what?" The screen door slammed as Wayne came in, shaking rain off a borrowed yellow slicker. Little Willy crowed and held out his arms to his father. Lucas reluctantly traded the baby for the raincoat.

"Susanna's staying here at the lake with Lucas," Maggie said as she brushed Wayne's cheek with a kiss. He raised his eyebrows over the rims of his rain-spotted glasses.

"Not exactly with *me*," Lucas quickly added. "She wants to rent one of the houseboats."

Wayne glanced from his wife to his brother, then warily at Susanna. He looked, she thought, like the overprotective older brother, instead of the younger brother he was.

"Susanna won't bother Lucas," Maggie said with the hint of a tease.

Wayne grinned sheepishly. "Some *bothering* is just what he needs. I was telling him that a while ago. He's getting to be a regular hermit."

Susanna flushed and glared at her sister. Maggie pretended not to notice. "He hasn't been to the house since the christening," she said, "not even for dinner after church."

Lucas shrugged, suddenly distant. He shifted from one bare foot to the other. "There's a lot to running a marina. It keeps me busy."

"You can take time out for my chicken and dumplings, Lucas Grant. It's a fair exchange for all the baby-sitting you do. Now take good care of my sister, please, the way you take good care of your nephew."

Susanna stepped back. "But my clothes, my books—"

"I'll drop them off later," Wayne offered at a nudge from Maggie.

Susanna submitted to a triumphant hug from her sister. She tugged at a lock of Maggie's curly brown hair and whispered in her ear. "You're getting as bossy as Mother," she said. Maggie just laughed and hugged her again.

Lucas carried the baby out to the car and handed him in when Maggie was settled. Susanna watched a stream of sunlight break through the clouds and light her sister's upturned face. How could Maggie insist she was plain? she wondered. Susanna had never seen her younger sister looking so radiant.

Lucas stepped back from the car and watched it pull away. He turned and mounted the steps of the porch where Susanna waited. The air between them seemed to vibrate.

"The cicadas are singing again." It was all he could think to say.

She nodded. A strand of her hair broke free from her braid. He wanted to tuck it behind her ear. Instead he reached for the screen door behind her. "The rain is over for the time being. I'll walk you down to the marina."

Lucas followed her eyes as she glanced down at her sandals. The turn of her ankle, he noted, still matched the delicacy of her wrists. "It's an easy walk," he said quietly. "The path is covered with pine bark. You won't get muddy. I'll just be a minute."

He left her standing on the porch and and returned a moment later wearing docksiders and a blue chambray work shirt tucked into his jeans. He handed her a set of sheets.

"You'll be needing these," he said. "Anything else, just pick it up at the marina store. Tell them to put it on my tab."

She hugged the sheets to her chest. *Cotton sheets.* They smelled like sunshine. "I'll settle with you at the end of the week," she said when she found her voice.

He caught her eye a moment, then quickly looked away. "I never charge for family, but suit yourself."

The thin material of his shirt hugged his shoulders as he swung down the steps in front of her. Susanna's heart rolled over.

This *can't* be happening, she thought as she followed him down the path. This crazy, itchy, totally unnerving feeling was something a girl would imagine, not something a grown-up woman actually felt for a man. She'd *never* felt this way about Daryl. Susanna wanted to laugh at herself, but something held her back. Could this be the way it would feel if the chemistry were really right?

Right? That *was* a fantasy. She was about as right for Lucas Grant as living in Wilamet would be right for her. She smiled grimly, thinking of Eleanor, predicting her mother's shocked reaction at either suggestion.

The rain had drenched the hillside and washed it clean, settling the red dust and sinking into the parched earth. The pyrite in the rocks glistened like gold, and the leaves of the pin oaks and scrubby bushes shone spring green again.

Susanna felt unexpectedly light, as though the rain had washed something out of her, too. At a fork in the path, she stopped to pick a daisy. A drop of water fell off the tree overhead and hit her nose. She laughed and brushed it off. Lucas paused but didn't turn. She picked another daisy and hurried after him.

A few minutes later, at the bottom of the gently sloping hillside, the marina came into view. The same man she'd seen before was hunched over the red gas pump, tinkering with the controls. He straightened and eyed them suspiciously as they stepped onto the dock.

"Susanna Foster, meet Dave Lonetree," Lucas said. "She's Maggie's sister. We'll be setting her up in the small houseboat."

The tall Indian nodded. He looked her over carefully. He didn't smile.

"You look more Cherokee than your sister, Maggie," Lonetree said.

"I have my great-grandmother's coloring."

Lonetree grunted. "Your great-grandmother? What was she, chief's daughter or something?"

Susanna drew inward at Lonetree's thinly masked hostility. Then she quickly dismissed it. *Another angry Indian.* She could deal with that. She'd had a fair amount of experience with them in Washington. She just wouldn't take his comments personally.

"My great-grandmother was an ordinary trading-post girl," Susanna said evenly. "She took care of my great-grandfather when he was sick. Everyone else was dying of typhoid fever. He pulled through, and they married. None of us would be here if it hadn't been for her."

A corner of Lonetree's thin mouth turned up in a subtle smile. Before she'd realized what she'd done, Susanna held out her hand to him. He looked at it, then up at her face. For a minute she thought he was going to offer her the stub of his arm to shake.

"Sorry," she mumbled.

"Yeah."

"I've seen worse," she added, trying to cover her gesture.

Lonetree's dark eyes narrowed.

"At a hospital in Washington," she hurried on. "I used to volunteer there on my day off. I've seen men with nothing left of their shoulder. You've got half of your upper arm. You're a natural for a good prosthesis."

"Don't want a goddamn hook."

"Lots of them don't have hooks anymore, Lonetree," she persisted. "Some are computerized, some have hands that look almost real."

"Don't want a goddamn hand."

Lonetree turned abruptly, his long hair swinging over powerful shoulders, and walked away. Susanna watched him stride toward the shore and felt vaguely displeased with herself. Washington was a world away. Maybe Lonetree wasn't *just* another angry Indian....

Suddenly Lonetree turned back. With his left hand, he saluted her.

"Congratulations," Lucas said beside her.

"For what?"

"Lonetree likes you. Anything you need on the boat, just mention it once."

"He *likes* me?"

Lucas nodded. "Most whites won't admit to their Indian blood, unless it comes from some high-ranking ancestor. You won him over with your straight talk, despite your interference afterward."

"My *interference*? I was only trying to—"

"Help him?" Lucas smiled wryly. "Like you tried to help those starving kids in China by standing at the doors to the cafeteria with that milk jug, begging for lunch money?"

Susanna felt her defenses rise. "Biafra."

"What?"

"They were starving in Biafra, not China. And I was only asking students to give up their ice cream, not their whole lunch. And since when is working for a worthy cause called interfering?"

Lucas stiffened. When he spoke, his tone was quiet but firm. "Lonetree doesn't need any help, Susanna. He's got a job here. The fishermen respect him. He's comfortable with his handicap. Don't make him ashamed of it."

She started to carry her protest further, but Lucas had turned and was walking after Lonetree. There was nothing for her to do but follow. Lucas was right, she knew, about the business of coming to terms with a handicap, but wasn't it possible to carry that acceptance too far? And she hadn't meant to treat Lonetree like a statistic. She'd been away too long, immersed in Washington policy-making and in weighing the special-interest groups that had to be pacified. Susanna picked her way along the shore between the puddles of ocher-colored mud.

It was too hot to think. The rain had done nothing to lighten the muggy air. When the sun managed to come out between the clouds, it served only to turn the fog to steam. The closer they got to the water, the more Susanna doubted her decision. A fat mosquito landed on her shoulder and took a bite before she could brush it away.

The short pier leading out to the houseboat wobbled as she stepped onto it. Three small boys were jumping off the end into the water, then climbing out and jumping back in again.

"You young 'uns pipe down," a harried mother yelled from the deck of the houseboat docked next to hers. The woman nodded to Susanna and then went back to hanging clothes on the line that stretched around her houseboat. Inside, a baby cried, and a man's cranky voice yelled, "Bonnie? Bonnie Sue, you out there?"

Susanna stepped aside just in time as the youngest boy shot by her, chased by his older brother. She teetered on the edge of the pier, but Lucas reached out and caught her hand.

Before she could thank him, the boys raced by again, this time behind her, forcing her closer to Lucas. His arm slipped easily around her waist, steadying her against him.

Susanna's heart thudded against her ribs. "Thanks," she managed. "I guess I'm just not used to kids."

"Lonetree will move you around the peninsula. There's a quiet cove on the backside of the hill. You'll get the afternoon shade."

He continued to hold her, not tightly, but just securely, with the same gentle pressure that had kept her from falling. "How...nice," Susanna heard herself saying. "The afternoon shade..."

She felt suspended in time. It was nothing more than the touch of his hand on hers, the press of her body against his hip, but both felt...*right*. Suddenly she was back in the world she'd known as a child, that world where things that felt right, *were* right. Where life was simple, unassuming and wholly predictable. And most of all, *honest*, like Lucas. He'd told her exactly what he thought of her suggestion to Lonetree, hadn't he? It had made her mad, but he'd said how he felt.

How was he feeling now? The touch of his hand seemed to contradict his distant, almost pensive smile. Susanna steadied herself and pulled away, self-consciously touching her braid. He handed her down the step onto the small deck of the houseboat, but didn't follow.

"I'll send Toby over with something for lunch. Tell Lonetree to wait till he comes before you head out to the cove."

She watched him turn and stride back down the shoreline, his long legs moving with the easy gait of a man in command of his body. If he'd felt anything when he'd held her, he certainly wasn't feeling it now. The skirt of her sundress billowed in the breeze against her bare legs, cooling them for an instant.

When she turned around, Lonetree was busy collecting paint cans, but the woman from the houseboat was staring at her, smiling a knowing smile.

Lucas kicked at the screen door of his cabin till it came unstuck and finally flew open. He went to the refrigerator and added the case of beer he'd picked up at the marina, keeping out one to drink. He flipped the tab and downed the beer in one long swallow, then tossed the empty toward the trash. He missed by a foot, swore to himself and went to retrieve the can.

Maybe the Liszt tape would soothe his nerves. He pulled a second beer out of the refrigerator and carried it to the living room, found the tapes with the silver color code and pulled out number twenty-seven. He put it on, then dropped into the easy chair beside the fireplace. He took another swallow of beer.

The day had started out normally enough. They'd pulled in a good-sized bass on the early-morning charter and gotten back soon enough for him to spend time with Wayne and Little Willy. The threat of rain might mean canceling the evening trip, but fishing had long ago taught him that nature was a lady who made her own rules. He'd learned to bend to them. Not that he always liked it.

Now Susanna Foster was back in his life, and he had no one to blame but himself. Susanna with her dark brown, almond-shaped eyes, hair like sable and those damn high cheekbones where the color sat when she got mad or embarrassed, like the sun rising over the hills in summer. She was a beautiful woman now, not just a pretty girl. He'd have noticed if he'd hung around at Wayne and Maggie's wedding, but he'd cut out early, his usual antisocial self.

He'd had a good look at her face this afternoon, though. That face from his hot-blooded teenage years he'd never been able to forget. And he'd had a look at the inside, too, there on the dock with Lonetree. She was just as caring as she'd ever been, though still intent on changing the world.

And she was just as far out of his reach.

Why hadn't he told her he couldn't read? Made sure she understood why he'd never answered her note? The whole thing made him feel dishonest. It would only get harder to say it, not easier. If he was going to lie, he ought to have told her that *all* the houseboats were rented. He crushed the empty beer can in his hand.

Still, she'd forgotten for a moment that Lonetree was missing an arm. That had to mean she hadn't defined the Indian by his handicap. Why should she define him by his illiteracy?

He almost wished that his disability showed, that he could wear it, like Lonetree and Toby. Then he and Wayne could both stop living a lie.

"Here I am, Lonetree. Lucas sent me. I brought food." The tall, gangly, freckle-faced young man, his carrot-red hair neatly trimmed in a crew cut, hopped first on one foot and then on the other.

Lonetree looked up from the engine pit on the deck of the houseboat. "Come on aboard, Toby," he said. "Those sodas you're carrying will explode if you don't quit jumping around."

Toby scrambled awkwardly over the side of the boat, teetered slightly, then stood on the deck at attention. Lonetree had gone back to tinkering with the motor. Toby stood there, ramrod straight.

Finally Lonetree looked up again. "At ease, sailor," he said. The young man relaxed and hurried into the houseboat with his bags. Susanna heard the refrigerator door open and started inside to investigate.

"He thinks we're all in the navy," Lonetree muttered as she passed him. "Damn nuisance."

Toby had neatly arranged the grocery items in the refrigerator and pulled Susanna over to show her. "Are you Lucas's girl? Huh? Lucas hasn't got a girl. Are you going to be his girl? I bet you are. I saw the two of you walking on the path. Lucas doesn't bring anybody down his path. He always comes alone.''

"He's taken you, Toby," Lonetree said, his tall frame filling the doorway.

"Awww. I don't count for a girl. Hey, that's funny, Lonetree. You sure are funny today."

Lonetree grunted and smiled at the boy. "You got your work done down at the store, Toby? You got those new minnow buckets stacked up neat? Lucas didn't give you that raise for standing around, you know."

Toby saluted. "Yes, sir!" Then he turned to Susanna. "Will you come and see my minnows? I'm in charge of the minnows. I've got three sizes. Little and big and bigger. I do a good job, don't I, Lonetree?"

"Yeah, you do a great job. You better get at it. If the weather clears, we'll have fishermen wanting those minnows tonight."

"I'll come in the morning, Toby," Susanna said. "I'd like to see your minnows."

"Tomorrow?" Toby seemed to study the word. "Is tomorrow a day that we come to work, Lonetree?"

The Indian unfolded his long, lean body from the doorway and moved inside. He was only a little taller than Toby, yet he seemed to tower over him. He touched a gentle hand to the carrot-red crew cut, then placed it on the young man's shoulder. "Tomorrow we work, Toby. It's Tuesday, remember?"

"Tuesday. Darn. I wish I could remember. But the lady will come to see my minnows?"

"Yes," Lonetree said, turning back to his work. "The lady said she would come. She will."

Susanna watched the young man's halting progress back toward the marina. Then she turned back to Lonetree. "How long has Toby been with Lucas?" she asked him.

The Indian took his time with tightening a bolt before he answered. "About two years. He came the year after I did. He's got an elderly mother up in Oklahoma City who's too sick to care for him. They were on their way south, to a home."

Lonetree made a last adjustment, then closed the hatch and gathered up his screwdrivers. He stowed them neatly in a green metal toolbox, then sat back on his heels to go on with Toby's story.

"The kid took one look at the marina and got this idea that he wanted to learn about boats so he could maybe join the navy someday. So Lucas took him in. We built him his own cabin last year. He can pretty well take care of himself. And the kid can cook. He can't remember what day it is, but he sure can cook. I eat with him most nights."

"What about school? He doesn't seem severely retarded. With a lot of individual attention, he might be able to—"

"Special education?" Lonetree interjected the phrase, then followed it with a cynical laugh. "You really believe in all that stuff, don't you? Toby's teachers said he was more than they could handle. And the only thing he learned in school was the meaning of the word *retarded*. The other kids taught him that in a hurry."

Susanna looked back toward the marina, thinking of Toby's carefree freckled face filling up with hurt. "He could learn to rise above teasing," she said softly.

"Maybe. Maybe not. Why risk it? Out here, he thinks he's somebody. He *is* somebody, to us."

Lonetree turned away to start the houseboat's engine, and Susanna held her tongue. She knew that he was talking about himself as much as he was about Toby. She thought of Lucas's admonition, *Don't make him ashamed*, but that was not the only reason Susanna kept her silence.

She understood the feeling, the need to *be somebody*, the desire to matter. She'd inherited that need from her father and had clung more tenaciously to it with each of Daryl's betrayals. Every time she put her name on a complicated bit of research for a piece of new legislation, she reached toward that feeling, welcoming the predictable high each time her bruised ego soared. Yet it had grown increasingly elusive. At best, it had always been fleeting. Not like the steady assurance that had shone in Toby's eyes when he'd talked about his minnows, or on Maggie's face when she'd shared the news of her pregnancy.

Her sense of usefulness had become as vague and unfocused as Lonetree's was sharp and clear. She read it now in the upturned corners of his thin mouth as he cocked his head and listened to the hum of the houseboat's engine.

She'd gone off to the nation's center of power, the place where her father had taught her that the differences you could make, if you worked hard enough, were monumental. Why, then, did they suddenly seem trivial, compared to getting a houseboat engine to purr like a kitten?

The question stayed with her as she lunched, leisurely for the first time in ages, on Toby's fresh rye bread and cheese spread, washed down by an orange soda. But it began to fade when she took off her sandals and settled on the shaded side of the deck, dangling her feet in the water. By the time the rain began again, she'd forgotten the issue completely, content to feel grateful that the day was cooling off.

She moved inside and puttered around the houseboat, sweeping the floor and checking in all the cupboards. In one, she found a beat-up portable radio, but all she could get was the local country-and-western station, its songs punctuated by static from the storm. She turned the radio down low, and hummed while she made the bed with Lucas's sheets.

Suddenly the feel of the fabric under her palms brought back her fantasy. *Cotton would cool the heat of their bod-*

ies. Warmth rushed over her, followed by a flood of apprehension.

It was one thing to fantasize about Lucas Grant when she hadn't seen him for years. But quite another, now that she had. Mixing daydreams with reality had blinded her once before, had made her see something in Daryl that had never been there. She'd *never* make that mistake again. She'd stick to reality. And nothing smacked of reality quite like work. She longed for it now.

Without her books and papers she couldn't even read, though that would end soon enough when Wayne dropped off her things this evening. Tomorrow she'd put herself on some kind of schedule, maybe working in the morning and sunning, swimming and relaxing in the afternoon.

Meanwhile, in the rain-darkened room, the freshly made bed looked inviting. She hadn't napped away an afternoon in years.

Susanna woke slowly and turned on her back, listening for the sound of the rain. But everything was still. Even the cicadas were quiet. They did that sometimes—stopped altogether, as though some invisible conductor had lowered his baton to silence them.

The air smelled fresher and lighter, and over her head, reflections of the late-afternoon sunlight on the water danced on the curved white ceiling of the houseboat, keeping time to the plop of the water as it washed against the side of the boat. Susanna lay, motionless, letting the peaceful rhythm seep into her body.

In the stillness, only the leaves of the oak trees on the bank seemed to move, caught by the whisper of a breeze. She closed her eyes and pictured their roots, gnarled, twisted and thick with age, hugging the red Oklahoma clay, holding on to what mattered, what kept them alive, just as she was doing now. The senator had been right. Home was the place where you could trust your feelings.

Finally the sunlight faded, and the song of the cicadas started again. Then, above their hum, she caught the sound of an outboard motor. The sound grew nearer. She sat up slowly, clinging to the sense of peace that had settled over her.

Lucas sat in the back of the boat, his hand on the tiller of the trolling motor. Over his shoulder, he watched the sun sink toward the horizon, rimming the random dark rain clouds with gold. Beyond, the deck of the houseboat was deserted. Then he saw her, leaning in the shadowed doorway. Tall and slender, she made him think of a supple young willow.

He cut the motor when he reached the cove and drifted quietly in toward the houseboat. A cooling breeze swept across his forehead and through his hair, then hurried on, catching the hem of her dress and lifting it softly away from her long legs. Lucas steadied his breath and focused again on the sunset.

A moment later, he pulled his boat up next to Suzanna's and passed a guide rope up to her.

"Loop it over that cleat on the stern, so my boat won't drift. I've brought you the bags that Wayne dropped off."

Her hand brushed his as she reached for the rope. It was warm. So were her eyes. He found them languid, vague and sleep filled. The top two buttons of her sundress were undone, and her feet were bare. His blood raced at the sudden, unexpected image of Susanna sleeping.

"I'll have these things unloaded in a minute, and then be on my way," he said quietly.

Susanna nodded. When his hand left hers to reach for her bags, she wanted to slow his movements, examine them and her response. The same electric pulse had rippled through her body at his touch, but its effect seemed different from their first encounter. It was softer somehow, and deeper, a gentle warmth that was none the less magnetic. Intimate.

"Are you fishing tonight?" she asked him. Her voice was hushed.

"No, not with the rain."

She weighed the warm, fragrant basket he handed up to her. "Maggie's sent supper."

"She said she wanted to make sure you'd eat." Lucas reached for the guide rope to release his boat.

Susanna laughed softly. "From the size of this basket, it's plenty enough for two." She took a deep breath. Then she looked back at Lucas. His hand was still on the rope. "You're welcome to stay. For dinner, I mean."

Lucas paused, his eyes on the lake. It was peaceful, not lonely really, just…empty. He thought of his decision, just hours ago, that the less Susanna Foster saw of him, the better it would be for both of them. Then he looked at her face.

Tentatively trusting, maybe a little wistful, her look fed the feeling that had haunted his thoughts. Didn't the *moment* matter at all, aside from whatever the future would bring? Did he have any right to let it go by? Did he have to keep on accepting the fact that she'd come and then leave, as she had in the past, often without his even knowing? Or should he make sure this time? Make sure they discovered what might have been possible between them.

Lucas let go of the last of his carefully guarded reserve and swung himself up to the narrow deck. His arm brushed hers. An ordinary, accidental touch, flesh against flesh, yet it triggered a wave of heat that went all the way to his gut.

"Thank you," she was saying, "for bringing my things. And for not teasing me earlier, about that silly note."

Then she was gone, disappearing inside the houseboat, and Lucas realized he'd lost his second chance to tell her that he couldn't read. But they had all the time in the world for confessions, didn't they? Why force it now?

She came out a moment later, carrying napkins, plates and forks, and a towel to serve as a cloth for the small deck table. He lifted the jelly glass she'd filled with daisies so she could set the table, and a petal fell on his arm, soft and delicate, like the shape of her ears. She'd brushed her hair neatly back from her face, exposing them.

His eyes traveled lower. She'd rebuttoned those top two buttons. Against her olive skin, the cinnamon color of her dress seemed part of the sunset. It slipped like sunlight down the curves of her figure, leaving hidden shadows. Lucas moved deeper into that other world, a world where nothing mattered but the moment and savoring Susanna in it.

They ate in companionable quiet, sharing Maggie's fried chicken and buttermilk biscuits. Susanna brought out ice, water, sugar and fresh lemons, squeezing them into their glasses at the table. When she passed him his, her fingers smelled fragrant.

"Could you check the radio, too?" she asked him after Lucas had lit the bug lantern on the deck.

"Classical okay with you?" he asked her.

"Preferable," she answered. "All I could get was country." Susanna nodded her approval when strains of Beethoven spread out in the air around them.

They stood at the railing and talked about nothing in particular, and everything, the way two people do who suddenly find that the years of silence between their meetings never really mattered at all.

She told him about the Elder Care Bill and her endless days of library research, and he told her how he'd fished for a week, catching next to nothing, before he pulled in his record-breaking catfish. She talked about building legislation and he about building cabins. And they both shared stories of hot, muggy summers, as common in Washington as they were in Oklahoma, and of rain that wouldn't end.

Finally a few stray stars struggled out of the clouds, dimming the lights of the country club on the far side of the lake with their brilliance.

"Daryl?" he asked her.

"Over," she answered, "it . . . he wasn't what I thought. Has there been anyone for you?"

"Nothing worth mentioning," he said. He tossed the toothpick he'd been chewing out into the water.

Beyond the boat, the evening deepened, turning the lake to a pregnant darkness. The wind picked up, and distant thunder echoed from down in the valley.

"Did Lonetree show you how to close the windows if the rain gets heavy?" he asked her. When she didn't answer, he turned to look at her. Her full lips had parted slightly, and her face was studying his.

With her eyes, she traced the smooth, sweeping line of his forehead, the slant of his authoritative nose, the firm yet conciliatory line of his jaw that said he might negotiate, but that he'd never give in when he knew he was right. So little had changed as the boy had grown into a man, except that the depth of conviction she'd only intuited then, from his quietness, had grown more pronounced on his face.

But something was different about his eyes. Still blue and clear and so bright they seemed to catch sparks from the stars, his eyes now held something bolder. A question, flagrantly intimate, but also tentative. One she'd dared to allow only in the safety of her fantasies. Until now.

"Welcome home, Cicada Princess," Lucas whispered. And then he pulled her into his arms.

Chapter Three

How would he kiss her? She had imagined it so many times. The thought came back to tease her now, in that long, protracted moment, just before it was finally going to happen. She'd measured everything that had happened to her later by that imagined kiss. When Daryl came along and it wasn't the same, she'd blamed herself for not knowing that grown-up love was never what you imagined, never what you dreamed. But now? Now she would finally know for sure....

His chest felt firm beneath her fingers as she steadied herself against him. Warmth rose up, escaping the collar of his open shirt, along with the same clean, fresh smell that had lulled her to sleep on his sheets. The warmth traveled through her fingers, up her bare arms and down into Susanna's body, moving steadily toward her heart.

His hand slid gently to the center of her back, his thumb lightly touching, then stroking, her skin where the back of her sundress ended. He exerted a gentle pressure until she settled against him.

Then her thigh met his thigh, and her breasts brushed his chest. The hand that pressed her back trembled, then stilled, then tensed, pulling her nearer.

At almost the same moment, she felt his other hand move, find the back of her neck, his fingers threading through the wisps of hair that always hid underneath her loose braid. Something almost apart from them both seemed to be bending her, lifting her, floating her up to meet his kiss.

His mouth covered hers, hard at first, and claiming, then gentler. Shifting, seeking, his kiss explored, fitting the firm edges of his lips to her more pliant, fuller ones. Coaxing, then urging, then coaxing again, he drew her own kiss forth from her, pulled it deep into his own, then deeper still, until nothing but the fit of his mouth on hers, his body arched over her body, his heart pounding into her heart, nothing else existed. Susanna's every thought was silenced except for one. *This was how it was meant to be.*

When she softened into him, Lucas felt his blood surge, hammer against his temples, throb in his neck, course through his body like a river of fire swept out of control. His kiss turned hungry, probing, reckless. And her mouth answered with equal abandon.

Suddenly a streak of lightning lit up the sky. At the clap of thunder that followed it, they pulled apart. Her eyes were wide, incredulous. She took a step back. The hand that still rested against his chest trembled. He brought her fingers to his lips and brushed them with his kiss. They tasted of lemons. He breathed the pungent aroma to steady himself, but his voice came out ragged when he spoke.

"Susanna, I—"

She pulled her hand away. "Please, Lucas, don't say anything. I...I'm not sure what came over me. The past...the things I've imagined...Lucas, forgive me."

Except for the halting tone of her voice, he might have believed her. Believed that she'd been, for a moment, just a starry-eyed teenager imagining him as a hero, which he wasn't, and all because the hero she'd lost had turned to clay in her fingers. But something in the way she struggled so hard with the words, and in the way she'd looked at him after they'd kissed, told him that there was more. He found himself hoping that when she found out what it was, she'd turn back to him, not farther away as she was turning now.

"Show me how to close the windows," she said unsteadily.

"Sure. Then I'd better get back to the marina and tie things down. These storms can be rough."

Inside, the tangle of sheets teased at the tension just barely within his control. It was all he could do to lean over the bed and show her how to fit the wrench into the louvered window and turn it till it closed.

"You'll be all right," he said to her. "The boat is tight. Just stay inside, away from the water, till the storm passes. It'll blow itself out by midnight. Tomorrow it's supposed to clear."

She studied the window wrench in her hand, still warm from his touch. "I'll see you tomorrow, then?"

"I'll be out on a charter all morning, but I'll be back by noon."

The tone of his voice had held a question. She didn't look up or answer, and then he was gone. The lake and the darkness and the sound of the cicadas swallowed him up like the end of a dream.

Susanna sat on the edge of the bed, listening to the fading sound of the outboard. Her thoughts moved neither forward nor farther back than Lucas's kiss. She tried to think how it had happened, but each time she did, she could only remember the taste of his mouth on hers and the incredible intensity of the feeling he'd roused in her. *Real*, too *real*. And risky. That feeling belonged in her fantasies where she could control it. Not in everyday life, where she'd wake up one morning as she had with Daryl and find it had all been a dream.

The rain began to pelt the houseboat in earnest. Tomorrow the weather was going to be calm. Calm, Susanna vowed, the weather *and* her raging emotions.

She rose and shut the rest of the windows, then restlessly paced the cabin till she spotted the bags that Wayne had left with Lucas.

But the contents of her briefcase had totally changed and none of her other bags held anything even remotely resembling work. Instead Maggie had predictably stuffed them with current issues of her favorite magazines, including a fat book of crossword puzzles. There were also half a dozen paperback romance novels, but unlike the ones that Maggie usually shared, these were all brand-new. Their shiny covers pictured rapt lovers lost to everything but the passion of their own embrace.

Just like Lucas and me, her mind accused. It was a signal, wasn't it? A sign that she ought to remember that happily ever after happened only in books. Not in real life.

She knew for a fact that there weren't any heroes. No perfect men like the ones in the books. She'd gotten herself into trouble once, by seeing too much of the hero in Daryl.... And yet? The quiet cadence of Lucas's voice as he'd spoken of the simple things he valued, his touch, the taste of his kiss on her mouth, all had moved her more deeply than anything she'd ever imagined.

No! her thoughts shouted back. *Never again*. Susanna shook herself and began to lay the books on her nighttable, making sure the romances were buried on the bottom of the stack.

"They're big as silver dollars, Toby. Where'd you get them?" Susanna stirred the surface of the water with the tip of a finger and watched the minnows scatter.

"These big ones come from the tank over there. When they get fat, I move them here." Toby stepped back to the neatly arranged wall in his corner of the bait shop and reached toward a hook that held a small net.

"This is my scoop." With a flick of his wrist, he captured the largest of the minnows and held it up for Susanna to see. Then he carefully released it back into the water.

"The ones over there come from the baby tank. They get moved, too, to the middle tank. I don't know where the babies come from. Wait! The babies come from their mothers! It's like Lucas told me, the babies come from their mothers, then they get big and have to move away."

Toby sat down on a crate of canned salmon eggs and hugged his knees. "Like me. I have a mother. But I grew up. I had to move."

The young man began to rock gently back and forth, hugging himself and humming. Susanna touched his slender shoulder lightly. "I'm sure your mother loves you very much."

Toby stopped rocking and looked up at Susanna. He smoothed his crew cut back with his hand. "That's what Lucas says. Only sometimes I forget."

Suddenly Toby jumped to his feet. "Do you want to come to my house for lunch?"

Susanna laughed. "I've heard you're a pretty good cook. What are we having?"

"I bet there's fresh eggs in the henhouse. I've got my own chickens. Wait till you see!"

Toby was pulling her along the dock, almost faster than Susanna could walk, when a boat turned into the cove. "It's Lucas," Toby crowed. He dropped her hand and hurried over to the dock.

Susanna stood still and closed her eyes for a moment, willing her jumping pulse to calm. But when she finally looked up, the scene unfolding seemed out of a dream. The sunlight, the sky, the shimmering green of the lake and the small, sleek boat moving toward shore. *Moving toward her?* She shaded her eyes.

She saw his head first, his sandy-blond hair whipping in the breeze. Before she could stop herself, she was thinking of the way it had felt last night, surprisingly soft as it tangled around her fingers. She watched as he stood to look over the prow and set his course parallel to the pier. Her fantasies had never done those strong, broad shoulders justice.

As the boat came nearer, Susanna's heartbeat quickened. Now she could see the muscle move in his bare arm as he reached down to turn the steering wheel, guiding the boat carefully toward the slip. His collar was open, and she could make out the cords of his neck. Susanna's own throat constricted with the feeling she struggled against.

Lucas cut the motor and tossed the guide ropes up to Toby. Then his eyes found hers and held them. Bluer than the cloudless sky above them, limitless as the horizon, they made Susanna give up her guard completely. The easy openness of his gaze conquered her resistance.

Someone coughed, breaking the spell. A heavy-set man stood and moved to the side of the boat. His expensive mauve jumpsuit stretched tight across his expanding middle and clashed with the fancy red fishing vest he wore. Bright new souvenir patches covered the front of the vest. From lakes he'd never even seen, Susanna guessed. When the man stepped up on the rim of the boat, she saw that he wore stylish cowboy boots, instead of sensible boating shoes.

Suddenly the man's foot slipped. He began to teeter precariously.

"I've got him, Toby," Lucas said as the man swayed back against him.

But Toby already had ahold of the fisherman's pudgy hand and was tugging hard. His freckles turned a shade redder with the effort. "I can do it, Lucas," he insisted. "I can help the man up on the dock. He's just got those funny shoes on, Lucas. You told me never to wear those shoes on the boat. I know about shoes, don't I, Lucas? There's lots of things I don't know about, but I sure do know about shoes."

Toby gave a yank, and the fat man fairly flew off the side of the boat, up the short distance to the dock. He fell flat on top of Toby. The two of them struggled there for a moment till the fisherman rolled off, leaving Toby gasping for breath.

"Tackled by a retard, well, I'll be damned," the fat man muttered. "First no fish all mornin', then this fella tries to break m' arm."

Lucas's lips were tight as he mounted the dock and bent over Toby. "He meant no harm, Mr. Tyler." He helped the young man to his feet. "Are you okay, son?"

"The kid's your *son*? You didn't say nothin' 'bout having a kid. Much less a half-wit."

Lucas looked into Toby's hurt eyes a long moment before he turned back to the fisherman. Susanna watched Lucas's face, searching for signs of the fury she was feeling herself, but it remained unreadable. Beyond, at the gas pump, Lonetree slowly rose from his work.

"Toby's not my son," Lucas said quietly, "but I'd be damn proud if he was."

The fat man shifted uncomfortably and glanced sidelong at Toby. Then he pulled out a wallet stuffed with bills. "Here's a couple of c-notes, Grant, t' cover the trip."

When Lucas made no move to reach for the money, the fisherman folded the bills and gingerly tucked them in Lucas's shirt pocket. Still, he didn't move.

Susanna wanted to scream. Why didn't Lucas tell the man off, or better yet, push him off the dock?

With the toe of his fancy boot, the fat man kicked at a stray paper cup that someone had left on the pier. "This place ain't nothin' like I pictured. No backwater bayous. No decent waterin' holes. No fish. They oughta give it back to the Indians."

Over the fisherman's shoulder, Lonetree's hulking form stiffened. His fist tightened, squeezing the wrench he was holding. But he didn't move forward.

"Guess I'll be cancelin' out of the evening trip and headin' on back t' Dallas. You can keep the extra hundred." The fisherman looked at Lucas and tapped his wallet.

The sour taste in Lucas's mouth made answering risky, but he knew by now that the man wouldn't recognize an insult if it hit him square between the eyes. He removed the bills from his pocket and passed one back. "Full payment won't be necessary, Tyler. Your charter fee only applies if we make the trip."

The man nodded and stuffed his wallet back in his pocket. "The boys said you was fair. I'll let 'em know you treated me right."

Susanna slipped an arm around Toby's shoulders when the man bent down to gather his gear. But used as he was to helping the clients carry things to their cars, Toby pulled away to offer his help. Lucas stepped swiftly in front of him, blocking his way.

He said it all with his eyes, *Don't lower yourself, Toby.* The boy nodded. For all he lacked, Susanna thought, Toby still understood the message. He stood a little straighter when Lucas stepped aside.

Lonetree turned back to his work. The fisherman struggled up the hill to the parking lot, carrying his gear alone.

"We don't need business like his," Lucas muttered. "Some people don't have the manners of a half-starved stray dog at supper."

Toby broke away from them and jumped down into the boat. He began to unload Lucas's gear, humming cheerfully, the episode already forgotten.

Lucas picked up the paper cup, smashed it in his hand and headed toward the trash can a couple of feet away. Susanna followed, her arms crossed tightly over her chest. The injustice of the episode burned in her throat.

"Why didn't you *say* something?" she asked him. "Why didn't you tell him that retarded people have feelings, too? He tramped all over Toby's. We don't treat handicapped people like that anymore in this country. We've come a long way. There are laws—"

"There's no law on earth that will prevent the kind of ignorance you just witnessed, Susanna."

"But that doesn't mean you don't fight it. You can't just stand there and let—"

The sudden set to his jaw and the flash of fire that lit his eyes stopped her protest midsentence. "Fighting isn't the answer, at least not in the way you're suggesting. Toby's retarded. We accept it, and we get on with our lives. Tyler won't be back. If he calls, the calendar's booked."

He shouldered by her, tossed the cup in the trash and went back to the boat. Susanna glared, her emotions a mix of frustration and anger.

Toby seemed determined to prove that he could carry twice the ordinary load of gear. As an orange life jacket fell off his arm for the third time in a row, his face turned almost a matching color.

Then Lucas said something that Susanna couldn't hear. The young man's face softened almost instantaneously as he turned it up to Lucas. With just a word to Toby, Lucas did what no amount of public education or fancy legislation for the handicapped ever could. It made her feel strangely inadequate. She shoved her hands in the pockets of her shorts and turned to go.

"Hey! Susanna! What about lunch?" Toby caught up with her as she reached the end of the dock. "We're having that egg thing," he said, nearly out of breath. "You were going to come and see my chickens. Don't go away."

A tear worked its way down Toby's cheek. Another swiftly followed. Susanna hesitated a moment, almost afraid to trust her instinct. Then she reached up and gently brushed Toby's tears away. Beyond, Lucas leaned against the piling, watching her, his thumbs hooked loosely in the pockets of his jeans.

Susanna straightened. "Of course I'm coming, Toby. I want to see your chickens, and not only that, I'm *starving*!"

Toby did a little dance, then called back to Lucas. "Susanna is coming to lunch. You come, too, Lucas. You like that pancake thing."

"*Omelet,* Toby," Lucas said, slowly moving toward them. "That *thing* is called an *omelet*." His eyes met Susanna's over Toby's head, unyielding, yet accepting.

"I never can remember," Toby said. "That word doesn't make any sense, anyhow. Why don't they call it an *egg*let?"

Lucas laughed with Toby, and then Susanna was laughing, too. Toby pulled her up the hillside, Lucas following close behind.

After a short climb, they rounded a turn and came upon a group of small A-frame cabins, each with a deck overlooking the marina.

"Lonetree lives there," Toby said, pointing to a cabin set apart from the others, a deer hide tacked to its door. "Here's my place. The rest we rent out to fishermen. Except the ones that aren't finished yet." Toby waved toward the bare pine frame of a cabin standing strong and sturdy in the sunlight. Next to it, a cinder-block foundation had recently been laid.

A bronze-colored rooster scuttled across their path, and Toby ran off to chase it, then came back carrying a basket with six brown eggs inside. His face was damp with perspiration, but he beamed as he handed the basket to Susanna. He tried to hide a huge green pepper and a bunch of spring onions, garden dirt still clinging to them, under his other arm.

"It's your turn to choose what goes in the pancake, Lucas," he said sternly.

"Peppers. Peppers and onions. And your usual herbs, of course."

"Coming up!" Toby shouted.

He led the way into his cabin, first to a small vaulted living room where Lucas stopped to open the drapes on the A-frame window. Susanna followed Toby into the little galley kitchen.

Lucas's eyes moved down to his marina and the lake stretched out beyond it. He'd looked at that view every day for the past ten years. It had always seemed complete. Now the sound of Susanna's voice as she exclaimed over Toby's kitchen settled around him, filling spaces he hadn't know were empty.

She was Toby's first guest from the world outside the marina. His, too, really, except for Wayne and Maggie. She'd end up changing things. She was trying already. Part of him minded, minded a great deal. And part of him wanted to help her. He heard her footstep behind him and turned.

For a long moment, they stood looking at each other, making a silent truce. The air between them calmed, but Susanna still felt hesitant. Finally she cleared her throat. "It must be the order that makes Toby feel so secure," she said.

Her tone had been as controlled as her statement. Lucas lifted an eyebrow. Then he nodded. "When Toby gets something new, he'll spend an hour deciding where to put it. He'll pester me or Lonetree to build him a shelf or put up a hook. Once he's hung the thing up, it never moves, except when he's using or cleaning it."

"That must be why he likes cooking. It's predictable. There are orderly rules to follow, and if you're careful, whatever you're making will always taste just the same."

His gaze moved from the vagueness in her eyes, down to the fullness of her mouth. Taste just the same? He thought of her kiss and wondered. His eyes slipped down, over the loose jersey T-shirt she wore, taking in the snug cotton shorts that hugged her hips above the long legs that yesterday's sundress had hidden.

Susanna shifted self-consciously and moved to stand behind a wingbacked chair. "If he can learn to cook, why can't he learn other things?" she persisted.

He looked up, meeting her eyes. "What?"

She colored, knowing he hadn't been listening. She wanted to keep the conversation on solid, familiar ground, on a subject real enough to keep her from slipping into some silly fantasy. "Why can't Toby learn math, or reading, or maybe even a trade?"

Lucas tensed. "What makes you think he can't learn?"

"Lonetree made a comment yesterday that Toby's dropped out of his special-education class—"

"He was *asked* to leave. And there's more to learning than what you get in school, Susanna."

He was echoing his father, Lucas thought uneasily. But he could name a thousand things his father had taught him, patiently, lovingly.

"Toby's learned plenty since he's been with us. He can tally a sale in his head. He can give out change to the penny. Checks and credit cards bother him some, but not just because he can't read—he thinks they're not real money."

"Not *real money*?" Susanna laughed. "We could all use a dose of *that* reality," she said, "especially in Washington. But what about reading? Have you ever—"

"Susanna..." Lucas interrupted again, but then he hesitated, searching for words. "Susanna, I don't—"

"Have time?" She finished the sentence as she thought he'd intended. "Of course you don't have time, but what about Lonetree, or one of the other guides?"

He'd watched the interest in her wide, dark eyes begin with simply idle conversation, then turn to something deeper. She cared. She cared a great deal. Her caring always seemed to avoid the individual and move quickly to the group concern, but that didn't mean her feelings weren't deep.

Supposing he went on and told her *he* was illiterate, too? She'd have him signed up for some government program in no time. Or else she'd feel sorry...but the last thing he wanted from Susanna Foster was her sympathy. Not that there was any need. He pulled out a chair, a little too quickly, at Toby's table for her, nearly upsetting the red plastic salt and pepper shakers placed side by side, exactly in the center of the table.

Susanna wavered. "I don't mean to interfere—"

"You're not interfering." He softened his tone. "I'll let you know when I think you are." He pulled out the opposite chair for himself, taking care to control the motion.

She was looking at him expectantly, waiting for him to go on with what she thought was Toby's story. He sat down.

"Lonetree tried to help Toby. We borrowed some books from the school in town."

"What happened?"

"He hid."

"Toby *hid* from you?"

"Under the shed. Squeezed himself into a six-inch clearing. It took us an hour to find him and two to dig him out."

"But I don't understand—"

"Toby's afraid if he learns too much, I'll send him away. His older brother went off to college. To hear his mother tell it, Toby almost died of loneliness. Then something happened. His brother was killed . . . a car wreck after a fraternity party, I think. Toby never saw his brother again. He gets these ideas. It's not that easy to change his mind."

Before she could question Lucas further, Toby set a steaming plate before each of them. The aroma of eggs and onions and peppers, and some herb she couldn't identify, chased away the sadness of the story. When Toby added a basket of hot rolls to the table and brought a tray with butter and honey, then tall glasses of iced tea, Susanna stared in quiet admiration. But Lucas and Toby launched into lunch as though they were used to the menu.

After lunch, Lucas took Toby back to work at the marina, leaving Susanna to spend the afternoon lazing around the houseboat. She started the first of the crossword puzzles but couldn't make any headway. She kept on thinking of Toby, wondering what more could be done for him.

The young man was happy. Probably happier than most retarded citizens. He had a job, a home and people who cared. All the schooling in the world wouldn't help him fit into Tyler's world. A world where people like the crude fisherman would see to it that he never got a chance. A world, she reminded herself, where it was easy to trust the wrong people, even if you weren't retarded.

Impatiently she set the puzzle aside and rummaged in her bag for her swimsuit. After she'd changed, Susanna waded out into the lake till she found a cool stretch of water. She floated and swam, then floated some more, letting the water flow over her body, feeling a part of the calm, still lake. Finally her thoughts stopped churning. And when they did, they settled on Lucas.

Lucas. Tremors of pleasure rippled down her back, demanding she remember his touch. She'd done her best all day to keep the memory of last night, and the chance for a repeat performance, at a safe distance. But the thought of his touch had been there, beneath the surface. The thought of a touch that really happened, not one she'd imagined.

Now the water flowing over her body was almost more than she could stand. Her teenage desires and even her foolish fantasies later had never been like this. Not like this burning, throbbing sensation that made her want to drown her doubts in a lake of sensation, pure sensation shared with Lucas.

She turned to her stomach and stretched out flat, pulling her body through the water with long, smooth strokes. She swam till she was tired, then flipped again to float on her back. The sky above her was blue, clear and fathomless, like Lucas's eyes. Could she trust them? Did she dare?

Chapter Four

Later that night the sound of the cicadas rose up on the hot, still air and hovered around Lucas and Susanna as they stood in the porch light outside his cabin.

"It's very warm," she said.

"The hottest night yet of the summer."

"It's humid, too."

"Unbearable."

"Lonetree says you ought to have air-conditioning put in the houseboats. After tonight I'm sure I'll agree, though it's been quite pleasant up until now. The breeze coming off the lake—"

"Susanna . . ."

"What?" she whispered, looking up at him.

"You don't have to come into the cabin if you don't want to. I just thought you might like to come up here where it's cooler . . . have something to drink . . . maybe talk . . . wait for the night to cool down."

He'd wanted to see her, that was all, Lucas thought. Especially after the way he'd let himself walk off and leave her last night. And then this morning they'd had that ridiculous argument over Tyler, and shared a distant lunch at Toby's. She obviously needed space. He could accept that. But he needed to see her, make sure that she was okay. The heat in the houseboat had to be suffocating. He'd told himself that, all the way back from McAlester.

"I'll walk you back down the hill."

"No," she said quietly.

She didn't doubt for a moment that he fully believed what he'd said. But at the same time, Susanna wondered if Lucas had any idea how much just the sweep of his breath on her cheek was arousing her. The silvered glow that had seemed to surround him on the moonlit path was gone now. In the harsh glare of the cabin's porch light, she saw the open, unassuming look that he wore daily with Lonetree, Toby, his other help and even with clients. Except that the lines in his forehead had deepened a little. He was tired. Tired from a last-minute charter he'd taken, and from the added trip to McAlester to drop the client at the airport. But he'd not been too tired to think of her discomfort at the evening's unrelenting heat.

"I'd like to come in," she said softly. "But let *me* fix the lemonade."

The tension around his mouth eased, and Lucas smiled. "That'd be great," he said. "I think I'll get a shower while you do it. All the dust from that highway traffic has gotten under my skin."

Susanna laughed as she followed him inside. "If you think our roads are bad, you should try to drive in Washington, D.C. There's nothing like bumper-to-bumper traffic at five o'clock on the Capital Beltway. You'd never survive."

"I hope I never have to try," he said. Whistling softly, he stopped in the living room to flip on the stereo. Then he headed toward the bathroom.

For a moment, Susanna stood looking after him, his off-hand comment settling in, tallying itself under other reasons why he'd never be happy in Washington. She'd started to list them that afternoon, after her swim in the lake. But she could better him at that game, she thought glumly. The list of reasons why Wilamet was a good place to be *from*, but not to *live in*, was as long as your arm, last time she counted.

Strains of something classical floated in to her through the kitchen speaker. They pushed away all thoughts but the soothing ones the music suggested. Was it Liszt? she wondered. She closed her eyes and sat on the kitchen stool for a while, just listening to the music.

Hauntingly simple, yet at the same time complex, the music mirrored the moment. Something was happening between her and Lucas. Something simple, yet so confusing she could not sort it out. She wanted, she knew, to be near him, yet she also wanted to keep her distance. At least till she figured things out.

Susanna got up from the stool and took out a can of frozen lemonade. When she turned on the blender, its noise interfered with the sound of the music. She shut it off and mixed the drink by hand.

Maybe Lucas would hate the traffic, she thought, and lots of other things about the city—the crowds, the exorbitant cost of living, the transience of even friendships in the face of political turnovers. But he'd love the music. She was sure of that.

She was filling two glasses with ice from the ample supply in the freezer when she heard him come into the kitchen behind her.

"The finest orchestras in the world play at Washington's Kennedy Center," she said over her shoulder. "The New York Philharmonic, Berlin, Vienna, Israel. I once heard Zubin Mehta conduct Mahler. I don't think I'll ever forget..."

Lucas reached out and shut the refrigerator door for her. She looked up to thank him, then stood there, suddenly speechless.

All of her senses sharpened. The smell of lemonade, pierced the woodsy scent of the soap he'd used. The glasses of ice felt frigid beneath her fingers. She could almost hear the splash of the water droplet that fell from his earlobe onto his shoulder.

Barefoot and bare chested, Lucas draped the cotton shirt he carried over a chair and reached for the pitcher. Beneath the towel he had hung around his neck, drops of water clung to the curling blond hair on his chest. The hair on his head was curling wildly, too. Sheepishly he gave it a swipe with the towel. "Sorry," he said. "I was so damn thirsty."

He lifted his glass and drank, savoring each swallow as Susanna watched. Visually she traced the line of his muscular neck, the swell of his throat, the rise and fall of his chest, then the matching contraction and relaxation of the hard muscles around his stomach. Her eyes were pulled lower, down the thin trail of hair that disappeared into his low-riding jeans.

But this time the top snap was fastened securely. Lucas set down his glass, and Susanna let go of the breath she was holding.

"Which of the Mahler symphonies did he do?" Lucas asked.

"What?"

"Zubin Mehta. Which one..."

"Oh, the Mahler. Oh, yes." She reached for the pitcher to fill her glass. "It was...it was...I can't remember!"

Lucas had covered her fingers with his, but he only took the pitcher away from her and poured her a glass himself. "You just said you'd never forget—"

"You distracted me."

"I'm sorry."

His tone was genuine, but a corner of his mouth had lifted in the hint of a smile. He reached for his shirt and began to put it on. Susanna took a long, calming swallow of the cold lemonade.

"Actually it wasn't the Israeli orchestra," she said. "It was the New York Philharmonic. Mehta divides his time between both orchestras, you know. And come to think of it, it wasn't Mahler. It was Tchaikovsky. The *Symphonic Fantasia*, opus 32.

Lucas raised an eyebrow. "'Francesca da Rimini,'" he said. The title slid easily over his tongue.

"You know the piece!"

Lucas reached for the pitcher and motioned for her to bring the glasses. In the living room, he set the pitcher on the coffee table as she settled into the sofa in front of it. Then he crossed the room to the wall of shelved tapes and pulled one off, almost, Susanna thought, with his eyes closed. He tossed it in her lap as he stood before her rolling up his sleeves.

She studied the tape, turning it from the color-coded spine to the picture and title on the face.

"This is the finest recording ever made of that piece," she remarked. "It's not that easy to find. Where did you get it?"

"I belong to several clubs. Wayne tracks them on the computer. He keeps a list of everything I'm looking for and orders whatever comes up."

Lucas buttoned all but the last three buttons of his shirt and reached for the tape. A moment later, the haunting music filled the room, carrying the plaintive cry of the ill-fated lovers. Susanna tipped back her head and drank in the sound.

"I guess we have something else in common," she said as he settled on the sofa beside her, "a love of classical music."

For a moment he didn't answer. Then he took the tape case from her lap, turned it over and stared at the words on the title, words that meant nothing to him. The operatic voices struggled to rise in the music. *He needed to tell her.*

He needed to tell her everything. What he was. What he loved. What he could never be. His unspoken promise to Wayne to keep quiet about his illiteracy seemed insignificant and even tawdry in the face of that need. But Wayne *was* his brother.

He tossed the tape case back in her lap and shifted his weight slightly away from her, till he could lean against the sofa's corner cushions, stretch out his long legs and prop his bare feet up on the edge of the coffee table.

"What I know about classical music comes from bits and pieces on public radio. I wish I knew more."

Susanna nodded. "That's how I got hooked, too. Public radio and TV, plus some reading and a class in college. Lucas, you should take an adult class in music appreciation. They've probably got them in Wilamet at the high school. You'd get a lot out of it."

He laughed dryly. "I don't think they'd let me in."

"Of course they would. You might have to pay a little extra since you don't live within the city limits—"

"Susanna, I never graduated from high school. I don't have the background to take adult classes."

She glanced, first at him, then down at the case in her lap. Absently she ran her finger down the strip of silver tape on its spine. *Lucas was not a high school graduate?* It seemed incongruous with what she knew of him. His love for classical music, the depth of his thinking, even the way he spoke, suggested an intelligent man.

An *intelligent* man? Had she come to equate intelligence with a piece of parchment from some school? The realization jarred her.

Susanna turned the tape case over again. "Maybe it doesn't matter," she said. "I don't think you're required to have a diploma for noncredit adult classes."

"It matters," Lucas said darkly, "to me."

Susanna looked up. He'd folded his arms across his chest. A muscle had tensed at the side of his jaw, setting it hard. She wanted to touch his arm, but Lucas seemed unapproachable.

"Why didn't you finish?" she asked him. "When I left for Washington, you were trying to catch up."

"I didn't get . . . far," he answered vaguely. "I guess you know about my father's illness. Then after he died, the government wanted the farm. They'd already taken most of the land when they built the dam and flooded the valley. I couldn't pay the taxes. . . ." Lucas paused for a moment, running his hand through his shaggy hair.

Suddenly Susanna saw the sixteen-year-old boy he'd been, saddled two years later with responsibility far beyond his years. "How did you manage?" she asked him softly.

Lucas grinned. "It wasn't so bad. In fact, it was kind of fun. Taking on the government usually is."

Susanna frowned. "You're talking about the people I work for," she reminded him. "Go on."

"I talked *your people* into a year of grace. Then everything happened at once. I had my hands full building the marina, hanging on till it made enough money to see us through, then trying to figure out what to do when it made so *much* money that the tax man was all over me again."

Susanna chuckled. "I bet Wayne's accounting education came in handy for that. Your putting him through school helped you both."

Lucas refilled their glasses and passed hers to her. "I owe Wayne a hell of a lot more than he owes me," he said quietly. "He gave me a reason to keep on going. But he's always felt indebted. I wish I could get him to see that he doesn't owe me a thing."

Susanna nodded. "It reminds me of my own relationship with Maggie. Maybe it's a complex of younger children who lose parents." Susanna settled back into the sofa and sipped her lemonade.

"When my father died and we came back to Wilamet, Mother kept herself busy with teaching. I studied like crazy, my head stuffed full of illusions about graduating and going back to Washington to pick up where my father left off."

She swirled the ice cubes in her glass. They had melted to thin crystal slivers. *Illusions?* She'd never thought of them quite that way.

"Anyway," she continued quickly, "Maggie was just a kid. I think she couldn't bear to go on having fun while Mother and I seemed to have such serious pursuits. I'd come home from school, and Maggie would be in the kitchen. At eleven years old, she was making dinner. By twelve she'd learned to bake. She seemed to be happiest elbow-deep in flour, concocting something especially for me. It was as though she was taking care of me, trying to make up for some sacrifice she thought I had made because I came home every day to look after her, took her out on Saturdays, took her, really, everywhere I went. Actually I enjoyed it. Years later, I found myself wishing . . ."

Susanna's voice faded just as the music crescendoed. The wistful solo matched the feeling that hovered on the edge of her memory.

"What did you wish?" Lucas's voice was husky.

Susanna smiled at him. Suddenly she felt she could tell him anything.

"I sometimes wished I'd chosen motherhood instead of a demanding career. Had a child. That's all." She lowered her eyes.

It was as if a door that had always been shut inside him opened a crack, letting in light. He thought of Willy and of all the times he'd wished his brother's child was his. Then the door in his mind slammed shut again. He'd never be a father. All the love in the world would not make up for a parent who couldn't make sure that his kid was learning to read.

He stood suddenly and reached for her glass. "I'll get you some ice," he said. But he didn't move. He stood staring past her, his eyes trained on the empty hearth in front of the sofa.

"Lots of women work and have children, too, Susanna. You'd be a good mother. You have a lot to offer. But kids can be a handful. I probably wouldn't have the time or the patience." He picked up his own glass and left her, heading toward the kitchen.

Not just his words but the tone of his voice rang in Susanna's ears. Desolate, final, almost cold. Was he telling her that *he* was the one who didn't want children? It couldn't be true. And that bit about his not having time and patience... Willy and Toby were testament enough to the contrary.

He was saying, she realized suddenly, that if she still wanted children, she ought to start searching for a father. But not in his cabin. Not in his heart. He'd answered her question before she'd had any idea she was contemplating it! And *why*? Had he guessed her secret? That she was a whiz when it came to public policy, but a miserable failure in private affairs?

Dazed, Susanna stood and crossed the rug to the fireplace where one of Little Willy's stuffed animals was caught between the hearth and the wood box. She pulled it out, straightened the bunny's floppy ears and carried it into the small guest bedroom where Willy slept when Lucas kept him. She was putting the bunny on the toy shelf when Lucas came into the room.

"It's been a very pleasant evening," she said tightly, "but you must be exhausted. And you probably have a charter early tomorrow morning. I'd better be getting back to the houseboat."

Lucas stopped inside the bedroom doorway and watched her try to prop up the bunny. It kept falling over. When she turned to him, her eyes held hurt.

She'd misunderstood, he suddenly knew. She'd turned what he'd said about his own inadequacy against herself. She actually thought that he wouldn't want her to bear his children.

"You don't need to walk me down the hill," she said. "Just lend me the flashlight. I can find my way." She forced a casual smile, but Lucas saw something else.

Wide, deep eyes filled with pain and longing and other feelings he couldn't name, and a sensititivy so finely tuned it would create an equally sensitive child. A boy, a girl, it didn't matter. *Their child.* Did he dare imagine it?

But she'd swept by him, aimlessly chatting about her afternoon swim, Toby's minnows, some silly crossword puzzle she'd been working on. He let her stride out to the living room, but caught her wrist as she reached for the flashlight that stood on the windowsill by the door.

"Susanna?"

She held her breath, then let it go in a rush as the heat of his touch traveled through her body. The ragged sound of her name on his lips made her own begin to tremble.

"Lucas, don't..."

His grip on her wrist tightened. Lines of concern had furrowed his brow, and his ordinarily clear blue eyes had clouded. But as suddenly as the troubled look had come, it faded. His forehead smoothed. And his eyes? Susanna could swear she saw them begin to twinkle. His grip on her wrist began to loosen, relaxing her tension with it.

"Actually, I *don't* have an early charter," he said. "How about filling it yourself? No charge since you're family. Except maybe *I'll* keep the catch."

She smiled, feeling the easy intimacy slip back around them.

He'd been smoothing his thumb over her wrist. Now he stopped and pressed gently. Susanna was aware that her pulse was pounding. He brought her wrist to his lips and kissed it, then let it go and leaned in the doorway.

Suddenly she didn't care whether what she was feeling for Lucas was real or something she'd imagined. She wanted to touch him, hold him, be held, flow with the feeling wherever it led them. Find out if it was real.

No. She'd done that with Daryl. If you closed your eyes and plunged into your feelings before you were sure, you'd never see the person clearly again. Her hand shook as she reached for the flashlight, then stilled as her fingers closed around it. Hadn't she learned *anything* with Daryl? The feelings that Lucas was rousing were a hundred times stronger than anything she'd ever felt before. Wasn't that all the more reason to be wary of them? She pushed through the door.

The blast of hot, humid air hit her full in the face as she stepped onto the porch, into the noisy drone of the cicadas. It was going to be a miserable night for sleeping, in more ways than one. And what would tomorrow bring? Then a thought occurred to her. The middle of Lake Eufaula was about as public as you could get, a safe enough place to be with Lucas, a place where she was sure she could maintain control. She turned back to him. "Let's *do* go fishing to-morrow," she said.

Lucas smiled. "I'll see you at dawn."

Susanna peered out across the lake into the quiet pre-dawn darkness. Beyond the houseboat nothing moved. Restlessly she crossed the deck to fill her mug for the second time.

Somewhere in the middle of the sleepless night, she'd come to an agreement with herself. She'd take things as they came, one day at a time, because that was what coming home was all about. But within those days, she'd keep up the snappy pace that she was used to. Whatever each day offered up, she'd throw herself into it, leaving no time for random thoughts and silly imaginings. There'd be plenty of time for daydreams once she got back to Washington.

She sipped at her coffee. Then she heard it—the unmis-takable *plop* of a jumping fish.

She leaned over the side of the boat and scanned the inky water. The edge of a widening circle crept with tantalizing slowness toward her. When it finally arrived, she could al-most feel it lick the side of the boat. Then she heard an-other *plop*, followed by a swishing sound that *had* to be a good-sized fish.

Where was Lucas? If they were going to fish, they ought to get at it. They were missing one right under their noses.

The sound of an outboard motor, then the quieter hum of the trolling motor, answered her question. Lucas's boat slid out of the darkness. As soon as he'd narrowed the space between them, the air turned vibrant. Her heartbeat quick-ened, but Susanna was determined to focus on fishing.

"They're jumping already," she said. "Where have you been?"

He watched her bend over the rail of the houseboat and reach for the guide rope. Her hair was pulled back into a freshly made braid, her flushed cheeks looked scrubbed and her dark almond eyes were lit with excitement.

"Well?" she persisted.

"I didn't realize I had such an anxious charter. I thought she might even still be asleep."

Susanna had passed the last of her gear over the side of the boat before Lucas had finished speaking. When she reached for the ladder, he held up a hand to stop her.

"I'll have a cup of that coffee, first. *If* you don't mind."

"Take mine," she said quickly, thrusting her cup into his hands. "It's still hot."

She hoisted herself down the houseboat ladder and stepped carefully into the narrow, streamlined bass boat. The space between them shrank to nothing. Her heart drummed faster. Susanna swallowed and backed toward the rear of the boat.

"Sit down behind the wheel and drink the coffee," she commanded. "I'll start the trolling motor and move us out. I know how to do it. I used to fish with my father."

"I didn't realize you were such a serious fisherman," Lucas said. He'd made no move to follow her orders.

"There are lots of things you don't know about me, Lucas Grant."

He watched Susanna bend over the small electric motor and flip the ignition switch. The cotton shorts she wore covered just enough of her bottom to set him on edge.

"For starters," she said, adjusting the rudder, "in my opinion, there's no sense in doing anything unless you do it right."

She seated herself decidedly in the small deck chair next to the motor. Lucas grinned and gave her a mock salute. "That's definitely a matter of opinion," he said. "Some things aren't worth doing *unless* you do them half-assed."

"You've got to be kidding. Like what?"

Grinning still, he moved to the front of the boat and settled in behind the wheel. He took a swallow of coffee. It was tepid. "Like waiting for fish. If you get too uptight, try too hard, they'll outsmart you every time. You'll find out before the morning is over."

Morning. At the moment, it was nothing more than a subtle warming of the air, a stirring in the bushes on the bank as the night creatures settled in their burrows to sleep, a slow diminishment of starlight. For a moment, Susanna forgot her resolve to control the pace of the day. She began to savor the long, slow slide toward dawn.

Her foot on the throttle of the little electric engine, she followed Lucas's motioned directions, guiding them out of the cove, around the peninsula and out toward the smooth, dark water. As they passed the dim light over the marina's doorway, Susanna saw Lonetree unfold himself and move to the dock. Slowly he waved to them, his good arm held high over his head.

Once they'd reached open water, Lucas started the outboard. Susanna turned off the trolling motor and worked her way up to the seat beside him. He gave her a grin as he threw out the coffee and passed her the cup. Then he revved the engine.

They were off! The bow of the boat rose for an instant, like a fish just clearing the surface before it jumps. Then it shot forward, slicing the water in a sheer wedge that left a roiling wake behind them.

Wind whipped across Susanna's face and slammed her back against her seat. *"What are you doing?"* she shouted over the roar of the outboard.

If he heard her shout, he made no move to slow the boat. One arm stretched out to guide the steering wheel, the other draped across the back of her seat, Lucas looked for all the world as if he was cruising down Main, not ripping the dickens out of Lake Eufaula. He didn't even seem to notice the wind in his hair and his eyes.

She could hardly see. What little scenery visible in the early light rushed by in a blur of green. The wind swept over the top of the windshield and snatched at her braid till it came undone and tangled her hair in front her eyes. And every half second, the boat slammed down on the water, jarring every bone in her body. Then as suddenly as he'd taken off, he cut the engine and stopped the boat.

Her ears kept right on ringing. Lucas swung himself over the seat to get to the back of the boat. Then he stopped and threw her a casual glance.

"Fast enough for you? I knew you were anxious to get down to business, and I usually make the ride out to work in half that time. Makes up for the hours of waiting for a bite that try your patience. The boat bucks a little, though. I wanted to give you a comfortable trip. So I went slow."

She opened her mouth to respond, then shut it again without answering as Lucas turned his back to check the trolling motor. She'd determined last night that she'd fish with a vengeance. If you worked hard at something, really gave it your all, there'd be no room left for unreliable feelings. She wouldn't let Lucas's teasing dissuade her.

"So what kind of bait are we using?" she asked him coolly.

"Plastic worms, of course. What color would you prefer?"

She'd never used anything but night crawlers dug by her father. Susanna glanced at the tangerine-streaked horizon grazing the treetops on the bank beyond Lucas. "Orange," she said. "I'll take an orange one, please."

He hesitated a moment, then flipped the catch on the top of a large tackle box. A fruity aroma rose up from the segmented compartments. Susanna leaned over the back of her seat.

Lucas rummaged in the box, then shook his head. "I'm sorry, I don't seem to have any orange ones. They all seem to be various shades of blue.

Susanna shrugged impatiently. "Just give me any old thing," she said. "Besides, are you really sure that bass can see colors?"

"Every shade in the rainbow, plus twenty-four tones in between."

He watched her brown eyes open wide, then try to appear unimpressed. He did his best not to smile. "Let's start with a medium blue," he said. "We may have to go pretty deep. It's morning, and they ought to be feeding in the shallows near shore, but as hot as it's been, we won't take a chance."

Lucas laid four of the thin, squishy-looking tubes on the rim of the boat beside him. Susanna grimaced. They really did look like segmented earthworms, except that they smelled like blueberries. Do fish like the smell of fruit? Do fish even smell? she wondered. She resisted the urge to ask him.

"Would you mind passing me the rods so I can bait these hooks?" He nodded toward the opposite side of the boat where four rods were tucked into holders.

Susanna climbed over the seat and handed him the rods, then perched on the side of the boat across from him. She watched intently as Lucas slipped a small cone-shaped sinker on the end of the first line, checked to make sure that it would slide freely, then pulled the line through the eye of the hook and tied it securely. Finally he pushed the head of the plastic worm over the hook, burying the point in its body.

"Aren't you going to pull it all the way through? My father always pulled the hook all the way through."

He held the rig closer so Susanna could see. He pushed the hook on through the side of the plastic worm, then barely drew it back. "You'll be far less likely to hang up on the bottom if we do it this way," he said.

"Of course, setting the hook will be harder," she responded. His eyes, inches from hers, held an unmistakable twinkle, but one of his eyebrows had lifted ever so slightly at her comment.

"You got it," he said. "You'll need a firm snap." Susanna smiled smugly.

She took the rod he'd finished rigging, stood and turned toward the side of the boat as she fed out a little line. She searched her memory one last time, recalling as much as she could of the subtleties of fishing. Then she cast.

The sweep of her arm and the hum of the line as it sailed out over the water brought back memories of the times she'd fished with her father, those joyful, stolen mornings of her childhood before he'd gotten so busy. He'd be pleased, she thought, that she still remembered.

Her bait hit the water with a gentle plop, and she felt it sink to the bottom. When it stopped moving, she slowly wound up the slack, set the drag, then relaxed, her thumb gently feeling the line, her eyes trained on where it had entered the water.

"Nice cast."

"Thank you."

"It won't do you much good, of course?"

Susanna bristled. "May I ask, why not?"

"There aren't any fish here. I just stopped to rig the lines."

He surprised himself with his comment. If she wanted to try a hopeless spot, she had every right. But something about her attitude was getting under his skin. She'd used that same tone in suggesting that Toby needed formal education, and yesterday afternoon when she and Lonetree got to talking about artificial arms again. Now she was using it with him. Next she'd be telling him how to do his job.

While Susanna was trying to think of a snappy comeback, she felt a tug on her line. Then it twitched a shade to the right. Quickly she jerked her rod, pulling it hard over her left shoulder. Her rod bent double.

"There he is!" she shouted.

She struggled to keep her line taut as the fish zigzagged forward, then back toward the boat. The repeated pattern made her so dizzy she nearly lost her balance. Suddenly the fish cut the water, leaping a foot in the air, its bottle-green back ashimmer in the first full rays of dawn.

"It's a largemouth! A nice one," Lucas shouted.

Susanna's heart rolled with the fish as it turned its white belly skyward and tried to spit out her hook.

The bass hit the water, hesitated for a moment, then zigzagged again. She'd lose the fish, she knew, if it managed to wrap up her line.

"Hang on!" Lucas yelled as he made for the back of the boat. He started the trolling engine, adding the weight of the boat to the drag on her line. Susanna stopped breathing as she felt her line go slack, then she gulped air as it tightened again. The fish made one last effort, straining hard with the fight it had left.

She pulled, reeled like crazy and pulled again. And then it was over. A long moment later, Lucas leaned over the side of the boat and netted her fish. The bass was a good fourteen inches long. He stared at the fish, and then he looked at Susanna.

"Where the hell did you learn to fish like that?"

"I didn't...I don't...I was only pretending."

He chuckled, then started to laugh. Susanna laughed, too. She had to sit down to keep her balance.

"I'd like to see what you'd catch when you're really trying," he said.

"Probably nothing," she answered, "unless someone tells me there aren't any fish."

Lucas gave her a sheepish grin and bent over the bass, working it free of the net. He removed the fish hook with a pair of pliers, then opened the live well. The fish nearly jumped from his hands as it tried to get into the water.

It hit with a splash that sent droplets of water scattering over them both. Then it discovered its confinement and fought to escape, sloshing water up over the rim of the well as it struggled.

Again and again the fish bumped its nose against the sides of the live well. Lucas started to close the lid.

"Wait!" Susanna said. "Please. I want to let it go."

Her hand rested lightly on his forearm. His skin seemed to burn beneath her touch. Yet he didn't want her to move it. Slowly he turned his arm and slid it up to catch her hand till he held it roughly in his, their fingers entwined and raised between them.

"Remember the terms of the charter?" he said, ticking them off in a husky voice on their clasped fingers. "One, you don't pay. Two, the catch belongs to me."

"Well, then *you* let it go," she whispered. He stroked the inside of her palm with the edge of his thumb.

"That, my fancy city angler, will cost you. Cost you dearly."

His mouth was inches from hers. His breath swept her face, and the smell of the morning mist and the masculine scent of musky desire rose up to fill her nostrils.

She flattened her other palm against his chest in a feeble attempt to stay his approaching embrace. "Maybe you owe me an explanation," she whispered. "What made you believe there weren't any fish?"

"It's all in the underwater structures, especially in hotter weather." With a brush of his thumb he erased the thin line of perspiration along her cheekbone, then tipped her face closer to his.

"The bass will hide in those bends of the old creek bed. Or you'll find them at the bottom of the ditches that used to border the roads. A rock bluff, a dropoff below a point..." He lightly brushed her lips with his. A whisper of flesh against eager flesh, yet it left Susanna breathless.

"I suppose you figured all that out with your sonar," she mumbled, nodding at the darkened screen of the small black box on the dash of the boat.

Lucas smiled, an easy, open, gentle movement that eased the corners of his mouth and softened his eyes. She felt that she could lose herself in his smile.

"I don't need sonar, Susanna. I fished this area when the stream and the land it was on were ours, before the reservoir flooded it. I have a very good memory of everything I've ever seen or felt . . . or touched."

His mouth moved down to cover hers, claiming it as her lips parted, helpless to resist his invitation. His kiss felt warm to her, familiar, sure. And so did his touch.

Chapter Five

Their lips lingered, lost in waves of warm, wet kisses. Kisses that left them breathless, then calm, then stirred again to a higher crest of passion.

His hands moved freely over her body, down the curve of her spine and up to hold her closer, then down again to the gentle flare of her hips. Wherever he touched her, she moved against him into his caress, fueling his passion.

Finally, at the approaching sound of another outboard, they drew apart. But Lucas couldn't take his eyes off Susanna's face. He cradled it between his hands.

The dawn's last light had settled on the ridges of her cheekbones, blushing them to a soft, warm pink. Her eyes were wide with wonder, an innocent wonder that told him everything. Told him she'd offered her bed and her body before, but she'd never been loved. Not the way she needed it, body, mind and spirit.

The passionate moves that her body made every time he touched her denied every word she spoke when she talked of holding back. But she didn't trust what was happening between them. Maybe she shouldn't, considering the limits of what he could offer.

The outboard drew closer, but he didn't give a damn who saw them. He kissed her again, gently brushing her lips, taking one more taste of what she was offering him without even knowing it. The chance to be the one to love her. *Really* love her. For more than just a moment. A chance he didn't dare take.

He let go of her abruptly and turned to watch the approaching boat. It was one of his guides with a client from Kansas City, a regular.

"Phone message for you from your brother, Lucas," the guide called out. "He wants to leave for Oklahoma City tonight instead of tomorrow morning."

"Had any luck?" the customer asked as the boat pulled closer. His question, Lucas noted, was directed at Susanna. His eyes, at her legs.

"The lady caught a fish," he found himself saying in a less than hospitable tone.

The guide gave a disbelieving snort. "In this godforsaken spot? Ain't no fish here. Ain't nothin' but a lot of mud and sand. Must a been some straggler. Little bitty thing, I bet."

The guy from Kansas City still had his eyes on Susanna. His smile was warming by the minute.

"How's the little woman, Mr. Bradley?" Lucas asked him before bending down and opening the live well. When he turned back, he held the fish, his fingers hooked in a gill. The long, shiny body jerked heavily from side to side.

The guide gave a whistle. Lucas tossed the fish into the lake, close enough to the other boat to make a good-sized splash. The client fumbled for his handkerchief.

"Throwin' 'em back now, are ya, Lucas?" The guide eyed Susanna and shook his head.

"The lady's fish . . . the lady's choice," he answered.

The guide shot Lucas a knowing smile, then turned his boat and headed out.

"My brother and I have an appointment with Toby's caseworker in Oklahoma City tomorrow afternoon," Lucas said to Susanna. "Wayne probably needs to take care of some other business first. Toby's mother will enjoy keeping him overnight. It'll work out well all the way around."

She waited, hoping he'd ask her to go, but Lucas was silent. She felt the heat rise up to her cheeks. Would he ignore what had passed between them? Why was he holding back? She thought of the way she'd welcomed his kisses, his touch. Or had she *invited* them? Recklessly thrown out a hook and hauled him in against his will, hardly knowing what she was doing, just the way she'd caught that fish.

He'd moved to the back of the boat and started the motor, then headed up the shoreline toward a rocky point not too far away.

"Throw in your line," he told her when he'd cut the motor to a crawl.

"What?"

"I said, throw in your line. You'll catch a fish."

"I've caught a fish. I don't want to catch another one."

She was back on the defensive. He'd put her there himself. Maybe that was safer for both of them. Without a word, he stowed the tackle and took his seat behind the wheel. When he turned the key, she braced herself. But there wasn't any need. He headed the boat back to the marina at half the speed he'd left it.

His mind was on the Kansas City client. He hoped when she chose the man who would love her, it would be someone with a little more class.

* * *

Susanna was heading up the path toward the campground showers when she met Lonetree coming down. He carried a pipe wrench, and a length of coiled hose was slung over his shoulder.

"Water's off," Lonetree said. "Lucas says to use his cabin. He'll be at the marina till five."

Susanna glanced at her wrist before she remembered she wasn't wearing her watch. The tall Indian grinned. Despite the hot day, he wasn't wearing the usual raggedy, camouflage cotton T-shirt that allowed him to flaunt his scarred stump. Instead, one long sleeve from his worn but clean western-style shirt was carefully pinned to cover it.

"It's only a quarter past four," Lonetree said. "You've got plenty of time to get in and out of there before the boss gets home. I got my hands full fixing a shower, or I'd offer to stand guard at the door for you."

Susanna felt her face turn crimson. It wasn't the first remark he'd made that told her he thought she was hung up on Lucas.

"Never mind, Lonetree. You certainly don't have to do that. In fact, maybe *I* could help *you*. I could pass you the tools . . . or something. It must be difficult. . . ."

Lonetree's dark eyes narrowed, and his thin lips drew into a tight line. "Difficult, but never impossible. Maybe you'd like to hang around and watch. We cripples have a passel of handy tricks. You might learn a thing or two, Miss Foster, just in case you ever lose an arm."

Stunned, Susanna took a step back. The Indian gave her a hard look and headed down the path.

She closed her eyes to erase the edge of pain she'd seen behind his anger. Susanna wanted to drop through the earth. *Why* did she keep on saying these things? If Lonetree needed her help at all, he needed it on a personal level. She wanted to offer it that way, yet everything she said to him came out sounding condescending.

"Miss Foster?"

Her eyes flew open. Lonetree stood before her. The hard look had eased in his eyes, though it still lingered around his mouth. He shifted the coiled hose farther up his shoulder and cleared his throat.

"I'm sorry," he said.

"*You're* sorry?"

"I've got a king-size chip on my shoulder. You seem to be good at knocking it off."

Susanna scuffed at the pieces of bark that covered the path. She stooped and picked one up. Then she looked up at Lonetree.

He'd squared his shoulders and tipped back his head till he seemed to be looking down his long, straight nose, waiting to judge her response.

Susanna fingered the chip of bark. She turned it over to the flatter side, then placed it carefully on her shoulder.

"I guess I've got one, too. Do you want to try to knock it off?"

The hint of a smile softened the edges of Lonetree's thin mouth. The tall Indian bent close to her shoulder. With one good breath he blew the chip away.

"We're even now," he said to her. "Until next time."

Susanna tipped her chin. "I hope there won't be a next time, Lonetree. Not for either of us."

The Indian didn't answer, but he nodded thoughtfully, then turned and started back down the path. Susanna headed in the opposite direction, toward Lucas's cabin.

"Susanna!"

Even with the noise of the pounding shower, Susanna heard every angry syllable of her name on Lucas's lips.

He banged on the bathroom door so hard with his fist, she was sure it was going to fly open. She turned off the water and snatched up a towel, hugging it to her body.

"Lucas, what on earth is the matter with you?" she shouted through the closed door.

"That's the same question *I'd* like to ask you. What the hell did you say to Lonetree?"

Hurriedly she dried herself, then reached for her clothes, all the while searching for words to explain. "I said ... I didn't say anything, really ... I—"

"Then will you please tell me why he's got himself locked in his cabin? He says the campground showers can go to hell. He says you gave him something to *think* about. Would you mind telling me what's more important to a man than his job? What's so all fired important that a summer visitor would stoop to—"

Susanna whipped open the bathroom door and stood almost nose to nose with Lucas's slouching form. He straightened and took a surprised step back. Her tangled wet hair was dripping water down the front of her cotton T-shirt, making it stick to the curves of her full, rounded breasts. He tried to lower his eyes, only to find them traveling up her long legs to where her shorts rode high on her thighs.

"*Stoop* to exactly *what*?" she shouted at him. "I offered to help him, that's all. Maybe I didn't do it so tactfully. If you didn't care so much about your darn marina, you'd see that people need time ... for other things besides work ... time to think ... time to ..."

Her voice had softened. Now barely a whisper, it drew his mouth to hers as surely as the pull of the moon on the summer tide.

She tasted liquid warm and clean. Her skin felt full of fire. At the force of his kiss, her lips gave eagerly. Her arms moved immediately up to his neck as his wrapped around her waist. He pulled her close, then closer still, till he felt the crush of her breasts against his chest and the urgency of her hips as they pressed against his.

At the knock on the front screen door, she jerked away. The fire in her cheeks had spread to her eyes. He read surprise, confusion and molten passion. It matched the volcano erupting within his chest.

"Lucas?" Lonetree called out from the porch. "Can I see you a minute?"

She backed away. The color had deepened on her face. It fanned out across her cheekbones, turning them a burnished sunset rose that swelled his heart near to bursting. Her dark eyes flashed all the brighter, their amber depths lit by that fire that had once again kindled between them. He wanted to keep that flame smoldering and then walk right into the middle of it. The knock came again.

Susanna watched his back as Lucas moved down the hall. Fingers trembling, she shut the bathroom door and reached for her comb. For a long moment she stood staring at her own reflection. What she felt for Lucas Grant was deeper than anything she'd ever spun out in her fantasies. Deeper and far more dangerous.

"I heard you're going up to the city this afternoon instead of tomorrow morning," Lonetree said when Lucas opened the door. The Indian stepped inside.

Lonetree had knocked on his door maybe half a dozen times in the three years since he'd come to the marina. Other times he'd needed to talk, he'd wait at the pier. And he'd never accepted an invitation to come into the cabin before. It was a hell of a time to start, Lucas thought as he shut the screen door behind him.

"Wayne got some last-minute business—"

"I'd like to ride along. I can pick up the engine we had overhauled and price out the load of cedar we need for the decks on the new cabins.'' The Indian looked away for a moment, shifted his weight and then looked back to Lucas.

"I thought you could drop me at the V A hospital, too, if there's time. It's been a while since I was there. Maybe too long. Thought I'd check out what they're doing...in the phony-arm department.''

The tall Indian squared his shoulders and leveled his eyes. Lucas searched them intently.

"You know you don't have to do this, Lonetree. I know how you feel—''

"Maybe that's why I'm going. Because you understand. And because of...'' Lonetree broke off and looked over Lucas's shoulder.

Lucas turned and saw Susanna. She'd braided her hair, pulling it back sleek and smooth from her face. A bit of the color still rode on her cheekbones, a remnant of the passion he'd roused in her. But everything else about her was calm, even tranquil, almost remote.

"I'll have that shower up and running before I go, Miss Foster,'' Lonetree said. "And I've asked the handyman to finish the painting on your houseboat. There's not that much. It'll make it nicer while you're here.''

"Thanks, Lonetree,'' Susanna said quietly. "Good luck...tomorrow.''

The Indian nodded to both of them and then stepped back outside. Lucas turned back to Susanna.

She'd moved to the living room, close to the wall of glass. Beyond, the pin oak trees, the raspberry bushes and snatches of meadow grass blended into one long swath of emerald green that turned a shade lighter once it reached the lake water. In the sultry scene, nothing moved except for the brush stroke of Lonetree's shirt as he headed down the path. Susanna hugged her arms to her chest.

Lucas watched her, trying to think of how he should start. Words wouldn't come. He opened the door to the small

closet beside the front door, kicked off his boating shoes and
pulled on his black dress boots. Still she hadn't moved from
the window. He pulled out his traveling bag and dropped it
by the door.

"He's going to take your advice," Lucas said.

Susanna spoke without turning. "I know."

"You don't seem pleased."

"I'm not sure I am."

The sunlight seeped through the window onto her bowed
head, turning her smooth, dark hair to glinting obsidian.
Lucas wanted to reach out and stroke it. Instead he crossed
the room to stand behind her.

"It's time Lonetree let go of his anger, Susanna. You were
right about that."

She turned. She stood so close he could smell the scent of
soap on her skin, and yet she seemed miles away.

"This is *your* world, Lucas," she said. "I'm not sure I've
got any business disturbing things."

"Look, I'm sorry I came thundering in here like that, ac-
cusing you of—"

She touched his chest. As quickly as her fingertips met his
shirt, she tried to pull them away, but he caught her hand.

"No, *don't*," she said. "You were right a while ago. In a
few short weeks, I'll be going back to a busy, complicated
life. A life where I do what I'm good at. I don't belong here,
Lucas. I'm a summer visitor, just like you said. Remember?"

He remembered all right. It all flashed before him. The
feeling he'd had when he first saw her again, the feeling that
something long dormant had suddenly sprung to life. Now
it had grown into an irresistible force that made him want to
reach for her whenever she came near, even a moment ago
in the middle of his anger. But she was right about their
separate worlds.

He felt the muscles tighten in his jaw, pulling his mouth into a hard line. He'd known it years ago. Nothing had changed. He ought to thank her for reminding him. They could meet for a moment, a week, a month, but that would be all. And it would never be enough. Lucas let go of Susanna's hand.

"You've still got a couple of days on the houseboat," he said dryly. "You'll get a good dose of peace and quiet. We won't be back till tomorrow evening. Let the man in the bait shop know if you need anything."

Susanna watched him turn and stride out of the room. Her heart felt leaden. Suddenly the scene outside seemed as flat and empty as his tone. It was what she had wanted, wasn't it? To put some distance between them? So why was she so disappointed that he'd welcomed it? She felt again as she had on the boat when Lucas had quietly withdrawn. Shut out, not knowing why.

"Feel free to use the cabin while I'm away," he called back from the hallway.

She watched him pick up his bag and sling it over his shoulder, then reach for a worn felt cowboy hat that hung on a peg near the door. It matched the dusty-blond color of his hair. When he jammed it down low on his brow, the brim nearly covered his eyes. But she knew she couldn't have read them, anyway. Lucas kicked open the screen door, and then he was gone.

"You told him *what*?" Maggie asked.

Susanna laid one last ribbon of bright green paint on the roof of the houseboat, then gathered up her brushes and the can of paint she'd forced the handyman to abandon to her. She climbed down the short ladder to the deck where Maggie waited with Little Willy.

"I told him yesterday afternoon, just before he left, that we're from two different worlds." Susanna went inside the houseboat to look for something to hammer down the lid of the paint can. Maggie followed her inside.

"Two different worlds? Susanna, you were *born* here, over in Wilamet, maybe, but close enough to—"

"I've been away too long." She grabbed a towel and wiped at the sweat on her brow. "Lucas understands. It's better this way."

"If it's better, why haven't the dark circles disappeared from underneath your eyes? And what are you doing *working* when you're supposed to be relaxing? I thought if I kept all those notebooks at home—"

"I *am* relaxing, Maggie. This is the most restful thing I've done in a month. And if I look tired, it's because I didn't sleep very well last night." Susanna turned away from Maggie's penetrating gaze. "The cicadas kept me awake. You wouldn't believe the noise they've been making."

"Susanna—"

"Maggie, I refuse to have a summer romance with Lucas Grant!"

"Who says it has to be just for the summer?"

Susanna spun around to confront her sister. But Maggie had settled wearily onto the bed. She seemed to gather up inside herself. Her flushed face was glazed with perspiration.

"Susanna, would you get me a drink of something cold from that refrigerator? I'm . . . not feeling well."

Wayne waved goodbye to Toby and his mother, then hurried out to the truck, mopping his brow. Once inside, he slammed the door.

"What's got into you, Lucas? Why didn't you come in? It's hotter than blazes in here."

Lucas pulled his hat down till it nearly touched the top of his sunglasses. He jammed the key into the ignition. When the engine turned over, he rolled up his window and flipped on the air-conditioning.

"I'll see Toby's mother this afternoon, Wayne. Our agency appointment won't take long." Lucas concentrated on working his way through the winding suburban streets, back onto the highway.

"You haven't said a word since we left Wilamet yesterday afternoon," Wayne persisted. "Was it leaving Lonetree off at the V A hospital? Are you worried that you're going to lose your number-one man?"

"Cut it out, Wayne. If Lonetree moves on, more power to him. I've had something on my mind, that's all."

Wayne grumbled and stared out the window as they passed a long line of cars on the divided highway. It was useless, he knew, to try to get anything out of Lucas when he was in one of his moods. Nonetheless, when Lucas missed the downtown exit, and they had to get off the freeway at an unfamiliar spot, Wayne made another attempt.

"It's Maggie's sister, isn't it?" Wayne watched his brother's big hands tighten on the steering wheel. "I knew it! I knew the minute I saw the two of you together in the cabin, the day that she came with Maggie to pick me up. Don't get me wrong, I've got nothing against my sister-in-law. Susanna's a great person, and she's also a beautiful woman. But Lucas . . . she's not your type."

Lucas hit the brakes and made a sharp U-turn as they passed the short, squat, red brick building that held the agency for social services. Wayne grabbed for the dash and muttered something about being grateful he'd worn his seat belt.

Lucas pulled the truck into the first available spot, jammed the gearshift into Park and turned off the key. He tossed his sunglasses up on the dash of the truck and slouched down in the seat.

"Just what sort of woman *is* my type, Wayne? Maybe you think I should hang around the Rebel Inn, pick up a fancy-dressed sweetheart who's tired of playing the field? Or head on into the city, find a nice, quiet waitress who'd do all her cooking just for me?"

"Lucas, I didn't mean—"

"I know what you meant, Wayne. You meant that Susanna Foster is educated, and I'm not. You meant that if I fool around with the kind of high-class fire she's got in her, I'll be sure to get myself burned. Thanks for your concern, but I've already decided that the lady's off-limits. But you've got her wrong, Wayne. She's not the kind of woman to care about what a person's lacking. I'm going to prove it. I'm going to tell her the truth about my illiteracy. She thinks *she's* the one who doesn't fit in. I'm going to tell her just how wrong she really is."

"Lucas, you can't..."

But Lucas was already out of the truck, heading into the building. When he got inside the door, he stopped at the building directory and tried to pick out the proper office from the confusing jumble of words. He shoved his hands into his pockets and looked down at his clean but faded jeans. He ought to have changed, he thought. Worn something a little more citified. He'd been in such a hurry to get out of the cabin.

A few minutes later, a thin-faced, middle-aged woman glanced at Wayne and then at Lucas as they settled into chairs in her cramped office. She pushed at a mountain of papers that cluttered her desk, pulled out a file and tapped her pencil on top of it. When she finally spoke, her tone was terse.

"The new test results are *very* clear, Mr. Grant. Toby is less retarded than we thought originally. That's all the more reason for him to be moved into the group home."

Lucas shifted in the metal chair that was far too small for him to sit comfortably. "Let me get this straight. You're concerned that if Toby stays with us, he won't advance enough, won't stretch his mind. You think that marina work is too routine, too simpleminded—"

When Wayne interrupted, Lucas was glad. He could feel the anger rising in his chest. In a minute it might choke his words. His brother would do better.

"Perhaps there's an alternative," Wayne suggested. "The home you're recommending does have special classes, and there's nothing like that at the lake or even in Wilamet. But what if we did some private tutoring with Toby? Made sure that he got as much enrichment as he could handle?"

The social worker tossed her pencil on her desk and leaned forward. She looked directly at Lucas. "You're certainly not intending to do that yourself, are you, Mr. Grant? I'm sure you're not qualified—"

"Me, teach Toby?" Lucas laughed. At the cynical sound of it, the woman sharpened her gaze. Beside him, Wayne drew in a sharp breath. "To tell you the truth," Lucas went on, "it's been the other way around. I've learned a hell of a lot from Toby since he came. And I couldn't teach him if I wanted to. I don't even know—"

"We're well aware of our limitations," Wayne interrupted. "But there are several qualified teachers in town. We can see that Toby gets the very best instruction on a regular basis."

"That kind of help is certainly superior to a classroom environment," the woman answered. "Toby might progress further than expected. Basic reading might not be totally out of his grasp. But tutoring is very expensive. I'm sure you're aware that the state couldn't possibly pay for it."

"Money isn't an issue," Lucas said coldly. "It never has been."

The woman studied him a moment longer. Then she put on a pair of reading glasses and flipped open the file. "I can see that. Apparently our check goes directly into a savings account in Toby's name, along with certain other funds, for menial chores at the marina, I presume."

Lucas felt the muscles tighten in his neck, but this time Wayne spoke before he had a chance. "Then we're agreed? Toby will continue to live with Lucas, and we'll arrange for tutoring. And the issue of formal guardianship will be postponed."

The woman stood. She was even thinner than her face and her voice had suggested. She needed some of Toby's cooking, Lucas thought.

"I think that's appropriate," the woman said. "I'd like to interview the mother again also, if her health will allow it. Let's meet again in a couple of weeks."

She turned toward Lucas and offered her hand. When he took it, her grasp was limp. "I'm sure you understand that we have our rules, Mr. Grant," she said. "I can understand your attachment to Toby, but we must make sure that what we do is for Toby's benefit, not ours. Don't you agree?"

The woman didn't wait for an answer, but sat back down and began to sort through her papers. As Wayne and Lucas left her office, she spoke into the intercom, telling her secretary that the next appointment would have to wait till she'd had her lunch.

Out in the hallway, Lucas eyed the long bench filled with waiting people. He considered telling them not to waste their time. Before he could make the first move, Wayne pushed him down the corridor and out the door into the heat. The muggy air felt downright good after the stuffy coolness of the agency office. Lucas took a deep breath and started across the parking lot.

"See? I *told* you," Wayne said. "You almost blew the whole thing, Lucas. If you'd let that woman know that you can't read, she'd have had Toby off the marina faster than a jumping catfish hits the water.''

''Maybe that would be best for Toby.''

''Then two years of the relationship you've built with him, not to mention your promise to his mother, would be just so much water over the dam.''

Lucas stopped dead in the center of the hot asphalt parking lot. ''Wayne, the woman almost asked me about my schooling. Don't you think she's going to do it again when it's time to sign the papers? I've seen those forms. I'll never be able to fill them out. I can read just enough to know that.''

''We'll fill them out together, Lucas or I'll coach you beforehand, like I did for your driver's license exam.''

He looked over Wayne's shoulder, squinting into the blinding noonday sun. ''I don't like lying.'' He turned away and continued walking.

Wayne caught his brother's arm as they approached the truck. ''You've never actually *lied*, Lucas. Besides, don't you see? It's probably what you've given Toby that made the difference when he was tested this time. Who knows where *I'd* be if you hadn't . . . Lucas, just let me help you awhile longer. *That's* what's best for Toby.''

Lucas moved to the opposite side of the truck and reached in on the dash for his sunglasses. He put them on, then stood for a minute more, looking over the cab at his brother.

''Is it, Wayne? Is it really best for Toby? Where the hell are we going to find anyone to teach him? And what happens after he's mine? Suppose there's a chance that he could learn to read, Wayne? I'd be a damn poor example. . . .''

''We'll find a way.''

Lucas shook his head, smiling wryly at Wayne's determination. That attitude had gotten his brother through school and was helping him build the best accounting business in southeast Oklahoma. It wasn't Lucas's financial help and parentlike support but Wayne's own perseverance that had gotten him where he was today. Wayne didn't owe him anything. But how could he make him see?

Lucas swung himself into the truck and stuck the key into the ignition. "It's your show, little brother," he said. "I hope you know what you're doing."

"I know that the best place for Toby is at the marina with you, Lucas. Now there's one more thing. You'll have to wait to tell Susanna. You know how small towns are. If you told her the truth, and someone asked her, you wouldn't want *her* to have to lie—"

"It's okay, Wayne. Forget it. You're in the driver's seat. I won't interfere."

"Susanna, stop fussing over me. I just had to get out of the heat, that's all, and I can just as easily wait for Wayne here. If you want to do something, Little Willy needs a change. Look in the chest in the small bedroom. Lucas always has a big supply of diapers."

Susanna adjusted the cool cloth she'd laid on her sister's forehead. Then she scooped up Willy from the rug in front of Lucas's fireplace where he'd been happily playing with the most accessible objects—his toes.

The diapers were right where Maggie had said they'd be, and to her surprise, she found everything else she needed, including a fresh undershirt and a clean cotton blanket.

"Does Lucas keep him often?" Susanna asked as she returned to the living room.

Maggie laughed. "As often as we let him." She sat up on the couch and then moved to the rocking chair opposite it. "I'm all right," she insisted when Susanna protested. She reached for Little Willy. Susanna hugged the baby close, then passed him to her sister.

Maggie smiled down at the child. "Lucas can't resist his nephew," she said. "But then he was always that way about kids. He'll stop on the street to talk to a five-year-old, when he passes the grown-ups with barely a nod.''

"And then there's Toby," Susanna said.

"Yes, and there've been others. Lucas always seems to know who in town needs a boost, and somehow he quietly sees that they get it." Maggie held the baby against her shoulder, rocking him gently. "Lucas Grant has a tender streak a mile wide."

"I know," Susanna said softly. She avoided Maggie's penetrating look. "Just look at this room. The furniture isn't cold and modern like at Daryl's bachelor friends' apartments."

She trailed her hand along the back of the plump and comfortable paisley sofa. The matching easy chairs beside the fireplace invited curling up with a book. Except there were no books. Susanna wandered over to the wall between the living room and the kitchen. Lucas had no room for books. Floor-to-ceiling shelves were filled with cassette tapes. Their color-coded spines held only numbers without titles. She wondered how he ever found what he was looking for, and glanced around for a catalog.

"What are you going to do about Lucas, Susanna?"

She turned quickly and faced her sister. "*Do* about him? I've already told you, I'm going to keep him at arm's length, make sure there's always somebody else around when we're together, get through this vacation the best that I can—"

"I think you're making a big mistake."

Susanna crossed the room and sank into the couch. "Maggie, I'm good at making mistakes with men. I proved that with Daryl. I'm *not* going to make one with Lucas."

"But you're attracted to him. You can't deny that. And I know he feels the same about you. I can see it every time—"

"Maggie, stop it," Susanna begged. She hugged her arms to her chest, trying to quiet the racing in her heart that thinking of Lucas created. She was *attracted* to him all right, drawn to him past all reason, past all ability to see the truth. Drawn into a make-believe world of her own creation. Maggie would never understand. She'd sized up Wayne, the first man that she'd loved, with her heart *and* her head, and she'd been right on both counts.

"I'm sorry," Maggie said half-heartedly. "I didn't mean to push you."

Susanna couldn't help but laugh. "Not much, you didn't," she said. Then she grew pensive again. "I'm not so sure that Lucas does feel the same about me, Maggie. There are moments when he draws away. Moments when I feel...I don't know...like I don't measure up somehow. He's special—"

"So are you! After all, you *were* the Cicada Princess."

Susanna laughed out loud and tossed a cushion at Maggie. "I have a life of my own in Washington. Even if it's not so rewarding right now, it puts bread on the table and it keeps me busy." *Too busy for romance,* she thought.

"And Lucas has a life here. He cares about Wilamet. You're right about that. You know him better than you think you do. You know that he cares about people, about things that matter."

"Maybe he cares too much."

"So much that you'd end up caring again, too? Caring about faces instead of just causes?"

Susanna sighed. "You have this way, Maggie Grant, of hitting a person's vulnerable spot." She stopped, alarmed. "Maggie?"

"I...I'm okay. Just take Little Willy. I think I'd better lie down again."

Susanna took the drowsy baby and carried him to the cradle, then hurried back to Maggie. Her sister's face still felt warmer than it should.

"There's another alternative, you know," Maggie was saying. "You could throw caution to the wind for the summer and see where it blows you."

Throw caution to the wind? Hadn't she done that already? She'd fallen into Lucas's arms at every opportunity. "Then I'd end up asking for a leave of absence for the fall. End up not wanting to go back at all. I'd never get out of this place."

"You're believing too many of Daddy's old stories," Maggie said. "Wilamet is not so bad. Besides, we could use you. We've got plenty of projects that need a good head." She yawned and snuggled into the sofa. "Life's too short to always be doing the things that you think you should ... instead of ... the things that you care about...."

Maggie had fallen asleep, and Susanna covered her lightly with the quilt from the back of the sofa. Her sister's cheeks felt cooler. Maybe a nap was all she needed. It must be exhausting, being pregnant and taking care of Little Willy, too, all in the middle of the hottest summer on record.

Susanna curled up in the easy chair and leaned her head into its high pillowed back. Even over the hum of the air-conditioner, she could hear the distant rise and fall of the cicada's cadence. Like background music to Maggie's gentle breathing, it lulled her senses.

Supposing she did let go? Let things with Lucas take their natural course. How would she know what she felt, *really* felt, for him if she didn't?

Her heart began to hammer out a warning. *No.* She already knew what she felt. A crazy, helpless, physical abandon whenever he took her in his arms. A recklessness that pushed her out of reality and into a dream. A dream of her own creation. A dream she didn't dare trust, even if she was beginning to trust Lucas.

But Maggie was partly right. When she saw him with Willy, with Toby, with Lonetree, even with his brother, she saw that Lucas had his feet firmly on the ground. He knew what mattered, what was worth caring about. He'd never make foolish mistakes or get carried away by his feelings. He was far too honest for that.

And she wasn't his match. She couldn't pretend that she was, even just for the summer, just for the pleasure....

Susanna yawned, feeling her eyes grow as heavy as her thoughts. She tried to push them away and focus on something more immediate. *Maggie.* Her sister could certainly use some help. And if she ended up needing to stay till the baby came, the senator could send her work to Wilamet. She closed her eyes a moment, imagining it. She could get a modem and rent a computer. Wasn't everybody doing that? It seemed so simple. For a moment everything seemed so simple.

Chapter Six

The sound of Little Willy's jabbering woke her. Susanna stretched lazily. Across the room, Maggie sighed and started to sit up.

"Stay where you are," Susanna ordered. "I'll get him."

The late-afternoon sunbeams streamed in through the bedroom window and fell on the baby's cradle. Little Willy opened and closed his fists, trying to catch them. Susanna picked him up and hugged him. "How come you're so happy, kiddo?" she crooned. "How come you don't fuss like all the babies I've ever known?"

Susanna checked her thought. She'd known exactly two babies, both children of Daryl's friends. And she'd always suspected that they were better than the office stories Daryl brought home. *He* was the one, she thought suddenly, who'd said that children were a bother.

"Do you want something more to drink?" Susanna asked Maggie as she settled Willy on the rug. "I thought I might fix us a pitcher of iced tea."

"What I'd really like," Maggie answered. "Is something to eat. It's nearly five o'clock."

Time for the men to return, Susanna thought with a start. "I've got some hot dogs down at the houseboat," she quickly suggested.

Maggie wrinkled up her nose. "Let's look in Lucas's pantry. The last time he and Wayne were working late and I made dinner, the cupboard was filled with spaghetti sauce. I could use a big bowl of buttered noodles, smothered in marinara. Maybe Lucas has some of that wonderful sausage made over in Krebs."

Maggie was halfway to the kitchen before Susanna could stop her. By the time she'd picked up Little Willy and followed, her sister was pulling mushrooms, peppers and tomatoes out of the refrigerator and talking about adding a salad.

Susanna pushed Maggie into a kitchen chair and dumped the baby in her lap. "You can sit right there and supervise," she ordered.

"I don't have to rest *all* the time," Maggie protested. "Just because the doctor said..." Maggie's voice faded. She ignored Susanna's questioning look and hurried on. "Maybe you'd better make enough spaghetti for Wayne and Lucas. Wayne hates to eat on the road. He says the fast-food places always smell so good that he overeats and then—"

"Maggie, tell me right now. Exactly what did Dr. Gurley say? And when did you see him last?"

Maggie played with Little Willy's hair, pushing it up to a curl on the top.

"Maggie?"

Her sister's fingers stilled. There was no sound in the room except for the hiss of the gas flame beneath the pot of water on the stove. Even Little Willy was quiet, his blue eyes fastened on his mother's face.

"I went in yesterday. Dr. Gurley said so far, so good."

"And?"

Maggie paused, went back to curling Willy's hair and then continued. "Susanna, I want this child. You know the doctor said I'd never get pregnant the first time, what with that infection I had when I was a child. And then I did get pregnant, right away, with Willy, and Wayne and I were so happy. And now it's happened again. If I don't have this baby, there might not be another..." Maggie broke off, her voice tight with held-back emotion.

Susanna went to the back of her sister's chair, leaned down and wrapped her arms around Maggie's shoulders, holding her tightly. Then she lifted Little Willy into his high chair, gave him a spoon to play with and settled down opposite Maggie. She took her sister's hands in her own.

"Does Dr. Gurley think there's a chance you'll lose the baby?"

Maggie nodded, her eyes downcast. "He'll do all he can to prevent it. He's a good doctor. He delivered Willy. He even came out to the house that time when Wayne was sick—"

"Maggie, I know you love Dr. Gurley. He's taken care of us since we were kids. Just trust him. Do everything he advises and try not to worry. Now have you told Wayne?"

Maggie looked at her hands. "Not yet. I keep waiting for the right time. He's been so busy. And he was gone with Lucas by the time I got back from the doctor's office yesterday."

Susanna stood to stir the spaghetti into the boiling water. "Lucas and Wayne spend a lot of time together," she mused.

"It's always been like that, but I've never minded. It's not just that Wayne is Lucas's accountant. They're very close.

Lucas means everything to Wayne. That's part of what I want for Willy—a brother to love and stand beside always, or a sister, who's there for you."

Susanna turned the burner up a notch. She carried the salad ingredients over to the table. Halfway through slicing a tomato, she laid down the knife and looked at her sister. "I haven't done much to help you lately," she said.

"But you were there when I needed you, last year when Willy came. You've always been there when it mattered."

"Maybe it matters now, Maggie. Maybe I could talk to the senator...ask for more leave. Stay around a little longer, to help you out. Heaven knows Mother is too busy with her committees and all her volunteer work. I could help you till the baby is born...." Susanna hesitated.

But Maggie had jumped up from the table and she was hugging her hard. A strong, sure feeling flowed over Susanna. A feeling she knew she could trust. Her place was here with Maggie.

Little Willy banged his spoon on the tray of his high chair, making a terrible racket. The spaghetti was about to boil over. And just at that moment, Lucas opened the kitchen door. The song of the cicadas swelled into the room.

He'd imagined the scene a hundred times. Susanna Foster, cooking in his kitchen, color riding on her high cheekbones, not from anger or embarrassment but just from simple pleasure. Wisps of her dark hair had escaped her braid to feather around her face, framing it and her flashing dark eyes, eyes that widened with warmth when she saw him.

He took off his hat and tossed it on the counter, then ran one hand through his shaggy hair. Wayne came in the door behind him and stepped between them a moment, then headed toward the refrigerator with a case of beer. When Susanna filled his eyes again, feeling, strong and simple and undeniable, poured over Lucas. It was as though a circle that had been nearly complete with Maggie, Willy and Wayne had opened up and let her in.

"Looks like we're home just in time for supper," Wayne said. He shoved the last of the beer in the refrigerator and crossed the room. After a tug at Willy's ear and an affectionate hug for Susanna, Wayne pulled Maggie into his arms and kissed her soundly on the nose.

"What's all the excitement?" he asked, turning to scoop Little Willy up in his arms. He passed the baby to Lucas, who held him so high he began to squeal.

"Oh, Wayne, I'm so happy," Maggie said. "Susanna's going to try to stay for a while. She's going to ask for more time, so she can stay here and help me..." Maggie hesitated, her eyes bright.

"That's great, Susanna," Wayne said. "Willy's gotten to be a handful, and Maggie's been pretty worn out lately."

The air in the room held expectancy. All their eyes were on Susanna. Something had been left unspoken, everyone knew it. Beside her, almost imperceptibly, Maggie shook her head.

"I...I'm missing all of Little Willy's firsts," Susanna said. "Soon he'll be walking, and talking. I want to watch my nephew's development. Washington can wait."

She'd moved nearer to Lucas and the baby as she spoke. Willy reached down and grabbed for her braid. Lucas laughed as the baby tried to put the end of it into his mouth. The warmth of his breath brushed down her upturned cheek. His clear, blue eyes held an open question. It matched the question she was asking herself. *Was she staying, even partly, because of him?*

Behind her, the spaghetti started to sputter. Susanna turned back to the stove.

"Did Toby and Lonetree get something to eat?" Maggie asked as they settled around the table.

"Lonetree wasn't hungry," Lucas said.

Susanna tensed as she slid into her chair. "Did something go wrong at the hospital?"

Lucas watched her a moment before he spoke, weighing her almost palpable concern. "Nothing bad happened at the hospital," he said. "One of the doctors took Lonetree out to lunch. They went to some barbecue place and overdid it, that's all."

Relieved, Susanna picked up her fork and started on her salad. "What did he say he found out about artificial limbs?"

"Not much. He was quiet most of the way home. It seems, midway through the meal, the doctor admitted he was wearing an artificial arm and also an artificial leg. Lonetree hadn't noticed. Then they got to talking about the war."

Everyone was silent for a moment. Then Maggie spoke. "It's easy for us to forget," she said. "The Vietnam war was so far away and so long ago."

Lucas nodded. "I guess Lonetree's afraid that if we do forget, we might have to worry about another one. One that could take Willy, a lot of Willys, away from us."

The thought of losing Willy was more than Susanna could manage. She pushed it down the only way she knew how. "Vietnam vets gave enough for their country," she snapped. "They shouldn't have to carry the burden of *our* responsibility, too. Lonetree's got potential. The government has any number of programs that could help him. Seeing a man with a handicap worse than his own who was able to go through medical school must have—"

"Must have made him ashamed of what he does for a living? I hope not." Lucas jabbed his fork into his spaghetti.

"I didn't mean it that way—"

"Susanna, there's more to Lonetree's situation than shows on the surface."

She glared at him. His sandy eyebrows were knit in frustration, and creases lined his forehead. He wanted her to understand, she knew. But why couldn't he see her side of it?

"And there's more to life than just accepting your handicap and never trying to overcome it," she argued.

Lucas stopped, his fork halfway to his mouth, and looked at her. Wayne coughed and held up his glass. Lucas pushed back from the table and began to pour the wine.

"Speaking of overcoming handicaps," Wayne said, "Toby actually lowered himself to carry-out pizza."

"He must have been too tired to cook," Maggie said, picking up on Wayne's effort to change the subject.

Wayne groaned. "How anybody can stand that stuff—"

"You're just spoiled by my fresh dough," Maggie said. She covered her glass when Lucas offered to fill it with wine. "How did the meeting at the agency go?" she asked him.

He took so long answering that Susanna thought he was going to start arguing about Toby's handicap, too. She saw him glance at Wayne. His brother quickly looked away. "Fine," Lucas muttered. "It went just fine."

"Lucas always comes back from the social-services agency in the blackest of moods," Maggie said. "But it isn't his fault. You wouldn't believe the red tape."

"If I'd known what we were going to have to go through every month, I'd have thought twice about taking Toby in," Lucas said.

"No, you wouldn't," Wayne said. "You'd have taken him even if the red tape had been sticky on both sides."

Lucas shrugged without responding and continued pouring. Susanna watched her glass fill up and thought of Maggie's words. Lucas knew what mattered, and he had more than a streak of tenderness. She'd been dead wrong to suggest that he only cared about the marina.

"Now that the state is involved," Wayne continued, "we just have to live with it. Toby's mother had already turned him over to one of your government programs, Susanna. The only way to get him out is to take over legal guardianship. And the only way to do that, as we learned today, is to get Toby a tutor."

"A *tutor*?" Susanna glanced at Lucas, hoping that he'd admit she'd been right about formal education for Toby.

"The social worker thinks he could be learning more," Lucas said grudgingly. "She wants him to have that chance."

"She flat out demanded it," Wayne added. "It's that or send him south to that group home, just because they've got some special classes."

"Send him south?" Susanna was astonished. "But that would be cruel," she insisted. "How could anyone think that Toby would be better off away from people who care about him, away from the only normal situation he's ever known? Surely the social-service policies put a higher priority on the quality of life. They can't just take Toby away because someone says he isn't learning enough. I don't see—"

"Whoa! I didn't say we were giving in," Wayne said. "Lucas has no intention of seeing Toby sent away." Wayne nodded to his brother to pick up the story, but Lucas was staring hard at Susanna.

She'd taken up Toby's cause again. Lucas listened to her voice as it rose by the minute. He grinned. She was talking about *Toby*. Talking about him as a person, not just a member of mentally retarded America. He wondered if she realized the difference between that and her earlier comments. He reached out and placed a steadying hand on Susanna's clenched fist.

"It's going to be hard, that's all," Lucas said gently. "Hard to find somebody willing to start from scratch with a retarded, older teenager."

Susanna stared at Lucas a moment, puzzled yet feeling herself quiet at his accepting tone. Toby was the one who mattered. At least they agreed about that.

An idea formed. Susanna's eyes locked on her sister's. "What about Mother?"

"Eleanor?" Wayne was drowning his spaghetti in Parmesan. Maggie reached over and gently removed the shaker. "I can't see your mother tutoring Toby," Wayne said. "Lately she's been more of an organizer than a volunteer."

Like me and Daddy, Susanna thought. If she was best at shaping policy and felt more at home when the cause was public, she had her father's example to thank for it. But that had never been Eleanor Foster's way. Why had her mother changed?

"Wayne's right," Maggie added. "Mother has plenty of background, but she's long sworn off getting personally involved."

Susanna stared at her sister. "You can't be serious. I can't imagine Mother living without the close attachments she had as a teacher."

Maggie got up from the table and carried her wineglass to the sink. "She's doing it, but she's bored to death. The literacy center is just getting started. All she does is watch the phone."

"Lucas or one of the guides could take Toby in three times a week or so," Wayne said. "She could work with him right at the center."

Maggie filled her glass with water and carried it back to the table. She took a sip before she spoke. "It won't be easy to get her to do it. But Mother just might be willing to strike a bargain." Maggie eyed Susanna. "There's something she needs."

Susanna groaned. "You might as well tell me, Maggie Grant. What does Mother want me to do?"

Maggie laid down her fork and took a deep breath. "She was fit to be tied when she dropped me off at the lake this morning. She had to go back to Tulsa again to attend more meetings, one tonight and one tomorrow morning. She says they're pointless. She wants to put you to work the minute you get back to town. Something about government funding for the center."

Susanna listened with interest. Maggie met her eyes and hurried on.

"She's got tons of forms and no idea how to fill them out. And she's got something cooked up with Bobby Joe Richardson, too."

Lucas stopped eating and stared across the table at Maggie. "B. J. Richardson?" The tangle of spaghetti that he'd just wound around his fork dropped off of it and plopped back onto his plate. Maggie raised one eyebrow.

Quickly Lucas lifted his wineglass. "Here's to *government funding*," he said. "May we be spared the agony."

"You've been very quiet," Lucas said later as he followed Susanna down the path to the houseboat. He lengthened his stride to keep her hurried footsteps within the beam of his flashlight.

"I couldn't see the use of joining the discussion when it turned to politics," she said over her shoulder. "Ever since urban renewal, half the people in Wilamet have been trying to get additional government funding. The other half keep sabotaging their efforts."

"I guess I made it pretty clear which half I belong to," Lucas said. "As far as I'm concerned, we can do without the government's money *and* its control."

"And you know darn well that I'm on the other side. Or I would be if I lived here. But I don't. So I'm trying to keep my opinions to myself."

"You're on the other side because of your job?"

She slowed to catch her breath before she answered. "Yes and no. I've worked on a lot of policies that had government funding attached. Some of them were very worthwhile."

"*Some* of them?"

"*Most* of them."

"Did you *care* about them, Susanna?"

The deprecating emphasis he gave the word made her turn on her heels and confront him. At her sudden stop, he caught her arm to keep from running into her. His grip was firm, forcing her gaze to meet his.

There was an immediate softening around his eyes that cooled her irritation at his words. "Of course I *care*," she said. "I wouldn't be doing what I do if I didn't."

His grip loosened, but he didn't let go of her arm. He seemed to struggle with a need to explain something. Suddenly she thought she knew what it was.

"Lucas, I'm sorry I said what I did before you left for Oklahoma City. I know now that you care about lots of things more than you care about the marina."

"And some things matter more to you than your job."

"Yes," she said softly.

"Then we aren't on opposite sides in everything."

He was standing so close to her that she could feel the warm, humid air tremble at his words. A rivulet of perspiration trickled down her temple. She fumbled in the pocket of her shorts for a tissue.

"Has running from me made you warm?"

"I wasn't running from you. I just don't want to keep Maggie and Wayne waiting. And it's past Willy's bedtime."

"Why go at all? You've got another night on the week you insisted paying me for. In fact, you've got the rest of the summer—"

"That's not settled yet," she snapped. "I'm merely considering taking some extra time. And going back into Wilamet tonight will save Wayne and Maggie another trip out to the lake. Besides, my sister needs me."

His grip on her arm tightened again, ever so slightly. His thumb moved back and forth, smoothing her skin. "And what do *you* need, Susanna?" he asked her.

His blue eyes had softened to pewter in the moonlight, and his hair was streaked with silver. She wanted to touch it, make sure it was real.

"It's too late to talk," she murmured. "And besides, the cicadas are making so much noise tonight, we'd have to shout to hear each other."

As if the insects had heard her, they suddenly hushed. Susanna smiled wryly. If she didn't know better, she'd think it was some sort of conspiracy.

"Talking wasn't exactly what I had in mind," he said.

The hand that held her arm slipped around her back, while the other one guided her waist as Lucas drew her into his arms. He held her body as he'd held her arm, loosely, gently, and yet with a surety that made escape totally out of the question. Not that she wanted to get away.

For one brief moment, Susanna fought what she was feeling. She clung to the thought of hurrying back to the cabin and the safety of too many people, too many eyes. And then the song of the cicadas crescendoed and closed in around them.

His first kiss settled behind her ear and hovered there. His touch seemed almost cooling as he slid his hand under her braid to cradle her head. Her hands moved up the firmness of his chest to his shoulders, drawing him closer, until, against her breast, Susanna felt his heartbeat quicken.

Then his mouth covered hers. First cool, then warmer, and finally scalding hot, his kiss laid siege to her mouth. Susanna surrendered any thought of running away, in fact any thought at all, and lost herself in Lucas's embrace.

He kissed her, again and again, as though trying to make up for all those years they had lost. And Susanna responded, reaching across time to him with the pent-up hunger of both the girl she'd been and the woman she had become.

When they were breathless with the effort, his kiss moved back to explore her ear, then traveled down her neck to her collarbone and crossed it to the throbbing hollow of her throat. Lingering there, he tasted the salty dampness of her skin.

But it wasn't enough, not nearly enough. His mouth moved back to hers. Then his palms nudged at the thin straps of her T-shirt, sliding them down her shoulders. His large hands trembled and then gentled as he realized that she wore nothing underneath.

She sighed and pulled him closer. His mouth traced tender circles over the curve of her breast, drifting lower. She buried her face in his thick, soft hair.

Her stomach tensed exquisitely, then tightened. Ripples of passion coursed through her body, and a small, soft moan slid out of her lips. It was merely a whisper of the deeper cry that her body was dying to utter.

But the sound spoke like a warning in her ears. She stiffened. She fought submission, not just to Lucas, but to her own desire.

"This...isn't...going...to work," she said raggedly.

His kisses stopped, and his caressing hands grew still. Susanna stepped back out of his arms and straightened her clothes.

"I...have to get my things," she said. "Maggie and Wayne are waiting."

He didn't move from the middle of the path. When she tried to pass him, he blocked her way. He had no idea what to say to her, no idea how to ask her to stay with him when only another day was all he had to offer. And so for a moment, Lucas said nothing.

"I've put off seeing Mother too long," she said. "It's best if I'm there waiting when she gets back from Tulsa. Maggie needs help with little Willy, and there are some reports that I promised to—"

"Susanna?" The sound of urgency mixed with longing in his voice jarred a secret corner of her heart.

She stared at him. Time stood still and then spun backward. "You said my name just that way, thirteen years ago. That day in the street, after my father's victory parade. I've never forgotten."

She'd hung on to the sound of her name on his lips and the bittersweet memory of leaving him. And she'd built a storybook romance around it. Now it was drawing her back, like an invisible ribbon of the strongest silk, marking the page where their story had ended.

"I didn't want you to leave."

"I had no choice. None of us did, in the face of Senator William Foster's exuberant desire to serve his country."

"And now?

The song of the cicadas rose and wrapped around them. She was home, home where it was safe. Home with a man she could trust. She let Lucas cradle her gently in his arms.

"Let's take it a day at a time," he whispered.

Hadn't she vowed to do just that? And wasn't that how one lived in Oklahoma? One day at a time. Patient with the summer heat, knowing it would cool in time. Grateful for the oil when it was there, welcoming the peacefulness when it was gone. You forgave the droughts, accepted the rains and cherished everything, even the return of the cicadas. How could she have forgotten? And yet . . .

"I've been away a long time, Lucas. It's not that simple. I don't belong here anymore. I can't go back to believing—"

"Let it be simple. Just for tonight."

Susanna trembled, but Lucas tightened his arms around her until she stilled. "Yes," she whispered, "let it be simple."

If she was going to figure out where her life was headed, it was going to happen here, Susanna thought as they headed up the path. Maybe it would happen tonight, maybe tomorrow, maybe out there on the lake. When the answer came, she didn't want to miss it. Especially if it included Lucas.

Wayne had the car engine running when Susanna and Lucas reached the cabin.

"I've changed my mind," Susanna said. "I might as well stay till tomorrow."

She hugged Little Willy and kissed his sweet-smelling cheek. Then she passed the sleepy baby into the car to her sister. She tried to ignore Maggie's mischievous look and Wayne's more skeptical one.

"Lucas can drive me in around noon tomorrow. Mother won't be back from Tulsa till then. I can get one more night of peace. And tomorrow I'll talk to Toby. I'll have a better idea of how to approach Mother about the tutoring."

Wayne tapped his fingers on the steering wheel. "Are you sure you don't want—"

"She's sure," Maggie interrupted her husband.

Susanna thought Wayne would never stop scrutinizing, first her and then Lucas, but finally, after a nudge from Maggie, he put the car in gear and headed it down the road. Susanna and Lucas stood on the porch, watching the car disappear.

Then his hand reached for hers. She gave it, hesitantly, and let herself be turned to meet his embrace. His touch trailed lazily over her back, down to the slimness of her waist. He drew her closer.

She sighed and slackened against him, her own hands traveling to the back of his neck, threading into his hair. His head began to bend toward hers, his warm breath sweeping down her upturned face.

When their lips met, the force of her pent-up desire tore through Susanna, a jagged streak of raw sexuality. Its force both amazed and frightened her. She tensed, ever so slightly, and drew back. She needed time.

"Let's go for a swim," she whispered. Her heart was hammering in her chest.

Above them a summer moon drifted in and out of the clouds. Lucas looked up at it and smiled, then kissed the top of her hair. "Sounds like a good idea," he said.

"We can swim off my houseboat pier. I brought a suit...."

His arms tightened around her waist. "Do you really need a bathing suit?" he whispered into her hair.

By the time they reached the small dock alongside her houseboat, Susanna's heart was thundering in her breast. But suddenly Lucas pressed her hand, stopped cold and hushed her.

"There's someone on board," he whispered.

She held her breath. The undulating song of the cicadas fell for a moment. Before it crescendoed again, she heard a sound. Someone was crying.

"It's Toby," she said.

They found him sitting on the edge of the deck, his thin arms hugging his drawn-up knees. When he saw them, his shoulders shook with the effort to hold back tears.

"Toby, what *is* it?" she asked him, dropping to her knees beside the young man.

He swallowed and brushed a hand across his cheek. "Lucas took me to visit my mother. She gave me this."

She took the cedar box Toby handed her and lifted the lid. The book inside had a worn leather cover, soft to her touch. Turning toward the dim light she'd left on in the houseboat, she read the faded gold imprint.

"It's a Bible," she said to Lucas. Her tone held a question.

Lucas knew its answer immediately. He knew from experience what the gift of a family Bible meant. He stooped down to join them, his large hand covering Susanna's smaller one where it rested on Toby's shoulder.

His voice sounded deep and resonant, despite his struggle with the words that he knew the young man needed to hear. "Your mother loves you, Toby, you know that. Whatever happens to her, she'll still go on loving you. Some things last forever."

"But lots of things don't," Toby choked out the words.

Lucas tightened his grip on Toby's shoulder. "That's right. That's part of living. That's why it's so important that we take good care of what we have, of those we love, for as long as we have them."

Feeling, pure and simple and true, washed over Susanna. Feeling deeper than anything she'd ever known. Lucas had held her body and awakened a passion she hadn't known she was capable of. She'd been afraid to trust it. Afraid it would betray her and leave her playing the fool again. But now, here in the moonlight as they knelt over Toby, Lucas was holding her heart again. Holding it, warming it, gaining her trust, as he had so many times before, with nothing more than the honesty of simple words.

Toby rubbed his eyes with his fists and reached for his Bible. "I came down to ask you to read me a story," he said to her. "My mother always reads me stories."

"Come on in," Susanna said. "We'll read till the cows come home if you want to." She glanced at Lucas, sure that he would support her offer, but his eyes were fastened on Toby.

Once they'd settled inside, the young man knew exactly which stories he wanted to hear. He found them by the pictures. While she read, he studied them, making her turn back again and again.

When she had a chance to look up, she saw the soft light pouring across the table on Lucas. The pain that had washed off Toby's face seemed to have gathered in his, along with the fatigue of his trip.

"Why don't you go on back to the cabin?" she suggested gently. "You must be exhausted. We can...swim some other time."

"Sure," he answered. He kissed her lightly on the top of her head and touched Toby's shoulder one more time. Then alone with his thoughts, he headed up the path to his cabin.

He hadn't known. Or maybe he hadn't wanted to know. In either case, it had never occurred to him that Toby's mother had read to him. A distant memory washed over Lucas...winter evenings...a fire on the hearth...his mother reading stories to his father...and to him. Lucas shrugged. It had been a long time ago.

It was almost eleven by the time Lucas finished with his morning charter. Susanna was waiting by the marina with her bags. On the trip into Wilamet, he stuck to the back roads, buying time. Still, he'd pulled the truck to a stop in front of her mother's house before he'd said what was on his mind.

"I want to thank you for what you did for Toby last night."

"But it's not what *I* did for him. That's what I've been trying to tell you ever since we left the lake. Reading to Toby made me feel great—better than lots of other things I've done that supposedly had a bigger impact."

"Sure. I'm glad." He swung himself out of the truck, slammed the door a little too hard and grabbed her bags from the back. He headed up the walk to the porch.

Susanna followed. "What's the matter, Lucas?" she asked him when they reached the porch. "If it's about last night, about our missed swim..."

"No." Lucas set her gear down at the door and took off his hat to stand beside it. He started to toss it on one of the white wicker porch chairs, then noticed the fancy cushion and didn't. He put his hat back on his head and tipped it low over his eyes, then hooked his thumbs in the pockets of his jeans.

He'd been going to tell her that she'd been right all along. That those two different worlds were too far apart. He'd planned to just let it go at that, then walk away.

He'd been kidding himself. He knew it now. He thought he'd adjusted to being illiterate. Thought it didn't matter. But it mattered all right, a hell of a lot. It made the future just a series of limits that got closer and closer till they shut him out.

So why couldn't he say it? And if he couldn't, why the hell didn't he just get in his truck and leave? *He wanted her back at the lake, that's why.* Not tonight, not tomorrow. *Right now—*

"I think I left my toothbrush," Susanna said as she stood. She'd been fidgeting with her bags, halfheartedly checking to see if she'd gotten everything.

He took her by the shoulders and lightly ran his hands down her arms. "When you get tired of things in town," he said, "and you want to get away for a while, keep in mind that the small houseboat is yours for the summer. I'm not going to rent it to anyone else."

"Lucas..."

He tightened his grip on her wrists to quiet her. Susanna sighed. Of all the things she thought she knew about Lucas

Grant, there was one thing she was sure of. He was generally flexible, sometimes too much so, but when he made up his mind, he didn't negotiate. But just what *had* he decided? Whatever it was had put some distance between them. A distance mocked by the shrinking space between their lips.

He was about to kiss her when Eleanor Foster's car turned into the driveway. Lucas touched his hat to tell Susanna goodbye and was down the walk and into his truck in half a minute. He'd be damned if he'd let Eleanor catch him courting her high-class daughter, looking like something the cat had dragged in. *Courting* her daughter? What the hell was he thinking?

DISCOVER FREE BOOKS

& FREE GIFTS

From Silhouette

S	D	A	V	R	Y	B	X	N	M
G	I	F	T	N	C	A	S	P	Y
Z	D	L	N	B	U	L	T	R	S
R	T	N	H	N	E	F	T	A	T
D	H	I	A	O	V	K	D	M	E
N	W	E	K	H	U	O	W	S	R
O	C	T	M	U	T	E	D	D	Y
I	L	P	F	L	P	B	T	I	E
P	E	A	J	S	M	H	I	T	P
S	E	N	S	A	T	I	O	N	E

As a special introduction to Silhouette Sensation we will send you:

4 FREE SILHOUETTE SENSATIONS

plus a

FREE TEDDY

and

MYSTERY GIFT

when you return this card. But first - just for fun - see if you can find and circle five hidden words in the puzzle.

THE HIDDEN WORDS ARE:

SILHOUETTE • SENSATION
TEDDY • MYSTERY • GIFT

Now turn over to claim your
FREE
BOOKS & GIFTS

FREE BOOKS CERTIFICATE

YES! please send me FREE and without obligation, four specially selected **Silhouette Sensation romances**, together with my FREE teddy and mystery gift. Please also reserve a Reader Service Subscription for me. If I decide to subscribe, I shall receive 4 superb Sensations every month for just £6.60, post and packing FREE. If I decide not to subscribe I shall write to you within 10 days. The FREE books and gifts will be mine to keep in any case. I understand that I am under no obligation whatsoever. I can cancel or suspend my subscription at any time simply by writing to you.

FREE TEDDY

MYSTERY GIFT

Mr/Mrs/Miss _____
(Please write in block capitals)

Address _____

_____ Postcode _____

Signature _____
I am over the age of 18.

3S1SS

Reader Service
FREEPOST
P.O. Box 236
Croydon
CR9 9EL

NO STAMP NEEDED

Chapter Seven

Eleanor Foster pulled her car to a neat stop in the exact center of the driveway, then reached for the door and got out.

"I suppose Lucas had to get back to his fishing," she called out cheerfully to her daughter.

Susanna gave up staring after the disappearing truck and went out to meet her mother.

"Fishing is his job, of course," the small woman chattered on. "And yours is helping to run things in *our nation's capital*. What are you doing home a month early, dear?"

The soft silver page boy swept her face as Susanna bent her cheek to her mother's. The familiar scent of *L'Air du Temps* lingered as she drew back.

"The senator was homesick, and *our nation's capitol*, as you always insist on calling it, is overrun with tourists. The air in Wilamet may be just as hot and humid, but at least we don't have to fight for it."

Eleanor laughed gently. "It's good to see you, baby. You've cut your hair!"

Susanna shrugged and lowered her eyes. "It goes with being newly divorced, Mother. The hairdresser told me."

Eleanor started to touch her daughter's arm, then hesitated and drew back. "At least you got a decent cut," she said lightly. "Georgetown?"

Susanna nodded. "Sorry I'm late. Did you just get back from Tulsa?"

"Oh, no," Eleanor answered. "I left first thing this morning. I've checked in at the center and read all the mail, and I'm ready to spend the entire afternoon with you. Now what is this Maggie's been telling me about you and Lucas Grant?" She linked her arm in her daughter's and started up the walk.

"Maggie's got such an imagination—"

"Baby, don't fib. You know you were standing *very* close to Wayne's brother when I drove up to the house. I hope that whatever it was you were saying was no indication you're thinking of—"

"Mother, I'm twenty-seven years old. I've been out on my own, had a job, been married and divorced. I'm *not* a baby."

Eleanor stopped, reached up and touched her daughter's cheek affectionately. "Oh, sweetie, you're so darn sensitive. Now hurry and get your shower. Maggie's got fresh yeast rolls and chicken salad for lunch, and we've got appointments with Della at two."

Her mother blew her a kiss at the door, then gave Susanna that little wave that meant the conversation was over but not forgotten.

Why hadn't she stayed out at the lake? The air was cooler and lighter there. So were the questions. Her mother had tried to ask a big one. Susanna wasn't sure how to answer it.

Last night she'd been so sure of her feelings. Sure enough to let go and follow wherever they led. But now...

It was hot, that was all, and terribly humid. She was back in the house that had been home to four generations of Fosters. Back where her mother still sailed through life believing that everything would work out beautifully. When it didn't, it was only because someone hadn't listened to her advice or hadn't tried hard enough to follow it.... And Lucas had been distant.

Inside the door, Susanna kicked off her sandals and then stood looking down at them. She'd thought she'd stopped following her mother's rules ten years ago. Now, being home had made her heed them again. If she wasn't careful, she'd soon be performing all the other little routines she'd fought so hard to leave behind.

In her room at the top of the stairs, Susanna dropped her books and her bag on the bed and glanced in the mirror over her dresser. The oval glass in a golden oak frame with carved-out daisies all around was the same mirror she'd had when she was a teenager. Eastlake, her mother had called it, antique but not too expensive. It went with the white eyelet curtains and the matching spread that still covered her bed.

Other mothers made sewing rooms out of their daughter's bedrooms as soon as they went off to college. Not Eleanor Foster. It was Maggie and Wayne's house now, and Eleanor had insisted that Maggie do over the house from top to bottom when they married. All except for Susanna's old room. Her mother had suggested that they keep that room ready and waiting—a contradiction, Susanna thought, since all she'd ever wanted was to send her daughter back to *our nation's capitol*.

"There you are," Eleanor crowed. "Come and sit down by me, dear. Maggie's got everything under control. Now look at this article I've been reading in the *Wilamet News*.

Is it really true that drugs and all those awful things are taking over even *our nation's capitol*?'' She bent back over the paper.

Susanna grimaced. From across the kitchen, Maggie shot her a stern look of warning. Her sister was right. Their mother would never believe that the capital city had its seamier side. So why upset her?

"Washington's not quite like it was when we were there with Daddy," she said as nonchalantly as she could. She smiled at her sister and passed her mother the basket of fresh-baked rolls. But Eleanor ignored them.

"Aren't they *doing* something about it? Aren't they passing some laws or setting up a special committee or something?"

Susanna buttered a roll for her mother and placed it on the edge of her plate, all the while thinking of how she could answer. Eleanor Foster seldom knit her brows. But when she did, both she and Maggie took her seriously.

"It's a very big problem," she said. "And I guess, sometimes, a new law isn't the answer."

In a rush, Susanna remembered Lucas's words when she'd protested the fisherman's treatment of Toby. *There's no law on earth that will prevent the kind of ignorance . . .*

Little Willy began to reach for the basket of yeast rolls. In a moment, Eleanor was fussing over him, buttering him little tidbits, the newspaper story forgotten.

"He's such a good boy, Susanna. And Maggie's a wonderful mother. Much better than I ever was."

Susanna looked up in surprise at the wistful tone in her mother's voice, but Maggie shot her another quieting glance.

"Perhaps you'd better finish your lunch, Mother," Maggie said gently. "Della called back. She really needs the two of you there by one-thirty."

* * *

Susanna matched her mother's hurried pace down the steaming sidewalk. "Why did you make an appointment for me, Mother? I just had my hair cut."

"But, dear, how was I supposed to know that? I didn't even *see* you before Maggie whisked you away." Eleanor dabbed at her temples with a white linen handkerchief, avoiding Susanna's eyes. "And you always come home looking all harried and tired. I thought a good do from Della would perk you up."

Susanna stopped in the middle of the sidewalk. "All right, Mother, who are you showing me off to this afternoon? Is it the book club or the retired teachers' association or what?"

Eleanor pursed her lips and pushed her daughter up the walk to Della's Delightful Hairdos. "I'm not showing you off, dear. My, what a thing to say. I've just arranged a little gathering at the club this evening. I knew you'd want to look your best. After all week on the lake, without even a shower in your houseboat . . . I do declare, I can't imagine why you wanted to stay out there with all those bugs."

Susanna thought of Lucas and felt a blush creep up her cheeks. "There were showers at the campground, and I enjoyed the peace and quiet, and I've never minded the sound of the cicadas." She stopped for breath.

Eleanor shivered and sidestepped a careering insect. It was close to the height of the mating season, and the fat bugs seemed to be everywhere. "It's all that research you did thirteen years ago. You've been brainwashed into believing the best about these creatures."

Susanna thought of the blanket of privacy the singing cicadas had spread at the lake every time Lucas had taken her in his arms. Deep in the memory, she almost missed the step up to the door of the beauty shop. Her mother caught her arm.

"Who's going to be at the club?" she asked to avoid explaining her misstep. Before she'd gotten her mother's answer, Della Dickers was pulling her into the shop.

"Haven't seen you around these parts in a blessed month of Sundays, Susanna Foster. Sit right down, and let's get you all fixed up. Your mama's gonna get you smack dab in the middle of that campaign, so you'd better do her proud."

"What campaign?" Susanna asked to the empty space left as Della darted by.

The hairdresser had a reputation for working as fast as she talked, and in two minutes flat she had Susanna's head under the faucet. The sound of rushing water blurred her conversation. She caught just snatches of Della's chatter with her mother when the hairdresser wrapped her head in a towel.

"And Bobby Joe Richardson is hinting he'll provide one of those big new Chevy trucks," Eleanor was saying. Della's animated answer was lost in the sound of the blow dryer.

Susanna gave up and closed her eyes. If Bobby Joe Richardson was going to be at the "little gathering," she was going to get suddenly, violently ill. Hairdo or no, Eleanor Foster could have her meeting without her daughter.

"I'm simply not going if B. J. Richardson is," she said an hour later, on the sidewalk outside the beauty shop.

"Oh, don't be silly, Susanna. You're both all grown up now. Bobby Joe Richardson has been active on most of the major Wilamet projects. With your government know-how and his ability to work with the businessmen, the new literacy center is a shoo-in."

"Mother, you *know* B.J. has always been after me. And ever since he hung up that funeral wreath and closed his dealership the day of my wedding, the whole town knows it, too." Susanna strode along the sidewalk, two steps ahead of her mother. "I still can't believe that the *Wilamet News* actually put that in the paper."

"It did seem a trifle out of place at the end of the story about your wedding. But, of course, Bobby Joe's brother owns the paper. Even then, it's not like the whole town's on his side."

Susanna stopped in the middle of the sidewalk and turned to face her mother. "But can't you see? I'm divorced now. It's like he'd be saying 'I told you so.' Besides, I'm just not interested...he's so pushy...he's not like..." Susanna swallowed the end of her sentence.

Eleanor lifted a tiny corner of one eyebrow, then tucked it down and patted her daughter's arm. "Maggie told me that nonsense about your discouragement with men, Susanna. Is your marriage really over, dear? Isn't there any hope? Maybe if you tried again with Daryl—"

"Mother, there are lots of things you didn't know about my life with Daryl. Things that made it impossible for us to live together. But apart from that, there was never any real feeling. Not like..." *Not like with Lucas?* She'd almost said it out loud. "Believe me, Mother," she hurriedly added, "it isn't *worth* trying again with Daryl."

Eleanor bit the bottom of her lip. Then she looked straight at her daughter. "I'm sorry, Susanna. I'm sorry I ever gave Daryl Dobson your Washington phone number."

"*You're* sorry?" Susanna stood staring in disbelief as her mother hurried down the sidewalk. She could *never* remember Eleanor admitting that interfering in her daughter's life had been a mistake. Shaking her head, Susanna started after her mother, toward the row of shops that marked the beginning of Wilamet's small downtown.

"I hope you've brought something suitable to wear tonight," her mother said. "You know how fussy the club can be."

"Fussy? The club enforces the dress code only when there's something special going on. Is there, by any remote chance, going to be a dance band there tonight?"

Once again, her mother conveniently didn't have time to answer. But this time, it was for a reason that Susanna welcomed. As they rounded the corner and passed in front of Murphy's Hardware, Lucas Grant was coming down the steps.

He slung the bag of cement mix he'd been carrying on his shoulder down to the sidewalk, hastily brushed off his hands and took off his hat. Beneath it, his hair seemed twice as shaggy and sun streaked as she'd remembered it. Susanna thought of how it had felt beneath her fingers, thick, yet surprisingly soft. Over the top of her mother's diminutive form, she met his eyes. She felt herself color, but she didn't look away.

His gaze swept down her face, taking in the transformation. A brush of curls pinned up the back of her neck and replaced the braid. And a yellow sundress covered the long legs he'd gotten used to seeing below her shorts. Like most of the women in Wilamet, she probably wouldn't be caught dead uptown in anything else but a dress. Already she looked part and parcel of civilization. Except for the color riding on her cheekbones.

"Lucas, I want to thank you so much for taking care of Susanna last week. She always comes back from Washington so weary. Apparently a week at the lake was just the thing to relax her." Eleanor paused for a breath, then hurried on. "Are you planning to visit Wayne? He was just arriving for lunch as we finished. Why don't you stop in?"

Eleanor slowly but surely pulled her daughter down the sidewalk as she spoke. "We're off to shop for something nice to wear to the club tonight. We'll start with that new boutique on Main. Come along, dear."

Susanna watched Lucas's mouth turn up in a wry smile as her mother pulled her away. He replaced his hat and tipped it low, over his eyes. As he lifted the bag back to his shoulder, her throat caught at the way the muscles in his arms flexed beneath the rolled sleeves of his shirt. Those arms had held her just hours ago.

He touched his hand to his hat, saluting her, and headed toward the truck.

Susanna had tried to hurry her mother through shopping, hoping that Lucas would still be there by the time they'd finished, but when they finally turned up the walk, his truck was nowhere in sight.

Maggie settled them at the kitchen table with tall glasses of iced tea. "The first word out of Willy's mouth is going to be 'uncle,'" she said. "Lucas brought him another one of those little toy boats that he carves. Willy wouldn't take his nap without it."

"He's spoiling that baby," Eleanor protested. But her affectionate tone contradicted her critical words and made Susanna wonder if her mother felt softer toward Lucas than her earlier effort to avoid him had indicated? Or was it that anyone was welcome to spoil her only grandchild? She settled on the latter explanation.

"Have you two talked about Toby yet?" Maggie asked.

"I couldn't get a word in edgewise," Susanna answered. "Mother was either filling me in on Willy's latest accomplishments or making not so subtle suggestions about what she wants me to say at her meeting."

Eleanor took small sips from her iced tea. "But you can help the committee so much, Susanna. You know how those men are when it comes to fund-raising. They'll get all engrossed in their games and raffles and forget the whole purpose of the project. *You* have the expertise—"

"Have you met Toby, Mother?" Susanna interrupted impatiently.

"Toby? Lucas's retarded ward?" Eleanor paused to stir her tea. "I can't for the life of me imagine how anyone could take on such a heavy responsibility."

"Lucas doesn't see it as just a responsibility. There's something special between him and Toby. It's his wonderfully sensitive way of..." Susanna's voice trailed off at Maggie's teasing look and her mother's lightly veiled, skeptical one.

"And there's something almost refreshing about Toby," she hurried on. "He's down to earth."

Maggie set her glass on the table and settled herself into a chair beside her sister. "Wayne and Lucas were wondering if you'd be willing to tutor Toby, Mother. Apparently his social worker thinks he needs more stimulation."

Eleanor picked up her napkin, folded it carefully into quarters, then laid it down again. "Maggie, I retired early to leave all that behind me. You know I don't—that is, I haven't tried in some time...to help individual students. And, besides, I'm busy getting the literacy center off the ground. Wilamet needs a place where all those adults can come for help...the ones who've been left out somewhere along the way."

Eleanor's chin began to tremble, and Maggie's voice softened. "You know that's not the whole story, Mother. You've taken a bit of a detour, that's all. It's high time you talked about it."

Susanna leaned forward and placed a hand over Eleanor's. In spite of her mother's invariably cheerful face, Susanna knew that, like Maggie's ability to change the subject, Eleanor's demeanor was sometimes a cover for deeper pain. "Mother, what is it?" she asked.

Eleanor didn't answer. She kept folding and refolding her napkin, blotting at the circle of moisture that had seeped into the kitchen tablecloth.

"Mother thinks she's directly responsible for the fact that so many adults in Wilamet either can't read at all or read so poorly that they are functionally illiterate."

Susanna drew back. "Mother, you can't be serious."

"I taught in this system for thirty years, girls, less the three years we spent with your father in Washington. Half the children in Wilamet passed through my first- and second-grade classes. We teachers have to take some of the blame."

Susanna frowned. "But that's ridiculous. You only taught what the curriculum dictated. If anyone is to blame, it's the state, or even the county, not to mention the confusion over the new public laws on the education of the handicapped—"

Eleanor shook her head. "I knew that there were children who were having trouble," she said. "We all did, but we just didn't talk about it, even with one another. We thought that if a child wasn't quite ready to read or not trying hard enough, he'd catch up, perhaps do better with his next teacher. We didn't want to send him on with a label."

"But some children never caught up," Maggie said. "Sometimes a youngster went all through school without learning adequate reading skills."

Eleanor nodded. "If only we'd known what we know now—the importance of phonetics, the fact that children all learn differently, that many of them need global or tactile or kinesthetic approaches—"

"*Kinesthetic* approaches?"

"It means that half the children don't learn just by hearing and repeating whole words," Maggie explained. "They've got to act out what they are reading, or play games with the sounds, or actually touch the words by drawing them. We were just beginning to introduce those ideas when I took my leave of absence for Willy.''

"Most of all, children must learn *all* the sounds, not just those of the alphabet," Eleanor said.

"Why not try out some of your new ideas on Toby?" Susanna suggested. "Though Toby's older, in ways he's like a first or second grader since he's never been to school."

"Surely there's someone else in Wilamet more qualified to help a retarded boy?"

"No," Maggie answered. "Wayne has been all over town inquiring. Everybody's either too busy or can't start till fall. Toby needs someone right now."

"I'd like to help, but . . ." Eleanor paused and took a sip of her tea. "I promised myself that when I quit teaching, I'd find some other way to help."

"So you've gone back to volunteering on committees?"

"Your father always said I did very well at that, during those years that we served in Washington. And he certainly made me see that one can make more of an impact, working on the broader scale."

"Oh, Mother." Maggie groaned. "You know you never really believed that."

Eleanor pursed her lips in protest. "Why of course I believe it. Susanna is living proof. The legislation she helps get passed affects thousands."

Susanna pushed a bit of spilled sugar into a little heap, then flattened it with a finger. She thought of the Elder Care Bill and Senator Stout's doubts about it.

"A tutor can only help one person at a time," Eleanor went on, "but by organizing and running the program, and working with the center's staff, one could help a whole passel of people. I really think that's where I'm better suited, girls."

"Oh, dear." Maggie groaned. "I told Lucas I was sure that you'd do it. By now he's probably already told Toby."

"Well, you'd better just call him up right now, Maggie Grant. Call your brother-in-law immediately and tell him that your mother is much too busy to start taking in private students."

"Too busy, or too afraid of failing?" Maggie asked pointedly.

Susanna smiled wryly. Of the two of them, Maggie had more of their father's directness. There was no escape from her razor-sharp questions.

Eleanor pursed her lips. "Well, I suppose I could try. And Susanna *is* here to help me on the committee...." Eleanor shot her daughter a questioning look. Susanna sighed and nodded resignedly.

"Perhaps I could try it for a week or so," Eleanor went on, "till they find someone else, someone better qualified for Toby."

As soon as Eleanor had left the room, Maggie broke into a grin and hugged her sister. "You can be the one to tell Lucas," she whispered. "Tell him he'd better get Toby down here this week, before Mother changes her mind."

"But I thought you'd already told him."

"I figured it wouldn't hurt to exaggerate a bit." Maggie busied herself with gathering up the glasses."

"Maggie Grant, just when I think you've got Daddy's directness, I see a *very* broad streak of Mother in you!"

In the Wilamet Country Club dining room, the big circular dinner table had emptied. Except for Bobby Joe Richardson, everybody was dancing.

Susanna considered returning to the ladies' room, but she hesitated a moment too long. B.J. spotted her, stood and waved her back to the table.

"C'mon over here and tell me all about Washington, Susanna. You had little enough to say at dinner. We all thought you'd be chock-full o' big-city notions 'bout how to get this thing off the ground.''

Susanna slipped into the chair that B.J. held out for her, then tried to scoot it a bit away. B.J. responded by moving his own chair closer. "It's not that easy to draw up a plan," she said. "We have to do a needs assessment, identify alternative approaches, do a *lot* of research...."

"Now you're talkin'. When do we start?"

He wasn't kidding, she knew. And his enthusiasm wasn't all attributable to the torch he'd always professed to carry for her. She'd seen his eyes light up that way countless times before. Even in junior high school, B. J. Richardson had liked leading the parade.

"I'm on vacation," Susanna mumbled. She wasn't saying it just for B.J.'s benefit. The talk at dinner had made her realize how right Senator Stout had been when he'd insisted she needed a rest.

"How 'bout a dance, then, just for old times' sake?"

"I don't dance anymore, B.J."

"But you did once."

"That was a very long time ago. I was the Cicada Princess and you were..."

B.J. lumbered to his feet without waiting for her to finish and leaned against the edge of the table. He sucked in his ever-expanding middle. "I was captain of the football team!"

He struck a pose and faked a pass. Heads around them turned. Wilamet's upper crust was watching. Faces she recognized smiled patronizingly and nodded. Susanna groaned. Tomorrow the story would be all over town that B.J. was about to score.

"As I was saying, we *had* to dance then, B.J. Now that we have a choice..."

B.J.'s ruddy cheeks fell, pulling the corners of his mouth down with them. She couldn't tell if his disappointment was real or merely pretended. Susanna gave in and rose to her feet.

"I hear you've made a big success of the Chevy dealership, B.J.," she said, trying her best to sound sincere.

His mouth slipped easily back to its confident grin. He took her hand and led her out to the dance floor. "It's those four-wheel drives. Everybody wants one. You'd think that Oklahoma wasn't civilized, the way folks want to tear around the country, blazin' new trails."

Susanna laughed. He wasn't her type. He never had been her type. But B. J. Richardson belonged to Wilamet, and something about him reminded her that she did, too.

She'd no sooner followed Bobby Joe onto the dance floor and settled herself at a safe distance in his arms, than her eyes were drawn to a commotion across the room.

"Otis gets a kick out of stressin' the code," B.J. said as he turned her away from the door. "Makes the members mad as hell."

B.J. turned her again, and this time Susanna got a better view. A red-faced Otis was gesturing wildly, his thin arms flapping up and down, shaking in the sleeves of his black suit coat like the wings on an angry crow. Dr. Gurley had his hand on one shoulder, trying his hardest not to laugh. Otis calmed down, shook his head and stepped aside. Lucas Grant was standing in the doorway.

Susanna missed a step and swayed against Bobby Joe. B.J.'s grip tightened around her waist, pulling her closer. He steered her around the dance floor, heading straight for the doorway.

Lucas had handed Otis his fishing vest and was rolling down his sleeves. His chambray work shirt was open at the neck, and he wore jeans and boating shoes. Even in work clothes, she thought, he was still the best-looking man in the room.

Several couples closed in around him, taking turns at shaking his hand. Dr. Gurley said something that everyone agreed to, then clapped Lucas on the back. Lucas looked down, then pulled his hand through his hair in that familiar gesture that told Susanna he was feeling self-conscious. Then he looked up. She knew that he saw her.

It wasn't even a particularly slow dance, yet B.J.'s cheek had moved close to hers. He hummed nonchalantly into her ear, and swept her around the floor...right past Lucas's riveting stare.

A moment later, Lucas stood at her elbow, a smiling Mrs. Gurley on his arm. "I'd like to cut in, B.J.," he said. "The doctor's wife wants to dance with you."

"She does?" In the split second before B.J. realized he'd been set up, Lucas maneuvered a change of partners and pulled Susanna into his arms.

"I didn't know you were coming tonight," she said as he swept her across the floor.

"That's pretty obvious."

"Lucas, I—"

"Is B.J. a part of that world that's between us, Susanna? I know he wants to get into politics, but—"

She leaned back far enough to eye him incredulously. "You're jealous!"

He pulled her back, then drew her closer till his lips brushed her ear. "Damn right," he said in a guttural whisper.

A rush of heat began at her temples and crept down her body, sensitizing the places Lucas touched her. Above the splay of his hand in the middle of her low-backed dress, the ends of his fingers seared her skin. The palm of her hand was held firmly in his, and the brush of her cheek against his shoulder began to burn.

The orchestra's tempo slowed, beginning a fifties love song, and Lucas pulled Susanna closer. He moved in perfect time to music she barely heard. Her hips felt liquid, her shoulders uninhibited, as he guided her around the floor. Helplessly, yet effortlessly, she followed him, her body flowing whichever way he led it. Other couples, whispering admiration, moved aside.

"Thought you didn't dance," B.J. teased as he and Mrs. Gurley glided by. The elderly woman winked at Lucas as she passed.

"I *don't* dance," Susanna whispered to Lucas.

He chuckled under his breath. "Pretending again?" he asked her. His breath swept the hair that feathered at her ears.

Before she could answer, he moved her close to the twin French doors that led to the deck overlooking the lake. Someone opened them wide as he swung her outside, then quietly pulled them shut. The back that moved away, into the brightly lit room, looked a lot like Dr. Gurley's.

The song of the cicadas hovered on the warm evening air, weaving a dissonant harmony between the bars of the muted music. Lucas pulled Susanna close and began to dance again.

His touch, the clean yet active smell of work on him, the sound of his steady breathing, even the taste in her mouth of remembered kisses, filled Susanna's senses. For what seemed endless moments, the music matched the flow of their bodies. His arms slid slowly down her back and Susanna's moved up to his shoulders. As she lifted her face, his breath swept her cheeks.

"Maybe you aren't pretending," he said jokingly. "You dance very well."

His eyes held that open look she'd grown to love, the one that made her feel as though she'd known him all her life. "If I *am* pretending," she answered lightly, "I'm not the only one this time. I thought you never came to town, at least not to things like this."

"I made an exception."

"For me?"

Lucas eyed her a moment, then slowed and steadied her, her back against the veranda railing. "I came to drop off a charter. A friend of Ben Gurley's who's staying at the club."

"Oh." Susanna looked down.

He tipped her chin so she had to look at him. He knew her face held that same embarrassment she'd felt when she'd handed him her note so long ago.

"I also knew that you'd be here," he said in a husky voice.

As he stared at her a moment longer, the blue of his eyes seemed to deepen to fathomless azure in the semidarkness. Susanna started to speak, then swallowed her words. Lucas moved a step closer, then stopped. He turned to look out across the lake. His tone was controlled when he spoke.

"I promised Toby I'd check on you. Find out when you'll be back for lunch."

She thought of their quiet lunch with Toby and compared it to the raucous dinner she'd just endured and the rambling meeting that had preceded it. She'd not been kidding when she'd told B.J. she was on vacation. She dreaded the work the committee was asking her to do.

Suddenly she wanted to be somewhere else. Anywhere but here, with commitments just a closed French door away. All those people with all those questions... She was good at research. But now? There were other things that mattered more. Things that mattered on a deeper, more personal level. Things that might not wait...

"Lucas... did you come by boat? I'd *love* to get out of here, go out on the lake. Just for a little while. Could we go for a ride?"

She had barely finished her question when he gave a low chuckle and pulled her toward the side stairway. Quickly she crept down the stairs after him, and crossed the dimly lit flagstone patio below. As they walked on the dark edge of lawn that sloped down to the water, the song of the cicadas rose around them.

Susanna hesitated only a moment at the edge of the shadowed lawn. Then she kicked off her heels and lifted her skirt, wriggling out of her stockings. The grass felt cool and wet and delicious beneath her running bare feet.

Then Lucas was leading her, laughing with her, lifting her up off the dock and down, into his waiting boat.

Chapter Eight

The boat moved silently out of the slip and into the darkened water. Susanna held her breath, half expecting one of the other two boats tied up at the pier to follow. But they just rocked gently, back and forth in Lucas's wake, almost in time to the hum of the little electric motor. Soon the boats were two white commas punctuating the lengthening stretch of inky water between them and the dim lights of the club.

Lucas cut the motor and moved forward. He leaned over the back of Susanna's seat. "Would you like to drive?" he asked her.

He'd rolled up the sleeves of his shirt again, so they were tight against the muscles that flexed in his forearms as he steadied himself against her chair, waiting for her answer. Susanna could almost feel the ropy hardness of his arms, could almost imagine them holding her close.

"I'd love to," she said. Her answer came out in a whisper.

Lucas smiled, then brushed her cheek with the back of his hand before making one last check of the boat. She slid into the driver's seat as he tied down two of the cushions and stowed a thermos in a compartment beneath them. Then he moved back to her, bent over her ducked head and reached for the windshield to fold it flat against the hull.

"Better take out your hairpins," he said, climbing into the seat beside her, "unless you don't care about losing them."

"I don't," she answered.

He laughed and tossed her the keys.

"Just aim for the middle of the lake," he shouted over the roar of the revving engine. "There's nothing between here and there but deep water."

"And freedom!" she shouted back.

She got a great gulp of it as the boat shot forward, slicing the water in one clean cut. Her hair streamed out away from her face, and a fine spray of water peppered her forehead.

Susanna's laughter burst out of her in one big explosion of joy. She gunned the engine to double their speed. Only then did she look at Lucas.

His head thrown back, he sat low in his seat with his blond hair whipping out behind him. The wind snatched at his half-open shirt, then plastered it against his chest till she could almost trace the swell of his muscles. A wave of desire swept over her, cutting as freely through her defences as the boat cut through the water.

He let her drive solo till they'd reached the middle of the lake, then he reached across her and guided the wheel, turning the boat with a touch of his hand over hers. The craft responded instantly, sweeping an arc as wide as a city block, first to one side and then to the other.

Her laughter was lost in the wind as she slid against him, pushed by the force of the turns to fit herself under his arm.

Susanna let go of the wheel and pressed her cheek against Lucas's chest. His heartbeat crashed in her ear.

She was vaguely conscious that the boat was drifting, that the wind had died, that the sound of the engine in her ears was only the echoed ring of its roar. Then silence slipped around them, warm, heavy, throbbing with pent-up desire.

He pulled her across him, into his lap, and covered her mouth with all the force of a claiming kiss that had been building since the moment he'd seen her dancing with B.J. She tasted like the water and the sweep of the wind, and she smelled like gardenias and nighttime and hidden things that had no name. Then she moved against him, and every desire that Lucas had ever felt rose up to battle his last shred of restraint and shatter it.

His hands touched her face, her throat, her shoulders, then moved down the fabric of her dress, caressing her breasts, lifting them, holding them, feeling them peak through the thin cotton that hindered his intimate touch. Then his hand slipped down, farther, then farther. She gave him room, let him touch her, begged him to touch her, moaned with the pleasure of his hands on her body.

She fought to keep him from leaving her mouth, then stilled and arched when she saw what he wanted, pulling his head to her breast, tangling her fingers deep in his hair as he fought for a taste of her body.

He tried to be gentle, knowing the rigid tautness of her nipple hid tender flesh underneath, but she pulled him closer, crying out for him to stroke her with abandon.

"Lucas...oh, Lucas...oh, Lucas..."

She was saying his name over and over, trying to find her bearings, trying to tell him that it was all right, that whatever he wanted could not come close to matching the want she felt for him.

She kissed him as deeply as she dared, as though in doing that she could quell the fire that was rising, burning, turning her body to liquid that wanted to flow around him and pull him deeper into herself.

Then suddenly, as though with a single thought, they drew apart. Susanna sat back in her seat and pulled her dress the rest of the way off, and then her slip, till nothing remained but the skimpiest panties he'd ever imagined. Lucas tore at the buttons on the front of his shirt and threw it aside.

She stood when he stood, and with one motion they moved to the open floor in the center of the boat. He pulled the cushions loose from the rails and laid them carefully on the floor. His fingers trembled with urgency as he spread a blanket over them. Then Susanna dropped to her knees on the makeshift bed and touched his knee, stilling his hands as he reached for his belt.

"Let me," she whispered. And he did.

The buckle of his belt felt hot to her touch, as though it had absorbed the heat of his loins and was signaling her, warning her, that the threshold she was bound to cross would sear them both. But heedless, she tugged at it till it came loose, then pulled at the snap that held his jeans and then at the zipper beneath it.

She touched him gently, through the fabric of his briefs, thrilling to the virile throb that answered her stroke. Lucas groaned and dropped to the cushions beside her, kicking his jeans off on the way down.

Their motions were synchronized as they each removed the last remaining barrier of clothing that separated their hungry bodies. On their knees, Susanna and Lucas reached out for each other.

Just when he thought he had some control, somewhere between the sweet, soft stroking he was giving her inner thighs and the brush of her lips across his chest...just when he'd decided they could go on like that forever... maybe not forever, maybe just for another moment...just then she shifted, settled beneath him and guided his hand to the center of her passion. Hot, wet, she ran like a river, her body begging for his.

"Lucas, please. *Please . . .*"

His lips silenced the last of her plea, and his thrust, the cry of her body. And then he was moving inside her, slower, then faster, then slower again, wanting again to hang on, wanting to give her all that he'd saved without even knowing he'd done it.

Finally Susanna cried out and let go, and he burst inside her, then surged and burst again, till he'd spread the last remnant of his seed in the hot, fertile moistness Susanna had offered.

She clung to him, rocking him gently, easing him down to cover her fully, till the sweet, warm sweat of their bodies mingled at every available place, and the crushing weight of him told her that this was real. No dream. Real as flesh and the pleasure they'd taken in it.

He turned and moved to his side, pulling her with him, guiding her under his arm, his leg across hers, pulling her nearer. Susanna tasted the salt of their lovemaking, mixed with a tiny bit of blood where she'd bit at her lip. Then he kissed her again and tasted her mouth, giving her the deep, warm recesses of his own. Her breathing became smoother then, and deeper, drawing out, again and again, into one long, endless sigh of release.

When at last he let go and lay back beside her, Susanna was reluctant to open her eyes. As long as she kept them closed, she could shut out everything but Lucas, everything but the perfect merging of reality with all her imagined dreams. Then, tentatively, he pressed her hand. She opened her eyes at last.

"Oh, Lucas! Look! Look up at the sky!"

He rose on his elbows at her excited command. The sky was its usual starry bowl of brilliance as it was on every clear night before the moon had risen. He'd always taken it for granted. But now? Tonight the sky seemed to dip into the water all around them, scattering extra stars, millions of them, more than he'd ever seen. Stars he was sure he'd never seen before. Stars he might never see again. He turned to look at Susanna.

"Do you see it? Lucas, tell me what you see."

"A dream. A moment in time. And stars. More stars than I've ever seen in my life." *And a face...a face that I thought I had lost...might still lose again—*

"Oh, Lucas, don't you see? It's not a dream. They're real stars. The same stars that shine everywhere—Washington, Wilamet, even over the marina, only we've just not seen them so clearly before. We've never had a chance. Never *taken* a chance. Lucas, I was wrong. It's *one world.*"

He touched her face and found it wet with tears. But the sound of his name on her lips as he cradled her in his arms was full of hope. Hope that wrenched at the realities he'd long ago grown to accept, pushed at the limits he'd placed on his life. Limits that excluded all but moments. Sacred moments, perhaps, but moments still. He held her tightly, willing the hope that stirred in her breast to pass into his.

Susanna hugged her knees and pulled the blanket around her shoulders. She didn't want to dress. Not yet. Lucas pulled on his jeans and moved about the boat. The snap hung loose, seductively, the way it had the day she'd first come home.

Home, she thought. She'd never understood before how much it meant to her. Now, knowing gave her confidence. She could *make* it all happen, she knew that she could.

She took the cup of cool water that he offered her and watched him put the lid back on the thermos. She tipped her head to one side. "You're not sure you believe it, are you?"

Lucas settled himself on the cushion beside her, taking time to choose his words. He took a long drink of the water, then emptied his cup over the side of the boat. He turned back to her and traced the cocky tilt of her jaw with the end of his forefinger.

"I've heard it takes a hell of a lot to satisfy a Washington woman."

Susanna laughed. "Lucas, I've never been so...so *satisfied*, in all my life. It was never like this for me...not with Daryl...not with anyone—"

"I didn't mean lovemaking, Susanna."

She caught the hand he'd run through his hair and kissed it. "Of course you didn't. I know what you meant. Lucas, there's *got* to be a way. I haven't been happy in Washington. It started long before Daryl. I've got to find some way to do what I'm good at, without giving up the things that matter."

"How—"

"I don't know!"

She stood abruptly, the blanket slipping off her shoulders. He watched her move to the front of the boat and reach for her clothes. For an instant, he framed the sight of her for his memory, the curve of her breast, the sweep of her slender arm, the bend of her leg. He could live on that picture a hell of a long time if he had to.

He tossed the thermos aside and stood. "There are things you don't understand. Things about me. It's high time I told you, Susanna. If you knew me better—"

"That's just what I *want* to do, Lucas. I want to know everything."

She had turned back to him, her shoes in her hand. He had instant recall of that moment on the edge of the country-club lawn when she'd taken them off, then hesitated, then run to his arms. Now he was the one who was holding back.

She took a step forward. The starlight sat on her high cheekbones and danced in her eyes, turning them as piercingly bright as they'd been that day on the dock when she'd wanted to fight for Toby.

Maybe her way *was* better. *Fight back.* You could accept what you had to just so long. Then you had to stand and deliver. Seeing her with B.J. had made him realize that. Lucas reached out and caught her arms and pulled her roughly toward him.

"You don't know what you're asking."

"I think I do."

She didn't flinch, though his fingers dug into her arms. His eyes burned into hers with a fierceness she'd never seen, a fierceness that matched her own, perhaps even bettered it.

He kissed her then, taking her mouth in a full, hard claim that erased any doubts she might have had that he was in it with her. In it all the way.

Lucas drove as they headed back across the lake. Susanna was content to snuggle under his arm. The boat moved smoothly and swiftly through the water. Too swiftly. He cut the engine when they drew close to the club and let the boat drift in toward the pier.

"I'll see you tomorrow," he said.

"Do you want me to drive out to the lake?"

"No."

"Where, then?"

"Tell Maggie I'm coming to the big house for dinner. I'll see you in church. Then I'm coming for Sunday dinner."

"Oh, Lucas!" She hugged him hard. Then suddenly Susanna drew back.

"What is it?" he asked her.

"Remember what you said about the houseboat? About keeping it for me all summer? I don't want that to change."

"Why should it?"

"People change when they're out of their element."

"Does it always have to be for the worse?"

"No, of course not. But tonight at the club I thought I would scream if Mother introduced me one more time as Wilamet's contribution to *our nation's capitol*. I kept on thinking of the houseboat, wishing I was there. It's like I became a different person at the lake. I'm having trouble snapping back. The same thing might happen to you."

Lucas laughed, then sobered when he saw that she was serious. "Look, Susanna, I am who I am. Coming to town more often won't change that."

"Maybe not just coming to town, but...Lucas, I'm going to have to get involved in the literacy center project. I promised Mother." She couldn't hide the look of hopefulness in her eyes.

Lucas shifted uncomfortably, then shrugged off the uneasy feeling and grinned at her broadly. "Committee work is *definitely* not my style, lady, but if that's where you're going to be, then I'll help you as much as I can."

Susanna laughed and hugged him again. She knew what his style was. Quiet, unpretentious, helping one-on-one behind the scenes. And doing it all with honesty. She thought of the moment on the club deck when she'd asked him if he'd come for her. He'd answered honestly. Another man would have hedged. But there weren't going to be any games between her and Lucas Grant. Not now. Not ever. And there would be plenty of chances for his style of help.

"We're going to be very busy."

"Never *too* busy," he growled. He feathered the edge of her mouth with kisses.

"You've got no idea what you're getting into," she tried to say when his lips weren't covering hers. "I hope you don't mind my tying up the phone...letters all over the cabin...your computer going day and night—well, maybe just days—not to mention the meetings. There'll be nights you might have to stay in town."

"In Maggie's spare room?"

"Surely you don't expect..."

Lucas laughed, a low and gravelly sound that stirred her quiescent passion. But his final kiss was quick and light.

"Just remember," he told her, "I've got a job of my own. Right now, if I don't get back to the marina, I'll never make it up at dawn for that charter."

She kissed him lightly on the cheek, then gathered her shoes and climbed up on the pier. Grateful that it was deserted, she stood alone and watched him move out.

"Tell Maggie to fix that chicken with dumplings she's always bragging about," he called back to her. "And one more thing. Tell my brother I want to see him. Tell him to meet me on the steps of the church about quarter to eleven. It won't take long."

There was so much more he wanted to say, but he'd give Wayne one more chance to support his decision. Besides, he'd drifted too far out from the pier. A shout might bring out the other club guests, and the rest of what Lucas had to say to Susanna was for her ears alone. And apart from that, he wanted this vision all to himself... the sight of her standing in the starlight, head held high, and waving slowly at him.

The final hymn was "Amazing Grace," and Lucas knew every word. He stood, as usual, somber and silent, at the far end of the family pew. Not singing at all was better than holding a hymnbook, pretending he knew how to read. But today Susanna stood beside him, the curve of her cheek showing beneath her broad-brimmed straw hat. Today he *wanted* to sing.

The organ swelled for the final stanza, and the small congregation paused for a breath. When they joined together to finish the hymn, just one more voice was added. But the rich, deep baritone of Lucas Grant made more than one head turn.

Susanna looked up in surprise and smiled.

Outside on the sidewalk in front of the church, Eleanor tapped him on the chest with her folded fan. "Lucas Grant, you ought to be ashamed. With a voice like that you belong in the choir! And to think I was sure you couldn't sing a note." He squinted into the sunlight and tried to look duly admonished.

Susanna adjusted her hat and took Lucas's arm firmly in hers. "Mother, there must be a million things we don't know about Lucas, but we're going to find them *all* out before this summer is over. Just you wait and see."

"Why, of course, dear. After all, Lucas *is* family." Susanna turned on her heels and marched Lucas up the sidewalk toward home. Had she only imagined that a little smile had tucked in the corners of her mother's mouth?

"What happened to Wayne?" Lucas asked.

"He said to tell you he's sorry he couldn't meet you before church. And I guess you noticed that he and Maggie slipped out early. He seemed really excited. I think, if I'm not mistaken, Wayne's got something to tell you, too."

"And *you* know what it is. I can tell by that bounce to your voice and the dance you're dying to do down the sidewalk."

He stopped as they rounded the corner and pulled her under the sweeping boughs of a white oak tree. A branch caught her hat and pushed it off her head, and a dozen cicadas shrilled, dislodged from their perch. Susanna laughed and shooed the bugs away. He bent to pick up her hat, but kept it, wanting to see more of her face.

Her hair was braided the way that he liked it. Bits of it had broken free, curling around her face. A thin film of perspiration glossed the color on her cheekbones. She smelled like springtime and something else. Something he remembered. *Gardenias?* Was she wearing that same perfume again, or had it just settled deep in his brain? He leaned a little closer, but Susanna laughed, grabbed at her hat and skipped away.

"You know very well why I feel like dancing," she called back to him.

He laughed, caught up with her and followed her home.

Half an hour later, Susanna stood behind her chair, facing Lucas across her mother's dining-room table, Maggie's bountiful Sunday dinner spread out between them. She could hardly stand to look away long enough to bow her head when Wayne began to say grace.

Not just her eyes had been full of Lucas, but her heart, her mind and her soul. Her entire being seemed filled to overflowing. *Home.* She was part of it again. And part of a family. Now there was someone to care about. Someone special. Someone to *love*? She squeezed her eyes shut tighter, but there wasn't time to add her prayer.

"Amen!" Wayne boomed, and everybody jumped.

Susanna looked up, guessing at what was coming. All eyes were trained on Wayne, except for Maggie's. She was looking down at her plate, trying not to smile.

Wayne tugged at his tie. The too-tight knot made his collar stick out and turned his usually serious face a shade of pink that matched his boyish grin. Halfway down the middle of his shirt, he'd missed a button. Susanna was sure if they checked they'd find that his socks didn't match.

He'd forgotten the family custom of asking everyone to take a seat, so they continued to stand there, awkwardly waiting. Wayne looked around sheepishly, then pulled out his handkerchief, removed his glasses and put them back on without wiping them. Finally he cleared his throat.

"Before we eat, Maggie and I have a little announcement. We are...that is, we will be...what I mean to say is..."

"Oh, Wayne, for heaven's sake, just tell them I'm pregnant!"

Eleanor flushed a brilliant rose and sat down in the chair that Lucas pulled out for her just in time. She fanned herself with her napkin.

"Oh, my, *another* one? Oh, my. Are you *sure*, Maggie? Of course you're sure! I'm going to be a grandmother again! Oh, my, my, my!"

Beside her, Little Willy banged his spoon on the tray of his high chair and sang along with Eleanor's repeated cries. Maggie scooped him up and hugged him, then dropped the baby into her mother's lap.

Lucas turned toward his brother and stretched out his hand. "Wayne...it's great. Congratulations. Oh, hell..." Lucas pulled his brother into a big bear hug. Over Wayne's shoulder, Lucas's eyes were wet and shining. Susanna looked away.

She tried to ignore the faint shadow that seemed to separate her from the others. She was going to be an aunt again. She'd give the new baby the same unqualified love she lavished on Little Willy. Her heart was already brimming with it. But something was missing, some measure of joy that she ought to be feeling, but wasn't.

"We'd better eat before Maggie's food gets cold," Wayne said. "There's no telling when she'll feel like cooking again."

Maggie had repeated all of Dr. Gurley's cautions, each in minute detail, when Eleanor finally acknowledged that she understood. Then she insisted that her daughter fetch the big kitchen calendar so she could see for herself exactly when the baby was due to arrive.

When Maggie came back, she brought not only the calendar, but another fresh batch of cloverleaf yeast rolls. She handed the calendar to her mother and the basket of bread to Susanna. The heady aroma was almost intoxicating.

"Take two," Maggie whispered. "You've hardly eaten a thing."

Susanna stopped pushing her mashed potatoes around her plate and looked up at her sister. "It's a wonderful dinner, Maggie. I guess I'm not used to more than a quick deli sandwich for lunch. I'm always so busy." She helped herself to an extra roll to make Maggie happy.

"It's January, by my calculations." Eleanor counted the months again just to be sure. "About the middle of January. Am I right, children? Oh, my goodness, how will we ever wait?"

"We could start by changing the subject, Mother. This is the first time we've had Lucas for dinner in ages." Maggie filled Little Willy's bowl with peas to make up for the ones that he'd pushed to the floor.

Eleanor took one last look at the calendar, then folded it and set it aside. But all she could do was sigh, between bites of Maggie's chicken and dumplings, and beam a smile from one face to the next down the table.

"When do you want to start bringing Toby in, Lucas?" Maggie prompted.

He'd been studying Susanna all through dinner, wondering what she was thinking. Her usual smile was there, for him as well as for the rest of her family, but her mind was miles away. Something was weighing on it. Something heavy.

"Lucas?"

He pulled his eyes from Susanna's face and gave her sister his full attention. "My morning charter usually gets back by eleven. I thought I'd bring Toby up right after lunch tomorrow."

"Come on over to the office after you drop him off," Wayne said. "We can review those new accounts. It'll save me a trip to the lake."

"You'll bring Toby every day, won't you?" Eleanor asked. "I've been reading a little about teaching reading to mentally handicapped students. Toby will feel more confident if we're careful to keep to a regular schedule."

"I'd like to bring him every afternoon if you can spare that much time, Mrs. Foster." Lucas's eyes slid from the elderly woman at his side to Susanna's face across the table. The same wistful smile played at the corners of both their mouths.

"It's high time you started calling me Eleanor, Lucas." Her tone had been almost intimate. Susanna looked up in surprise.

Eleanor's eyes were fastened on Lucas, and they lacked the usual demure reserve that she always wore around Wayne and even around her daughters at times. With Lucas, her mother seemed totally open. Susanna smiled and picked up her knife to butter her roll. He had a way of bringing that out in people. He'd brought it out in her. And so much more.

"I've got lots of time," Eleanor said. "I wish I had *less* time. Which is to say, I wish our initial notices for the literacy center had drawn a better response."

"But I thought your sample study showed lots of interest," Susanna said. "You mentioned those statistics last night at the meeting."

Eleanor shook her head. "Oh, the students are out there, all right. In the beginning, we received several calls. Now I get fewer. And none of them will give their names, even when I assure them they'll be confidential."

Lucas glanced across the table at Wayne. His brother shrugged and looked away. "How many people are you helping right now?" Lucas asked.

"There's the young mother who sweeps up for Della, and the man from the factory who lost his driver's license, and half a dozen others. And of course Maggie has the little second-grade reading-enrichment class."

"I think that class is part of the problem," Maggie said.

"It's an agreement we have with the school," Eleanor explained. "Since we don't have a budget yet, they're not charging us for the use of the room. In return, Maggie gives a special early-morning class for beginning readers."

"Why is that a problem?" Susanna asked. "Are you short on tutors?"

"Oh, no," Maggie answered. "People seem willing enough to help. Although if we don't get the program rolling soon, I think the volunteers may lose interest. The problem is *where* we're located."

"Maggie thinks that perhaps the adults are embarrassed, but I can't believe—"

"Mother, would you want to come back to elementary school, perhaps to the very same school you attended when you were a child, perhaps with your children and their friends, and have everyone know that you can't read better than they can? And look at the furniture. Mr. Purdy feels downright silly squeezing into that sixth-grade school desk."

"Maybe B.J.'s idea of a raffle is not such a bad one," Susanna said. "It would keep the project in the public eye and raise some money for books and furniture."

Wayne leaned forward, his elbows on the table, and took off his glasses. "Maybe you *should* put things on the shelf for now, at least till you get some firmer backing. Maggie's going to have to be careful…and, well, let's face it." Wayne glanced around the table. His eyes caught Lucas's riveting stare, then quickly slid back to Maggie. "You've given the center an honest try. Maybe people who can't read aren't that interested. Maybe they've got their reasons."

Maggie's eyes flashed. "Wayne, that's ridiculous. How would you like to go through life, spending an extra hour in the grocery store every trip because you couldn't find what you needed? Suppose you couldn't read the warning on the can of paint thinner you were using? And what if you got a chance to advance at your job but couldn't fill out the application?"

"I'm not saying they don't *wish* they could read, Maggie." Wayne put his glasses back on and pushed them up along his nose. "Maybe some of them have tried and given up, or been tested and told they'll never learn to read."

"But—"

"Now, Maggie, dear," Eleanor interrupted. "Don't get yourself upset. And don't be so hard on Wayne. He's just concerned about you and the baby."

"Are there people like that?" Susanna asked. "People who can never learn to read?"

"No!" Maggie said at the very same instant that Eleanor answered, "Yes." The women eyed each other with practiced toleration.

"Mother believes that there are certain disabled people, people with severe cases of mirror vision, for example, or people whose reading disability seems inherited, who will never learn to read."

"And you don't agree?" Lucas asked, leaning forward.

"No. First of all, nonreaders often test very high in IQ. Albert Einstein was a disabled reader, and so was Woodrow Wilson. And second, in all my teacher training and all my experience since, I've never met anyone who couldn't conquer reading with enough motivation and enough individual help. And as for reading disabilities being inherited, I think that's hogwash. Your father couldn't read, and look at you and Wayne."

Wayne pushed his glasses back up again and coughed. He looked from Maggie's determined face to Lucas's trouble one, and then, imploringly, back at Eleanor.

The older woman sighed. "Fortunately for them, Wayne and Lucas didn't inherit their father's disability, dear. When you've taught as long as I have, you'll see. There are a few people for whom the effort of trying to read is just too difficult. They're better off accepting their handicap and arranging their lives accordingly. We must put our effort toward helping the others."

Maggie sighed resignedly. "Mother and I are echoing two sides of a battle that's been going on forever between reading experts. But that's part of the reason we want to establish an adult literacy center. We need to stop trying to figure out why people never learned to read in school, and get down to correcting the problem. To do it we've got to get serious."

"Maggie's right about that," Eleanor continued. "We've got to get funding. We need books and furniture and a full-time staff. If Dr. Gurley puts Maggie on a restricted schedule, we'll need more volunteers. And we've got to find somewhere else for the center. Someplace where adults can get the help they need without sacrificing their dignity."

Suddenly the vague sense of emptiness she'd felt at Maggie announcement evaporated, and Susanna was back on familiar ground. "I guess this is where I come in," she said. "I'll start by having a look at those stats from the earlier report. We may have to do another survey, but we'll do it by phone if we have to. We can use the numeric phone listing and announce that we're calling the numbers in order, instead of by name, so people will feel free to answer."

Ideas flooded Susanna's head, and her fingers itched to write them down. "Wayne, I'm going to need a modem. Lucas said he thought you might have an extra one." She'd need to access FAPRS, the database with every federal program authorized by public law. It would get her to the sources of available funds twice as fast as the library. Senator Stout could help her get in.

"I've got the modem," Wayne said, "but where will you get a computer? The one at my office is busy day and night."

Susanna glanced at Lucas and felt a blush that rushed up her cheeks.

Lucas smiled. "She can use mine while I'm at work," he said. "I'll be at the marina all afternoon and out on the boat in the evening, the early part of it, anyway."

"I thought you didn't believe in going after public funding, Lucas." Maggie's teasing tone made Susanna want to kick her under the table.

Lucas's smile deepened. His eyes held Susanna's, clear and steady. "I've got a personal interest in this project, Maggie. Maybe more than one."

"Oh!" Eleanor uttered a little cry, and two bright spots appeared on her cheeks. But when she spoke her tone was even. "I didn't know you were interested in literacy, Lucas," she said. "Isn't that nice. Now the whole family's going to be involved."

"I can ride out to the lake with Lucas when he picks up Toby after his lesson," Susanna said. "I can spend the afternoon and early evening on the computer, then catch a ride back to Wilamet with one of the other guides."

"Why don't you just move back to the houseboat," Maggie suggested.

Eleanor coughed. "Don't you dare, Susanna. I've seen little enough of you already." She reached across the table and patted her daughter's hand. "Besides, I want to keep you here where we can feed you. You need to put on a little weight before you go back to *our nation's capitol.*"

Susanna resisted the urge to groan at her mother's phrase. "I can't move back to the houseboat. Maggie needs me."

She returned her sister's mischievous glance. "You're going to follow Dr. Gurley's orders to the letter, starting with taking a nap every morning. You can sleep again when Willy naps in the afternoon. I'll see you both safely tucked in before I'm off to the lake."

Eleanor let out a happy sigh and pushed her chair back from the table. "Now that we've got everything settled, you men take Willy and go to the parlor while we get these dishes cleared away. Maggie's made strawberry pie for desert."

"Susanna said you wanted to talk to me," Wayne said when he and Lucas were alone with Willy in the parlor. "I can guess what you're going to say. You don't want to wait any longer. You think you've just *got* to tell her."

Lucas nodded as Wayne passed him Little Willy and leaned back in the recliner. When he finally got the footrest up, he settled himself and reached for his son. But the baby had already fallen asleep in Lucas's arms.

Lucas shifted to make Willy more comfortable. "There's more, Wayne." He watched his brother take off his glasses and pull out his handkerchief.

Pursing his lips, Wayne cleaned the lenses far longer than was necessary. "I watched your face at dinner," Wayne said at last. "I suppose you've got some crazy idea, now that the literacy center is open... Lucas, isn't it a little too late for you to be going back to school?"

"Maybe it is too late, Wayne, and maybe it isn't. I've been thinking about it ever since our meeting with Toby's social worker."

"That's different."

"Of course it is. Toby's mildly retarded. We've always thought he couldn't learn to read. I'm not retarded at all. I'm actually pretty bright. You said so yourself last week. What we don't know anymore, not for sure, anyway, is that I can't learn to read."

"But the tests—"

"Tests can be wrong. They were wrong in Toby's case. Maybe they were wrong in mine."

"Lucas, you heard what Eleanor said. I don't want to see you bang your head against another stone wall. We've been doing okay, up till now."

"Yes, but didn't you even hear what Maggie said? I *know* she's right, about what it feels like not to be able to read. Only she just scratched the surface."

Wayne shifted uncomfortably. "I know it's been rough, Lucas. There must have been times when you resented—"

"No." Lucas stared hard at his brother. "It's not your fault, Wayne. It's not your fault that Dad and Mother didn't live. It's not your fault that I was in and out of school. And most of all, it's not your fault that you're an accountant and I'm a fisherman. I'd have been a fisherman, or a farmer if the government hadn't taken our land, whether or not I'd learned to read. I love what I do. And I'm happy with my life.

"But I can't read. I've let you protect me from the consequences of that because I thought you needed to. Or maybe I was just so ashamed of my illiteracy, I used your insistence as an excuse. But it's got to end. For your sake and for mine."

"It's Susanna, isn't it, Lucas? I warned you she'd stir things up. She won't take over where I left off. Mark my words, she'll go back to D.C. Then who's going to answer your mail, and read you the specs on all that equipment, and—"

"Wayne, *damn it*. I don't want Susanna around for that, or anybody else. I'm tired of just accepting my limits. I want . . . I want a *wife*, Wayne, and a kid, a kid of my own. But I won't feel right about going after either, unless I learn how to read."

Wayne kicked the footrest on the recliner and sat up straight. "Do you want me to quit right now? Just say the word, Lucas. Lord knows I've got plenty of other work."

Lucas looked at his brother, wishing he knew some better, kinder way to break his dependency on Wayne. Then he slowly nodded his head.

Wayne stood. He strode across the room and opened the glass door off the parlor that led to the garden and lawn beyond. "Tell Maggie I needed to get some air, will you?" When he went out, he slammed the door.

Little Willy woke with a start. His face turned red as he gave out a yell. Another followed and then another. Soon the baby was crying with full force. The sound seemed a fitting accompaniment to the pent-up frustration Lucas felt.

Maggie came through the door, followed by Susanna. Lucas handed the baby back to his mother. "The best thing about being an uncle instead of a father," Lucas growled, "is times like this."

"It's not so bad," Maggie said lightly. She cooed to Little Willy to quiet him. "You'll find out someday when you become a father, Lucas."

"Hey, look, I've got to get back to the lake. It was a terrific dinner. See you both tomorrow." Lucas turned and strode out of the room. The front screen door slammed shut behind him.

"He's had another fight with Wayne," Maggie said as they stood at the door, watching him go. "Wayne will be out pacing the garden. I'll put Willy down, and then I'll go find him."

"I'll take care of Willy, Maggie." Susanna put the fussy baby over her shoulder and rubbed his back to soothe him. Willy began to quiet as she carried him up the stairs. Susanna held him close, feeling the baby snuggle against her breast. But her own heart was filled with turmoil.

Lucas obviously felt uncomfortable about Maggie's remark that he'd have a child of his own. She thought of the desolate feeling she'd had at Maggie's announcement.

It wasn't that she didn't want children. She knew that now. It was that she knew she wouldn't be good at the closeness, the intimacy, the total responsibility for a single, individual human being. Weren't babies the ultimate one-on-one? It was something she had to accept, the fact that her strength had always been in numbers. Big projects, big policies.

Lucas, for some reason, must have decided that children were not for him, either. But if that was something else they shared, why did the pain in his eyes and the distance he'd forced between them with his sudden retreat wrench so desperately at her heart?

Chapter Nine

Lonetree took off his cap and wiped at his brow with his forearm. Then he leaned into the open window of the big silver truck, just as he had every day at this time for the past four days in a row.

"Toby, you *know* I can keep an eye on the minnows. Things went okay all week, didn't they, kid? And remember last year? That time you got sick? I did a good job, didn't I?"

"But you know what happens, Lonetree. You know. The minnows get too big. Then they get hungry. They eat up all the little ones. You've got to move them before they do that, Lonetree."

"Hey, *look* at me, will you?" Lonetree put his cap back on and pulled the bill low over his eyes. Then he straightened to his full height. "Do I look like I can protect the babies, or what?"

A smile broke through, erasing the worried lines at Toby's mouth. Lonetree stepped back, saluting, and Lucas started the engine. "Don't forget to check them every hour," Toby called out as Lucas backed up the truck.

When they reached the main road to Wilamet, Lucas switched on the radio and found a soothing classical station. "Roll up your window, Toby," he said. "I'll turn on the air-conditioning. We can hardly hear the music today over the sound of the cicadas."

"Do I have to, Lucas? I like their song. Susanna says those bugs are just doing what they're meant to do. They sleep for a long time underground, and then they come out and sing as loud as they can till their time is up. When will that be, Lucas? When will the cicada's time be up?"

"Soon," Lucas answered. "All too soon." He turned the radio off, and hung his left arm out the window, thinking of Susanna. She still hadn't said for sure that she'd be staying on through Maggie's pregnancy. She was always saying that she was too busy to think—

"Are you coming in with me today, Lucas? I want to show you my flash cards. Miss Eleanor gave me my own cards. I keep them in a box. So far I've only put *T* on the box. Miss Eleanor says that's the first letter in my name. I'm going to learn the rest of the letters and put my whole name on that box. Then it will really be mine, won't it, Lucas?"

Lucas glanced over at the young man sitting beside him and mustered a smile. "Sure, Toby," he said. "You just keep at it." Toby laughed and hung his elbow out the window, imitating Lucas.

Eleanor brushed the chalk dust off her hands and reached for a bright red folder with Toby's name written in big black letters on the front of it.

"It's going to take time, a lot of time, but I think there's a chance he can learn to read, Lucas. Does he talk about his lessons at home?"

Lucas laughed. "Nonstop. He's driving us crazy. He's got Lonetree convinced he's a poet. He goes around the marina day after day, pointing out things that begin with *T*. He's in love with the sound. We're wondering if he'll feel the same way about every letter."

Eleanor laughed. "Now that he's made the initial discovery, of the connection between the written letter and the sound it represents, we'll be going on. You can all prepare yourselves for words that begin with *B* on Monday."

At Lucas's wearied look, Eleanor chuckled. "You're not too old to remember. Try. Think back to first grade, or even before that, when you first learned the sounds of the letters."

Think back. "I'd rather not," Lucas said abruptly before he could stop himself.

A puzzled frown creased Eleanor's brow. "Why—"

"Lucas, come on," Toby interrupted. "I've got them all lined up. Come and see my cards."

He crossed the room to a low table where Toby sat in a too-small chair, spreading out several flash cards on the table. Each one pictured the letter *T* and an object that began with the letter.

"This is a clock, and this is a *T*. This one gets me confused."

Eleanor put her hand on Toby's shoulder. "Think hard," she said.

Toby squeezed his eyes shut and clenched his fists at his sides. Finally he opened them and looked up. "Help me, Lucas," he begged.

Lucas looked at Eleanor, who silently shook her head. Then he looked back at Toby. He felt the young man's frustration as if it were his own. He wanted to answer for

Toby. It was all he could do to stand there and watch him squeeze his eyes shut again. He thought of Wayne and understood something of what his brother must feel.

"Time!" Toby shouted suddenly. "Time, time, time! Clocks tell time." Toby quieted and sat very still. And then he turned to Eleanor.

"Tell," he said. "That's a *T* word, too, isn't it, Mrs. Foster?"

Eleanor stood still. Slowly she nodded. "Yes, Toby, *tell* is a *T* word."

"But there's no picture."

"No. Some words are hard to draw a picture of. Especially things we do. Like *laugh* and *sing* and *learn*. But we still have words for them. A word can be a kind of picture."

"Tell, tell, tell." Toby repeated the word over and over as he gathered up his cards.

Eleanor crossed the room to her desk and motioned Lucas to follow. "I want to write this down," she said, opening Toby's notebook. "Toby doesn't know it yet, but he's discovered the principle of abstraction. He did it all by himself. Lucas, in some ways I think he's farther along than we realize. If I could just find the key..."

"I think you've already found it. Toby trusts you. What you're doing is worth a lot to him, and to me. I'd really like to pay you. There's no reason why—"

"I won't hear of that, Lucas Grant. Besides, you're doing enough. Susanna's told me how you've been on the phone every night this week, helping with the survey."

Lucas smiled and stuck his hands deep in his pockets. He could feel his color rising. Had Eleanor guessed that there'd also been a time, every night this week, when it had grown too late to make phone calls? A time when Susanna had finally turned off the computer and come looking for him? Usually just for half an hour, just time enough for a couple of beers and some talk before one of the guides stopped by to take her home. Still, it had been time he treasured.

Lucas cleared his throat. "I'll be back in an hour for Toby."

"Fine. Don't forget to remind him all weekend that his lessons begin again Monday afternoon. We're over that period he was scared to death to come, but now he'll be worried he's missing something. He actually likes it here."

"Thanks to you."

"No, Lucas, it's thanks to *you*. Every teacher knows that it's what happens at home that matters."

Her words sunk in like stones. Maybe he'd had something to do with getting Toby to the center, but soon enough the young man was going to need more. More than he could give.

"Well, don't just stand there. Come in." Maggie held the kitchen screen door wide, but Lucas stood his ground on the porch.

"You're letting the bugs in, Lucas," Wayne mumbled. "Come on in." Wayne didn't look up from his newspaper.

Maggie took Lucas's arm and forcibly drew him into the kitchen. "Honestly, you two, how long is it going to last this time?"

Both men glanced at Maggie, shrugging off her question, then eyed each other darkly. She sighed and wiped her hands on her apron. "Sit down and have a sandwich, Lucas, and don't forget the one I've wrapped for Toby. He'll be hungry after his lesson. I'll go up and see if Susanna's ready."

Wayne read for a minute more while Lucas ate. Then he carefully folded his paper and tossed it on the table between them. "Where have you been all week? I thought you were going to stop by the office."

"I came on Monday. You were out."

"I needed a haircut, Lucas. You could have come by the barbershop. Or waited."

Lucas eyed his brother. Wayne had his head cocked to one side, the way he always looked when he was mad. He'd probably had it cocked that way since Monday. One side of his hair was cut slightly shorter than the other. Lucas smiled.

Wayne lifted an eyebrow and straightened his head. Then Lucas grinned. Wayne's haircut was definitely lopsided.

"Well?"

"Well, what?"

"Well, what are you grinning at, for one thing?"

"You shouldn't get your hair cut when you're angry, Wayne."

Wayne's face turned pink. Then he started to laugh.

Lucas began laughing, too, and nearly choked on his sandwich.

"That's one sure thing about Charlie Parker," Wayne said. "You get a straight haircut every time."

"Straight in direct relation to whichever way you happen to be looking," Lucas added.

"At least I stay away on Saturdays, when the bench outside Charlie's window is filled with waiting girlfriends."

The kitchen door swung open, and Maggie came in, followed by Susanna, who carried a cardboard box full to overflowing with computer printouts. Lucas stood to take it from her, and Maggie passed her the overnight bag she carried.

"What was that about *girlfriends*, Wayne Grant?" Maggie stood with her hands on her hips.

Wayne grabbed her wrist and pulled her down on his lap. "I was just telling Lucas about Charlie Parker's barbershop and how all you girls used to hang out, hoping to get lucky."

"Wayne, you know very well I never—"

Wayne stopped her halfhearted protest with a hug and a quick kiss. Maggie looked from him to his brother, smiling her approval. Lucas looked at Susanna.

She flashed him a dazzling glad-to-see-you smile, then turned to her notebook and busily sorted the papers. Her hair was pulled back in the usual braid, but she'd woven a ribbon through the length of it, a shiny yellow ribbon that matched the sundress she wore. And she smelled so good. The kitchen filled with the scent of soap and the hint of gardenias. He hardly heard his brother.

"I'll come by an hour early tomorrow when we drop off Little Willy. I'll get the accounts caught up and print out the checks," Wayne said as he followed his brother out the door.

"Toby's sandwich!" Maggie called after them. Susanna turned back to the kitchen.

"Have you...done anything yet?" Wayne asked his brother in a lowered voice.

"It's not that easy. I'd have to go through Eleanor or Maggie to get tested. I don't want—"

"Don't work too hard, you two," Maggie called after them.

Wayne leaned in as Lucas closed the door of the truck. "We'll work it out," he said.

Lucas nodded. There wasn't time to explain the rest of it to his brother. He wanted to tell Susanna first. He'd tried all week, but there hadn't been time. Tonight she was staying over, sleeping in the houseboat, presumably so she could work late and then start in early tomorrow. But there would be the evening. She didn't know he'd asked Lonetree to take over his scheduled charter.

"Did you have a chance to stop by the post office?" Susanna asked him before he'd backed out of the driveway.

Lucas grinned. "It's in the back. Do you want me to get it?"

"Oh, no, don't bother, I can wait till we get to the lake. How big is it? Did the senator's office send only one envelope? Is it heavy?"

Lucas laughed out loud, pulled the truck to the curb and left the engine running while he got out and swung himself up into the bed of the truck. Susanna's eager look turned radiant at the sight of two large manila envelopes in his hands. Lucas grinned and shook his head in disbelief.

"If I didn't know differently, I'd say you just hauled in a record fish," he said, climbing back into the truck.

"Better than that," Susanna crowed. She tore at the packages, and forms spilled out on her lap. Some of them slipped to the floor as he headed down the street. "I thought we'd missed the filing deadline for most of the fall proposals, but look at this. There must be fifty of them! If we get the prelims done by tomorrow noon and express mail them to Washington . . . what's the matter, Lucas?"

He'd pulled his hat down low over his eyes and slouched down in the seat, his arm stretched rigid over the top of the wheel. "You've worked all week."

Susanna scooted across the seat and brushed a kiss across his ear. "I know. I guess I was half hoping myself that there would be fewer forms. I thought we might have dinner together late, after you get back from the charter. I wore a dress. . . ."

"I noticed," he told her. "And I haven't got a charter tonight."

The feel of her leg pressed next to his, with just her skirt and his jeans between them was almost more than he could handle. Again the scent of gardenias rose up and filled his nostrils. Lucas took a deep breath. When he reached the school, it was all he could do to leave her to go in for Toby.

The young man hurried across the short, dry grass of the schoolyard, headed straight for the silver truck. "Look,

Susanna. Mrs. Foster let me bring home all my papers. I've got lots of *T*'s. Which ones do you like best?''

"In a minute, Toby, just let me check..."

She kept shuffling through her forms even after Lucas had started the engine. Toby was very quiet. They were out on the highway before she even looked up.

"I'm sorry, Toby. What was it you said?"

"It's okay. You're busy. Susanna's been busy, hasn't she, Lucas?"

Lucas nodded.

"Now wait—"

"You've got lots of papers, too. It's okay. You've got lots more papers than I've got."

Toby shuffled the scraps of writing tablet he held in his lap, folded them and tried to shove them into his pocket. But Susanna gently took them away. The envelope of forms slid off her lap and onto the floor. She didn't bother to retrieve it.

The "one more hour" she'd begged for had turned into two, and it was nearly four o'clock when Susanna looked up at the knock on the kitchen door.

"Lonetree, what's wrong...what—"

"Get Lucas."

The big Indian stood on the porch of the cabin, his bronze face glowing copper red, his dark eyes burning into her face.

"At least come inside where it's cool." She tried to pull him into the kitchen, but Lonetree shrugged her off.

"Is he here?" the Indian asked her.

"I...I guess so. I've been working...I—"

"Lonetree?" Lucas pushed through the swinging door to the kitchen, squinting into the sunlight. He was barefoot, and his shirt hung open at the chest. He'd obviously been napping. She'd been so busy working she hadn't even noticed him head for the bedroom when he'd come in.

"You'll have to take the charter, Lucas. I'm not in the mood to sub." Lonetree was halfway down the steps before Lucas got out the door.

"Will you get back up here and tell me what the hell happened," he said. "I'll take the charter out, but first I want to know what's going on."

Lonetree kicked at the chips of bark on the path and sent a few of them flying. Then he spun, rocked back on his heels and stood looking up at Lucas.

"There's a woman with them."

"So? You've taken women out plenty of times. I don't see—"

"I knew this one . . . before."

Lucas went down the steps and stood eye to eye with Lonetree. Neither spoke. Then Lucas turned back to Susanna as he buttoned up his shirt.

"Fix him something cold to drink, will you? And make sure he eats. Keep him here as long as you can, at least till I get out on the water. Get him to talk. He's been like this all week."

Lonetree came up the steps, his big shoulders swinging under his long, dark hair. She'd promised to trim it for him, Susanna remembered, before she'd gotten so busy. She held the screen door for him, then she went to Lucas.

She reached up to straighten the collar of his chambray work shirt, and let her fingers trail along his shoulder. Lucas caught her hand, and his eyes grew intimate. "You'll have to take a rain check for dinner," he said.

Susanna smiled but shook her head. "I've still got tons of work to do, anyway. I'm going to be up half the night."

His blue eyes narrowed a fraction as he looked down at her. His kiss barely brushed her cheek. "I'll be late. Don't bother waiting."

He turned away abruptly and then turned back. "You've had a hard week. A decent night on the houseboat, out of reach of that damn computer, might do you some good. The rest of that stuff can wait until morning.''

''The deadline—''

''The hell with the deadline.''

''But if we don't get these proposals in—''

''The hell with the proposals.'' He pulled her roughly into his arms and kissed her hard, the way he'd wanted to all afternoon. When he let her go, the last thing he touched was the yellow ribbon in her hair.

Lucas's eyes had blazed at her before he'd turned and headed down the path to the marina. The taste of his angry kiss still burned a warning. She'd neglected him. She'd let work take over again. Something in the back of her mind suggested that she'd been running. *No.* Couldn't he see that the time she'd been spending on the literacy center was necessary?

When she pushed through the kitchen door, Lonetree grunted. ''Looks like I'm not the only one with woman problems.''

Susanna spun on her heels. ''Lucas doesn't have a problem. Not with me, anyway. And neither should you with anyone else. If there are any *women problems* around here, they're probably with the both of you!''

She pushed him into a kitchen chair and shoved aside her books and papers. Then she opened the refrigerator. Fresh peeled shrimp were heaped on a bed of lettuce and a creamy dressing filled a bowl beside it. A split of champagne was cooling on its side.

Susanna stared at the food, knowing what Lucas had planned. It wasn't Lonetree's fault. If she'd left her work when Lucas had first returned . . .

She closed the refrigerator door. ''How about if I make us some lemonade? I think we both need cooling off.''

* * *

She filled Lonetree's plate a second time with shrimp salad and watched him tear off another piece of the loaf of French bread she'd found in the pantry.

"Was she somebody special?" Susanna asked him.

He took his time in answering, studying her across the table. "No. She was just a girl...a woman now. I knew her in high school. I knew a lot of girls."

Susanna laughed. "I bet you did."

Lonetree gave her a lopsided grin. "I knocked 'em dead. I was pretty good-looking, for a ragtag Indian kid, that is."

"You're not bad-looking now. Except you could use that haircut I promised you."

Lonetree speared another shrimp and stared at it on the end of his fork. "It doesn't matter a hell of a lot. Now nobody looks twice."

"I don't think that's true, first of all. And if it is true, why don't you do something about it? What happened last week when you went to the city? Lucas told me about the doctor you met."

"There's not a lot to tell. I can get an artificial arm with a hand that looks almost real. Hell, they can even make them *feel* like skin. But there's a trade-off. Any hand I get has got to be able to do more than just look pretty. For the kind of work I do, an old-fashioned hook is better." He popped the shrimp in his mouth and chewed thoughtfully. And then he laughed, but there wasn't any humor in the sound of it.

"I can see it now. Old Elaine what's-her-name would *really* have done a double take if she'd seen a hook sticking out of this empty sleeve."

"Lonetree, I don't think—"

"You don't *think*? Susanna, you don't *know*."

"Lonetree, what about the new experimental programs? When I was volunteering in Washington, I heard something about skin implants. I could use the computer to find out where they're doing the research.'' She was already reaching for her government data service directory.

Lonetree covered her hand.

"No," he said quietly. "I lent my body to the government once. Never again."

Still, after he'd gone, Susanna set aside her proposal forms and fiddled with the computer till she'd pulled up a data base. She didn't look up from the keyboard till midnight. When Lucas walked in, the computer was still spewing out addresses.

He glanced at the clock and then at the reams of paper covering the kitchen floor. Susanna looked tired, but her eyes were shining.

"Look, Lucas. There must be a hundred sources. Universities, research centers, lots of people are studying artificial limbs. They must have programs. If Lonetree doesn't want to send letters, I'm going to do it for him."

Lucas frowned. "Why?" he asked her.

Susanna started to answer, but words wouldn't come. It's what I do, she wanted to say. *It's what I'm good at.* Instead she watched him stride across the kitchen, pull a beer from the refrigerator and pop the tab. He slammed the refrigerator door, and a pencil she'd left on the top rolled off. He didn't bother to pick it up. His back still to her, he lifted the can and drained it in one slow draught.

"You're tired," she said.

"And hot," he added. "It's been one hell of a night." He all but brushed her aside, stripped off his shirt and headed toward the bedroom.

Susanna followed tentatively. "What did you mean when you asked me why I was trying to help Lonetree?" she asked him.

He eyed her darkly and sat down on the edge of the bed to pull off his shoes. He smelled like fish. Ordinarily he'd have been elated at the catch. Tonight the smell disgusted him. He grabbed a towel and headed for the shower.

"I only meant that it seems to me that Lonetree was a hell of lot happier when he wasn't thinking about getting an artificial arm. I've never seen him act the way he did tonight. Not with men. Not with women. Sure there are people who stare at his stump. And there are those who ask stupid questions. But he ignores them, or sets them straight. At least, he always has until now."

"And you think I'm to blame. He's started to wonder if he's adjusted too much. And you think I'm responsible for that?"

"Aren't you?"

"Lucas, I just can't help it. And underneath, I feel that he wants some help."

"*Help.*" Lucas spat out the word. He crossed the kitchen to the computer and thumped its top. "Is this what you mean by help?"

"It's one way. I know it's not the only way. I know you—"

"Did Lonetree tell you what else he found out in the city? Did he tell you about the surgery he's going to have to go through again? Did he tell you about the hell he went through when they cut off his arm? Did he mention the *guillotine* procedure that's common in wartime? Did he tell you any of that, Susanna?"

Susanna felt light-headed. She reached for the back of the chair for support.

"Susanna, for Pete's sake, he's a *man*, not just another statistic."

He slammed the bathroom door behind him, and a moment later she heard the rush of the shower.

She wandered back to the kitchen. The computer printer had stopped. She tore off the list and started to fold the paper.

If someone needed help, she knew every catalog of programs. She knew a thousand phone numbers. She knew every major support group in the country. What she didn't know was how to help, just by reaching out.

She knew very well what rejection felt like. An empty ring at the end of Daryl's office phone, or the female caller who quickly hung up when she answered hers. Lonetree had probably felt it a hundred times. He'd started to open up to her. And then she'd closed him off.

She was gathering up the forms when Lucas came back into the room. She couldn't meet his eyes. She spoke without lifting her head. "It's just a habit, I guess. At least, I hope it's *just* a habit. I hope I'm not really that uncaring—"

His arms were around her in a moment, pulling her close. "You're not uncaring. I'm sorry. I was tired. It was a long night. I wanted to be here with you."

"And you thought *I* wanted to work. Oh, Lucas, you just can't imagine what it's like in Washington. There's so much competition for the money. So many people are fighting for a piece of the action. I get so angry when I see people like Lonetree, people who could really benefit—"

"You're still the kid I remember who stood outside the cafeteria with the milk bottle. Tell me, Susanna," he said. "Did any of that money ever get to China?"

"Biafra," she whispered, just before he reached for the ribbon that held her hair.

Chapter Ten

Lucas pulled the yellow ribbon the rest of the way out of her braid and watched Susanna's hair fall loose and free around her shoulders. The single strand of silk felt warm and smooth against his palm. Slowly he drew it through his fingers.

"I meant what I said, Susanna. You need a quiet night on the houseboat."

She hesitated. What was he trying to tell her? Had he hoped she'd be gone by the time he got back? Had she missed one too many chances all week? She thought of how willing he'd seemed to leave her alone with her work when he'd gotten home that afternoon.

"I'm not the only one who needs some rest," she answered, trying to keep her voice even. "You've had early-morning and late-evening charters all week. And you've spent almost all of your afternoons helping me with the survey."

He took a step toward her, and Susanna stopped breathing a moment, but he only hung the ribbon over the top of the computer monitor. Then he looked up, riveting her eyes with his. "I don't have a charter tomorrow morning."

She looked back steadily, still unsure. "I could come up and fix you breakfast."

"No, I'll fix *you* breakfast. You're going to stay out of the kitchen. You're not going to touch that keyboard until noon."

"But, Lucas—"

"We had a date tonight, remember? Now I'm offering you breakfast instead of dinner. In fact, just because it's a little late—"

"I thought you were tired."

"I am."

"Me, too."

"We could sleep a little . . . first."

She wrapped her arms around his neck and buried her face in the soft terry folds of his robe. "Do we have a choice?" she whispered.

"We did a moment ago. But now . . ." His voice was low and throaty as he stroked her cheek with the back of his hand.

He flipped off the kitchen light when they passed through the doorway and turned on the intercom stereo, flooding the cabin with music. The same tape he'd played after she left last night started up again, the soft, delicate timbre of Liszt.

He turned out the hall light as they passed. Then only the light from the bathroom was left, a dim yellow glow from the rear of the bedroom. It fell on her back and her shoulders as she stopped to wait for him.

Susanna felt suddenly shy, but calm and certain. She stepped into the room and turned toward Lucas. A drop of water had slid down his cheek from his still-damp hair. She touched his face.

It wasn't the bottomless hunger with which they'd first shared each other's bodies. Not at first, anyway. It was more like the music that was filling the cabin. Rich, slow, languorous.

He carefully undid the tiny buttons that ran down the front of her sundress, letting the straps fall over her shoulders, pausing to kiss the hollows of each as he did it. He caressed her skin, luxuriating in the softness of it, enjoying the silky touch of her undergarments until they, too, seemed in the way. Then, half with her help, he slid them off her.

When she stood before him at last, he held her a moment with his eyes, caressing the silhouette of her body in the soft diffusion of light. Then he reached for the belt of his robe and loosened it. He took it off and stood before her.

The music swept over them, hushing all but the current of desire that pulled her body slowly toward his. She touched the firm line of his mouth, and he kissed her fingers. Then he reached his own hand out to her, touching the ridge of her cheekbone as though for the very first time.

Their fingers met, and he stroked her palms till she opened them wide, accepting his touch, then giving hers, up the sweep of his forearms, across his chest, through the rough, masculine hairs that covered it, to the smooth, taut muscles below his ribs, and lower. Susanna closed her eyes. Her hands moved lower, then lower. And then she touched him.

Lucas groaned, but he didn't move. She touched him again, stroking him, exploring that part of him that she knew would soon be plunging inside her, probing her to her inmost being.

He swept her up and laid her gently in the middle of his bed. For a very long moment, he just stood over her.

"I want you, Susanna," he said. "Oh, God, how I want you." He covered her mouth with his before she could answer that she wanted him, too, that *want* was hardly the word for what she was feeling.

His tongue thrust through her pliant lips, tasting the deepest recesses of her mouth, testing for warmth, drawing it up from the depths of her. He kissed her mouth, her neck, the hollow at her throat, her breasts. He lingered, taking the time he'd not taken before. Not just for her. Something in him wanted to worship, wanted to wait, wanted to smell, taste, touch, listen to the butterfly-soft beating of her heart.

He wanted it to be slow, to last forever, to make her remember, to make her so conscious of every sensation that she'd never forget, never push aside the memory of their lovemaking for anything else.

Susanna began to moan, to cry out for him. Lucas tried to stop her cries with his kiss, but instead they drew him closer to her, over her, into her. She arched with the force of his thrust, moved with him, against him, in perfect rhythm with the tempo of his hips against hers.

Then she was taking over. Caught in the sweet, dark, moist center of her, he was swimming, holding his breath against the explosion, trying to slow it as she drew it forth from him. He stroked his body against hers, till he burst inside her and gave her what she'd been crying for.

Flowing, flowing, Susanna became a river that welcomed him in her current. Together they moved past cities and valleys and towns, into the starlight of grassy banks and silence and sleep, then on. And somewhere in the night, they woke and loved again. The river simply carried them, half sleeping, on.

Her face felt warm, and the music was strange. Susanna opened her eyes. The window over the bed was open. Sunlight streamed in. The sound of the cicadas rose on the breeze of the billowing curtain, and fell, and then was quiet. Someone was whistling. *Lucas.*

She stretched, and thought of their lovemaking. Curling around the pillows they'd shared, she inhaled the musky fragrance that still lingered in the bed. Susanna wished she could stay there forever.

Finally she slipped into his terry robe and belted it loosely around her waist, then tiptoed, barefoot, off toward the kitchen, following the smell of coffee and the sound of his whistling. She stood in the doorway a moment, watching him work.

He'd been for a swim. He still wore trunks, along with a faded short-sleeved shirt. He had strong legs. Closing her eyes, she felt them again, pressing her thighs, holding her legs, spreading them apart...

"Kitchen's off-limits, lady. Remember?" His arms were around her, pulling her close. His kiss left a lingering taste of salt and coconut oil. His arm around her waist, he led her out to the deck.

She'd never seen the lake this early in the morning from this high up on the hill. Now, her back to his chest, leaning against him as his arms wrapped around her, Susanna looked out across blue water, silent and bright as a diamond nestled in a bed of emeralds.

"Even the cicadas have hushed. I can barely hear their song."

His arms loosened slightly. "It's getting on toward August, Susanna. They won't be out much longer."

"Oh, Lucas, *don't*." She turned in his arms to face him. "I said we'd find a way."

"And I believed you. I still do." He looked away, over her head, out toward the lake. "But I've seen you work, lady. You're very good at what you do. I'm not sure I could ever..."

She touched his lips to still his protest. "Wait. Wait one more week till I get through this project. Wait until the meeting. By next Friday it will all be over. Then we can talk. There'll be plenty of time, just for us."

He held her close, wanting to believe. He had so much to tell her, so much more he wanted to say. But she was right. The memory of the moment mattered more right now. He knew about that. How to make the moment matter. They were going to need these memories later. Maybe desperately. Last night, this morning, the boat ride, their fishing trip, stolen moments all last week. Lucas crushed her against his chest. The coffee could wait. *Everything* else could wait. He lifted Susanna and carried her back to the bed.

Susanna took one last sip of coffee and hit the switch on the computer. After a hum and a buzz, the little green light glowed ready. She looked up at Lucas.

"First things first. I've built an input screen, and I'd like you to help me enter the data from your calls. It would probably be faster if you just read me your notes."

Lucas took a long swallow of coffee and met her eyes across the table. "I didn't take notes."

"You didn't take—"

"I never take notes. But I can remember everything."

"You've got to be kidding. Lucas, I know you have a terrific memory, but you must have made a hundred calls."

He nodded. "Try me."

She picked up the numeric listing they'd gotten from the phone company, read a number at random and waited for his response.

"Woman, married with children, all readers, likes mystery novels and gardening books, some sympathy but no understanding of nonreaders, class two."

Susanna read a second number, this one from deeper into the listing.

Lucas leaned forward. "Woman, single, reads the *Wilamet News*, wishes she were a better reader. I gave her class five."

"Class five? Positive attitude and functionally illiterate? But she reads the paper."

"Only the comics. Dear Abby gives her problems. She gets mad at the answers, then finds out from her sister that she didn't understand them. Next?"

Susan glanced at Lucas then back at the computer terminal. "You are incredible. You make taking notes seem superfluous."

"Necessity is the mother—"

"Of invention," Susanna finished for him. But she gave only a passing thought to what he was saying. Her fingers were already flying over the keyboard.

Later that afternoon, Susanna reluctantly gave up the computer when Wayne and Maggie arrived with Little Willy. She and her sister left the men in the kitchen, pouring over Lucas's accounts, and headed toward the marina with the baby.

"Susanna, Wayne and I don't *have* to go out tonight. If it meant you could get a little further today and wouldn't have to work so hard next week . . ."

"Don't be silly, Maggie. I'll get it all done. I always do. Besides, Lucas has been looking forward all week to the two of us taking care of Little Willy. And heaven knows, you and Wayne can use an evening out."

Maggie patted her tummy. "The movie, yes, but the dinner is debatable. Dr. Gurley threatened to charge me double if I gain too much weight again."

Susanna stopped to pick up a pinecone and show it to Little Willy. Maggie settled down heavily on a big, smooth rock beside the path. Susanna eyed her sister.

"Maggie, tell me how you're feeling. *Really.*"

Her sister shaded her eyes and looked down toward the lake. Susanna couldn't see the expression on her face, but the tone of her voice was telling.

"I'm fine."

"You sound tired."

"I'm doing much better than Dr. Gurley expected."

"But not as well as you'd hoped?"

Maggie shrugged away her sister's protests. "You're there every morning, Susanna. It's really a help."

I don't do enough, she thought. *I've been so busy.* She touched Maggie's shoulder. Her sister sighed.

"Maybe I should think about giving up my class, at least till the baby's born. It's so blissful to sleep till eight. I could use just one more hour."

"Go ahead and do it. Mother's work with Toby has gone so well that I think she's got her old confidence back. She can take over the class for you."

"I know," Maggie said. "But I'll miss it." She linked her fingers through her sister's. "Funny, isn't it? We're all alike, we Fosters. Each of us wants to do 'something meaningful,' to use Daddy's old phrase."

Something meaningful? Susanna caught the pinecone just as Willy decided to taste it. The baby clung tenaciously and turned his clear blue eyes up to hers. Thank goodness, she thought, that Willy has a mother who can set aside her work for him.

"I think you've got your hands full right here for a while, Maggie." She tickled the baby until he let loose of the pinecone. "Someone else can teach the world to read for a couple of months."

"How about you?"

"Me? You mean tutoring?" Susanna laughed. "I haven't done that since—"

"Since you used to help me with my homework. Remember how all my friends would follow me home after school? You got us all through long division. I think my love of teaching comes more from you than from Mother."

Susanna smiled at the memory, then quickly shrugged it off. "If I started tutoring, who would finish the proposals?"

"How can you finish them when you haven't even been to the center or actually worked with some of the students?"

"Maggie, Washington doesn't care if I've seen a student or not. Only that I prove there's a need. The new survey and some careful analysis will accomplish that."

Her sister propped her chin in her hands. "It sure beats me. We *know* we have a problem. Why should we have to prove it?"

She started to explain, but Maggie interrupted her. "Susanna, it's just that it seems like such a tangle. Look at the time you've spent. You could have tutored a handful of students, maybe helped them advance by a month or more."

"But somebody's got to do the paperwork."

"Why?"

"Because the center needs funding. Because every worthwhile project needs funding. Because there's so much competition..."

"So if Wilamet gets the money for the center, some other project has to lose?"

When Maggie clucked in disapproval, Susanna didn't respond. She'd seen the list of turned-down projects. It bothered her more than she cared to admit.

Just then Little Willy succeeded in snatching the pinecone back and getting the end of it into his mouth. It took their combined effort to hold him down and pull it away.

"Come on," Maggie said wearily. "I promised I'd bring Willy down to look at the minnows. Toby will pester me all next week if I don't."

The cooler day, plus the fact that it was Saturday, had brought more than the usual crowd into the marina bait shop. Maggie took Willy back to the minnow tanks, and Susanna waited in the register line to speak to Lonetree. It was the first time she'd had a chance to watch him work with people. His ease surprised her.

"Okay, Jake," he said to an elderly man. "You've got your night crawlers and a box of those lightweight sinkers and a package of blueberry worms. Anything else?"

"Gimme some ice and a case of cola, Lonetree. I'll git 'em m'self."

"Hang on a minute, and I'll load you up." Before the man could object, Lonetree had maneuvered the case of cola, topped by a bag of crushed ice, up to his shoulder. He headed for the door.

Susanna considered holding it open and then thought better of it. She was glad she had when Lonetree caught the edge of the door with his foot and opened it himself. The tall Indian nodded at her as he passed, a smug smile playing at the corners of his mouth.

The old man shuffled after him, shaking his head. "That missin' arm don't slow him down a bit, eh, missy?"

Susanna smiled and nodded. Nothing seemed to slow down Lonetree, except maybe the suggestions she'd made that he needed to make changes. *Had* she only interfered?

"Where's Toby?" Maggie asked behind her.

Lonetree came back in time to hear her question. "He's out back, waiting for Lucas. I've been telling him that it's Saturday and he won't have another class till Monday, but you know Toby."

"I'll see what I can do," Susanna said. "Let me take Willy, Maggie. You come, too."

Sure enough, on the bench behind the marina, Toby sat alone in the sun, worriedly studying his watch. When he saw

Maggie and Susanna, his face brightened, then clouded again in confusion.

"Why aren't you at the school, Maggie? Have you seen Lucas? It's time we were going."

"I don't teach today, Toby. Remember? We all have Saturday and Sunday off. I brought Little Willy to see the minnows."

"Darn!" Toby kicked at the dry red dust in front of the bench. "Darn," he repeated in a softer voice. "I wish I could remember what day it is. I'm always forgetting. Why don't I remember? It makes me feel real stupid."

Susanna sat down on the bench and took Toby's hand in hers. She held her own wrist next to his, her red sport watch beside his Timex. "Look at our watch faces, Toby. Do you see any difference?"

Toby studied the two watches for a moment before he pointed to the calendar on Susanna's. "What's that?"

"The windows give you the day and the date, Toby. I'll tell you what. As soon as you learn to read, I'll get you a watch like mine. Then you'll always know what day it is."

Toby pulled Susanna's wrist up close to his nose and carefully studied the calendar. "There's a *T*!" he crowed. "I can read part of it! I can read the *T*!"

"It just so happens," Susanna said, "that *Saturday*, *Sat* for short, is the only day that ends with *T*. Maybe you're ready for that watch right now."

Toby looked from Susanna to Maggie and back again. Then his face broke into the broadest grin she'd ever seen him wear. He hugged her hard. "Maybe I'm not really stupid," he said.

"No," she answered. "You're not the least bit stupid, Toby. *Stupid* is for people who don't even try."

"I try hard," Toby said. "Have you got time to look at my papers now? I want to show you how hard I try. And I want to show Maggie's baby my minnows."

Toby ran ahead of them to the bait shop. Maggie touched Susanna's arm as she started to follow. "You're a natural, you know? Maybe you're wasted in Washington."

Susanna laughed. "What would Mother say if she heard you talking like that about—"

"About *our nation's capitol*?" Maggie made a face and headed for the bait shop. "You know, deep down, I suspect she just might agree," she added as she went through the door.

Wayne pushed up the glasses on his nose and looked over the computer terminal at his brother. "You've waited this long to tell her. Can't you wait just a little longer?"

"It's not that I've *waited* to tell Susanna about my illiteracy, Wayne. I've tried. A couple of times I've almost blurted it out. And now... I just can't find the right words, that's all. And the timing is crazy. She's either buried in those damn proposals or..." Lucas stood quickly and turned away from his brother.

"Or you're busy with charters, and chauffeuring Toby, and God knows what else. So why not just cool it? We'll go into the city for the meeting a week from Monday, and that will be that. Then you can talk to whomever you want and *do* whatever you want to do about trying to learn how to read."

Lucas turned back, intending to protest, but Wayne went on. "One more thing. I... I never meant to hold you back, Lucas. If you think I—"

"No, little brother." Lucas braced his arms on the table and leaned across it. "I won't have you blaming yourself, Wayne. It's not your fault. Maybe I just took it for granted the tests were right. Maybe, down deep, I didn't want to put out the extra effort."

"That's ridiculous! The harder the challenge, the higher you always rose to the occasion. Look what you've done *in spite* of not being able to read!"

Lucas's smile was pensive as he ran one hand through his hair. "It's only a start," he said. "I've got a hell of lot more on the agenda."

Behind him, the screen door opened. "Like what?" Susanna asked. "I thought we were taking the afternoon off. *Now* who's too busy for...?"

His eyes met hers and locked. She was smiling, but it was a smile so deep that her parted lips held only a hint of it. Color rose and sat on her cheekbones. She wore those shorts he loved, the ones with the cuff that made her legs look even longer, legs he'd caressed just hours ago...

"It sure is hot out there," Maggie said. She stepped between them and deposited Little Willy in Lucas's arms.

With effort, Lucas pulled his eyes from Susanna to the baby. The wiggling, laughing, blue-eyed bundle of energy that was his nephew suddenly quieted, nestled against his shoulder and popped his thumb in his mouth.

Suddenly the room was silent except for the far-off hum of the cicadas. Maggie stood behind Wayne, her arms looped around his neck, her cheek against his. Lucas kept holding Little Willy, rocking him gently against his shoulder.

The whole scene blurred in front of her eyes as Susanna's heart grew large with love. It was a quiet love that filled her up with longing. She stepped across the empty space between them and reached for the baby.

"Let me put him down, Lucas," she whispered.

Her cheek was wet as she reached for Willy. Lucas's eyes met her full ones and held them fast. A silent question passed between them, and then its answer. And suddenly Susanna's longing had a name. *This,* it said as the baby passed between them, *a child like this is what we really want, you and I, together.*

He gave her the baby, then turned and stood in the doorway, watching her carry him into the bedroom and bend to the cradle. His throat caught then. When Maggie spoke, he wasn't sure he could answer.

"Are you sure you don't mind keeping him tonight, Lucas? I know you and Susanna have a lot to do...on the computer, that is."

The tease in Maggie's voice brought Lucas back to reality. He turned and grinned at her, then crossed the kitchen. "Susanna will probably want to enter all the data you brought her. If it weren't for keeping Little Willy, I'd probably be bored out of my mind."

Had she been wrong? Susanna wondered as she caught the last of Lucas's answer from the doorway. Did he still see her as the Washington woman who'd choose a career and give herself over to it at the expense of anything personal? *Was* she really that kind of woman? *I'll think about it later,* she decided. She glanced at the pile of surveys that Maggie had brought. She'd enter the last of the data and then get started on the needs assessment for the proposals.

Wayne flipped the lever on the computer port and pulled out his disk, storing it in the file that contained Lucas's accounting records. "The computer's yours, Susanna. Good luck with your work."

She nodded absently. A quick hug from her sister, then the soft swing of the kitchen door closing behind them, left Susanna and Lucas alone in the kitchen.

"I thought you wanted some help with taking care of Willy." Susanna kept her voice level, her eyes trained on the kitchen linoleum near his feet.

"You can work while he's sleeping. We can still all go for a swim later."

His voice gave no hint of the distance she thought she'd read in his answer to Maggie. She looked up at him. "It's not that important for me to get started. One afternoon won't make a difference...."

"It might make the difference between midnights all next week." He took a step toward her and gently took her hands. "Look, Susanna, you said there had to be a way. How will we find it unless I try to be more understanding about the pressure you're under?"

She let him pull her into his arms and hold her close. Her eyes squeezed shut, and she tried to push down the sense of panic. She didn't really *want* him to be understanding. She wanted him to keep reminding her, keep *insisting*, that lots of things mean more than work. She realized, in a sudden flash of understanding, that work was a way to avoid taking risks, a way to avoid making choices, choices she'd rather Lucas made for her.

As long as he was forceful, she was strong enough and brave enough to reach out for what she wanted for herself, and for them. But when he gave her room, gave her the freedom to choose for herself... it was then that her old patterns surfaced, her slowness to trust, her need to be sure about every detail, her distance till she had that surity, her preference for safe generalities. And most of all, her workaholic habits. They always stood ready and anxious to take over whenever she began to doubt her feelings.

Just then Little Willy stirred. Lucas kissed her ear and let her go. "I'll get him," he said. "He probably needs a change before he'll settle down for good."

She stood in the middle of the kitchen and hugged her arms to her chest. She wanted to follow him. Wanted to watch him change the baby, watch his big, rough hands grow gentle and tender as the baby's fists curled around his fingers. She took a step forward, brushing the stack of notes as she moved. One of the papers fell to the floor. She bent to pick it up.

The stack was twice as fat as she'd expected. Maggie had brought Eleanor's surveys, too. Lucas was right. She'd better get started. She'd get some work done on entering the statistics. Then there'd be time for Lucas and the baby.

But there wasn't time. Within an hour she knew that there wouldn't be time for anything else all week, except the proposals and her report for the literacy center committee. Just entering the data from the rest of the surveys took all afternoon and evening. She ate a hurried bite with Lucas and the baby and then returned to the terminal.

At midnight, she went home with Maggie and Wayne, then back to the cabin with Lucas after church the following day, begging off Maggie's Sunday dinner. When he came in from his evening charter, she was still at work at the terminal.

"How's it coming?" he asked her.

"Slow," she said. "The data is in. Now I can start on the needs assessment. Once that's done, I'll have several bases for alternative approaches to present to the committee, as well as some recommendations on sources of funding. Once they approve them, and hopefully they *will* approve them, I can have the final proposals signed and get them in before the deadlines."

"Supposing they don't approve?"

"Not approve? They wouldn't do that. We've got all the data. Preliminary analysis has targeted the needs, and I've already got some good matches. There's a special private foundation out of California, for example, that likes to give educational assistance to mothers who are raising their families alone. It's a natural target for our project."

"California is half a continent away."

"So is Washington, D.C., but that doesn't make any difference. Money is money."

Lucas searched her eyes a moment longer before they slipped away from him, back to the computer terminal. He kissed her lightly on one cheek. For a moment, Susanna inhaled the smell of the lake and the tangy scent of his skin and wished she could leave her work.

"Later..." she whispered.

But later never came.

The whole next week seemed one endless session at the computer. Even her mornings with Little Willy grew shorter and shorter as she borrowed time for pouring over last night's printouts. Sometimes she didn't even hear him cry till Maggie appeared in the doorway, rubbing the sleep from her eyes. She'd jump up then and start for the bedroom, but Maggie would hear nothing of it.

"You've only got till Friday. I'll get along."

"I'll make it up to you, Maggie, honest I will."

Afternoons, when she rode with Toby and Lucas back to the lake, Susanna tried to concentrate on Toby's papers and offer encouragement, but by the middle of the week, even Toby had figured out that her mind was totally absorbed by her work. Lonetree, too, had stopped by the cabin once to talk but hadn't come again.

Susanna worked on, oblivious of everything else around her, except for the hurried kiss she shared with Lucas every night on the porch after he'd driven her home. It was always late, too late for anything else. But the feel of the kiss would linger, filling her senses as she slipped into bed, making her wish that she'd had more of him, much more, to carry into her dreams.

Friday morning dawned gray and cloudy, but Susanna was up at six, assembling last night's computer printouts to add to the reports for the noontime meeting. She wanted to finish before Little Willy woke up. Maggie needed the extra sleep, especially since she was coming to the meeting to speak on the current work of the center.

At seven, she looked up briefly as Wayne went through the parlor where she was working, on his way to work. "Good luck on your presentation," he said. He hesitated in the hallway, as though to add something, then went out the door, closing it softly behind him.

It seemed only a moment later when the clock in the hall struck eight and Eleanor hurried out of the kitchen. "I'm late again. Just can't get used to that early-morning class. How did Maggie ever manage?" She sipped the last of her coffee and handed her mug to Susanna.

"See you right before twelve," Eleanor said as she gathered up her books. "If Lucas and Toby get here before I do, be sure Toby understands that we're having our lesson here today so I can baby-sit Willy. Tell him I'll bring his box of flash cards. There's leftover chicken in the refrigerator. And do try to see that Willy gets fed, so I can put him down for his afternoon nap while Toby and I have our lesson. Now have I forgotten anything?"

Before Susanna could answer, Willy let out a muffled wail. "I've got to get him before he wakes up Maggie," she said.

"He's teething again," her mother called after her. "He'll want his ring from the freezer. Top shelf."

The front door closed and her mother was gone. For a moment Susanna stood in the hallway. Should she carry the cup into the kitchen and get the teething ring before she picked up the baby, or the other way around? Or what about this last report that needed assembly. Was there time to—?

Willy let out another wail and Susanna hurried off to his bedroom, coffee cup, report and all. As she passed Maggie's room, she quietly closed the door.

When she reached for Willy, her hair swept forward and brushed his face. The baby laughed and grabbed for it, then cried, and stuck a finger in his mouth.

"Poor boy," she crooned. "We'll get your ring and make ourselves a nice hot breakfast. Then you'll have a bath and I'll have a shower, and you can play with your toys while I braid my hair and finish the reports. And last of all, we'll wake up Mommy."

But nothing happened the way that she'd planned it. The teething ring was not in the freezer, so she had to use ice cubes wrapped in a towel while she hunted it down and waited for it to freeze. Then Willy fretted and cried and wouldn't eat his cereal, and finally decided to dump out the bowl. Sticky oatmeal continued to drip off the tray of the high chair and into Susanna's hair as she bent to the floor to clean up the mess.

It was almost eleven by the time she'd finished Willy's bath and put him down for his morning nap. Then he didn't want to go to sleep. Susanna stood over the crib, gently rubbing the baby's back, wondering what to do next. She felt almost relieved when her sister appeared in the doorway.

"I don't know how you do it, Maggie. The house, the cooking, looking after us all, and now with another baby on the way..." She stopped as her sister reached for the door-jamb to steady herself. "Maggie? Maggie, what's *wrong*?"

Her sister's face was pale and drawn, and as Susanna led her back to her room, Maggie hardly spoke. Susanna made her lie down. Then she sat on the edge of the bed and took her sister's hand in hers. Maggie's eyes filled up with tears.

"Maggie, what *is* it?" Susanna pleaded.

"I'm tired that's all. And I had some spotting last night, not that much, but—"

"Oh, Maggie, you should have told me. I'll call Dr. Gurley right away."

"I already did." Maggie plucked at the coverlet.

"What did he say?" Her sister just looked at her, and another tear spilled out of each eye. "Tell me the truth," Susanna insisted.

"He said that I shouldn't get out of bed for the rest of today and tomorrow, and that if it didn't stop..." Maggie tried to rise up on her elbows. "I don't want to lose this baby," she said fiercely.

Susanna gently pushed Maggie back down onto the bed. "You aren't going to lose the baby. And you'll do exactly as Dr. Gurley says, or you'll have me to answer to, young lady."

"But the meeting—"

"The heck with the meeting. It can go on without us. I'll just have Lucas deliver the reports."

Maggie tried to sit up again. "But they won't understand it. They'll fool around till it's too late. That center means a lot to Wilamet, more than we ever imagined. I couldn't believe the things that I heard on my survey calls. Mother said the same thing. The committee needs to hear about them, too. We've worked so hard to be ready..."

Too hard, Susanna thought. Just then she heard the front door open.

"Anyone home?" Lucas called out.

"Up here," Susanna answered. Suddenly she had an idea. If going to the meeting meant that Maggie would stop worrying, then Susanna would go, and present the material the best way she knew how. Lucas would have to help.

"Promise me you won't get out of bed," she said to her sister. Maggie nodded, and Susanna hurried out the door and down the stairs.

Chapter Eleven

One hand skipping over the banister and the other clutching at the flying skirts of her robe, Susanna ran down the stairs to Lucas.

"Sexy outfit," he whispered in her ear as he caught her. "But what the hell have you got in your hair?"

"Oatmeal," she said.

Lucas felt the brush of a hurried kiss before she pulled away. Lately she was always pulling away. He couldn't even remember the last time he'd held her, *really* held her, in his arms.

In a quick sweep of the parlor, Susanna had gathered up the finished reports and was piling them into Lucas's arms. "I'm going to take a shower," she said. "There's chicken in the refrigerator for Toby. Rock Little Willy if he won't go to sleep. And whatever you do, *don't* let Maggie get out of bed. She isn't coming to the meeting with us."

"With *us*?"

"You'll have to cover for her."

Lucas watched her ankles fly up the staircase, the slender calves flashing above them under her hiked-up robe. He had half a mind to follow her up the stairs and make her *really* late for that damn meeting. Instead he looked down at the reports in his hands. A blob of oatmeal was stuck on the cover of the first one. He was almost sorry it peeled off so easily.

"Where did you get the tie?" she asked him as he backed the truck out of the driveway. It was dark blue knit. Against his clean chambray workshirt and jeans, it looked almost preppy.

"Borrowed it from Wayne's closet. Sorry I couldn't add a jacket. Maggie said they were all too small."

"You saw her? Then I guess you know."

Lucas nodded. "She'll be okay. She's tough. And Eleanor will keep her down for the afternoon. Even Toby's helping out. Little Willy likes him."

Susanna sighed. "Little Willy likes everybody these days but me. When it comes to teething babies, a twelve-hour work day on Capitol Hill doesn't look half-bad."

Lucas shot her a sideways glance as he turned the corner at Main and headed toward the bank.

"*You* look like Capitol Hill today," he said. He tried to make it sound like a compliment. She wore high heels, a high-necked blouse and a tailored suit the color of honey. It made her olive skin look as lustrous as the small gold earrings she wore. Susanna slid her hand down her braid.

"Did I get all the oatmeal out?" she asked him.

"Yeah," he muttered. "Every bit."

She looked at him. The set of his jaw told her something was wrong. "Lucas? What is it? You're not uncomfortable with this, are you? I know meetings aren't your style, but so much depends on—"

He pulled the truck to a sudden stop at the bank, and she grabbed for the dash to keep the reports from sliding off of it.

"I know how important this meeting is, Susanna. I'll try not to let you down."

"Let me down? Of course you won't let me down." She hesitated a moment, knowing from the edge to his voice that there was something more that he wanted to say. But there wasn't time. "Just answer any questions that might come up about the people who are likely to use the center. I've got great stats and solid information, but I don't have the personal side. You and Maggie and the others got in touch with that when you did the surveys. I don't have a feeling for—"

He turned in the seat till he could look her full in the face. "You've got all the feeling you need. You just run away from it sometimes."

She stared at him. "I don't understand—"

"Come on. It's after twelve."

The blue of his eyes looked like tempered steel as he opened the heavy glass door of the bank. He took her elbow, almost possessively, she thought, and ushered her across the marble floor. Tellers and customers turned their heads as he steered her toward the glassed-in conference room in the rear of the bank.

Dr. Gurley saw them coming and opened the door of the conference room. "Lucas, Susanna, good to see both of you."

Five men rose from their seats at the long polished table, three of whom she knew. B.J., Bob Barlow, the bank's president, and Jay Thomas, head of the board of education, had all been at the club dinner. The other two men were strangers. But only to her. Each of them greeted Lucas by name.

"Meet Susanna Foster, from Washington," Dr. Gurley said. "She's really a hometown girl who just goes East when she has to." Susanna smiled at the round of chuckles and turned to Lucas, but he had crossed the room and was talking quietly to B.J. Whatever rivalry the two had felt seemed nonexistant now. Or had she only imagined it . . .

"I'm Lou Byers." The shorter of the two men stuck out his hand to her. "I'm Wilamet's new eye doctor."

"Don Dickers," the taller man said. "You know my wife, Della."

Susanna nodded and quickly shook the outstretched hands. She was anxious to begin the meeting. Across the room, B.J. laughed, his head bent amicably toward Lucas. She caught the end of the joke's punch line. Susanna smiled wistfully. *She'd* never heard Lucas tell a joke. She still had a lot to learn about him, she realized.

"Gentlemen, please be seated," Dr. Gurley said. "Susanna?"

Half an hour later, Lou Byers took off his glasses and set them carefully on the table. "I'm most impressed with your report, Miss Foster, especially the financial section. I'm sure our bank president would agree?" Across the table, Bob Barlow gave an emphatic nod.

"There's one thing I don't understand, though. You've included a cost center titled Evaluations and Disseminations. Could you give us some idea of what that category will include?"

"Of course. As I've explained, our primary sources of money will be public funding and private foundations. Section two of the report lists those grant moneys that I feel we should pursue. Provided we do receive their funds, each of the sources on that list will require periodic reports. We must measure our progress constantly, analyze our results and report on our effectiveness."

B.J. stubbed out his cigar and leaned across the table. "What Miss Foster means is this—if we take their money, we've got to play their game."

Susanna bristled. "Bobby Joe, funding isn't a *game*. Corporations have every right to know what we're doing with their money, and the government has to be able to answer to the taxpayers."

"Seems to me it's usually t'other way 'round between us and the government, 'specially come April," Don Dickers added.

While everyone had a good laugh at that, Susanna tried to gather her thoughts. "Look in the appendix, page twenty-five," she suggested. "I've included a possible work sheet for the evaluation process."

Around the table, every head bent over her report, except for Lucas's. He simply watched her through the curling smoke of B.J.'s cigar, his blue eyes calm and slightly narrowed.

Dr. Gurley shook his head. "Looks like some of those forms I have to fill out for medicare. Susanna, you have my sympathy. I don't think there's a man or woman in all of Wilamet who could manage this sort of analysis."

"That makes me wonder who is going to serve as our so-called 'evaluation coordinator', provided we get the funds, that is." B.J. looked around the room.

"The important thing is to get the funding," Susanna emphasized. "Once we have that, we can locate someone experienced—"

"You sure are optimistic," Bob Barlow interjected. "I've had an opening here at the bank for going on three months.

Can't find a soul who wants to process those complicated new government forms.''

Jay Thomas cleared his throat, and everyone turned to look at the mild-mannered head of the school board. ''I wonder,'' he said, ''if we aren't putting the cart just slightly before the proverbial horse? That is to say, I never recommend that we add a new course to the curriculum before I'm sure I've got someone qualified to teach it. What I'd be interested in knowing is this—how many of those people on your survey actually said they'd be willing to be volunteer teachers?''

Susanna rose to her feet and leaned excitedly forward. ''That was one of our surprises, Mr. Thomas. A full forty-two percent of our class-two respondents expressed an interest in primary involvement in the center.''

Blank faces stared at her from around the table. ''What?'' Don Dickers said.

Susanna started to repeat herself, then looked beseechingly at Lucas. He held her eyes a moment before he answered.

''Seventy-five people are willing to tutor, Jay, and our survey was only a sample. What she's trying to say is that almost half of the people we interviewed who are qualified to teach are willing to volunteer some time at the center.''

Every head turned Lucas's direction. ''I'd say that's a pretty positive response,'' Dr. Gurley said. ''Surely there'd be *one* among them who'd do this evaluation stuff.''

Their eyes followed Lucas's as he leveled them at Susanna. ''Possibly. Provided the center *gets* any clients to evaluate.''

Susanna sucked in her breath. Lou Byers put his glasses back on. B.J.'s tipped chair snapped forward.

"Maybe we should ask Lucas to explain his comment," Bob Barlow said. Heads around the table nodded. Susanna sat down, but on the edge of her seat.

Lucas loosened his tie. "I'm a stand-in today since Maggie Grant is ill. You all know that she and Eleanor and B.J.'s mother and a few other people have already started volunteering at the center. We all agreed to do a portion of the survey. If you look at Susanna's report, you'll see the results of our study. *Most* of them, anyway."

Lucas paused and glanced around the table, his eyes catching hers briefly, before moving on.

What was he saying? she wondered. Did he doubt the validity of their survey? All her recommendations hinged on that data!

Lucas poured himself a glass of ice water and passed the pitcher over to B.J. "There's no question that we need an adult literacy center. You can also see that a lot of people who don't have a problem have a lot of sympathy with those who do. According to Susanna's analysis, those two things alone give us a really good shot at the money." He paused and found her eyes again. He was on *her* side, damn it, she *had* to see it.

Dr. Gurley tapped his pencil on the table. "Then I don't understand. Why do you suspect that the center wouldn't be used?"

Lucas stood. He turned his back to the conference table and looked out through the glass wall to the people milling around the bank. A little boy had his nose pressed to the glass, making funny faces, and Lucas grinned at him. An embarrassed mother hurried the child away. Lucas turned back.

"Nearly every person I talked to who'd be interested in using the center wanted to be sure that he, or she, could do it in private. Illiterate people don't want their handicap advertised. They don't *want* to be counted. They're ashamed."

Lucas sat down. For a moment there was total silence around the room. Then Dr. Gurley spoke. "It seems to me that it would be pretty hard to manage a literacy center that guaranteed everyone total anonymity."

"'Specially in Wilamet," Don Dickers added. "Della can vouch for the speed news travels up one side of Main and down t'other."

Lou Byers nodded. "If people don't want to be counted, and tracked, and analyzed, your evaluation coordinator's got a heck of a job on his, or her, hands."

"And if you can't evaluate," B.J. added, "you can kiss outside funding goodbye."

All their eyes turned toward to Susanna. Hers, in turn, were blazing in fury at Lucas. "If I'd had access to this *opinion* sooner, I'd have had time to—"

"I just confirmed it myself this morning." Heads turned back to Lucas. "I had thought maybe I was the only one whose survey respondents seemed concerned about confidentiality. I thought maybe...I'd let personal feelings influence what I was hearing. But there have been indications since the center first opened that people were uncomfortable about the possibility their literacy problems would become public. And this morning when I dropped off Toby, Susanna's mother brought the subject up. She'd had a lot of questions when she made her calls. When I checked with Maggie—"

Jay Thomas waved his hand for attention. "I don't understand. This is a learning situation. We have them all over town. Why would anyone be ashamed to admit he needed help?"

Lucas leaned forward, his big hands splayed on the conference table before him. He nodded over his shoulder.

"Look at those people out there. Ordinary people like you, like me. How would you feel if you were standing in that line, worried that the teller was going to ask you to sign some new form. Some form that you'd never seen before, or not had time to show to your surrogate reader, provided you had one. How would you feel? Would you calmly announce that you couldn't read?

"And then supposing you took your money and you headed across the street to Murphy's Hardware, back to that corner of the store where he keeps those bags of dog food. Only Murphy's been doing a little rearranging, and what you reach for *looks* like dog food, same green bag with big black letters, only you get it home and open it up, and if you're lucky, the smell tells you it's not dog food at all, but pellet fertilizer.

"And supposing your kid is standing around, a boy about six or seven who's maybe just started to read himself. You know he's having a hell of a time, maybe the same rough time you had. Now he's looking hard at you, wondering what's going on. Would you tell him the truth? Tell him you made another dumb mistake because you tried your damnedest but never could learn to read?"

Dr. Gurley shook his head. "I never thought—"

"I did," Don Dickers said quietly. "I'm not that good a reader myself. I'm not illiterate, but I got some feeling for them that are."

Lucas stood a moment longer, emotions warring inside him. He wanted to tell them all that *he* was illiterate. That *he'd* been that seven-year-old kid. That he'd seen his father brush away hasty tears when he'd tried to say that reading didn't matter. That he, Lucas, had just begun to deal with his own sense of shame.

But he wanted to tell Susanna first. He wanted to try to make her see. Slowly he sat down in his chair.

B. J. Richardson tossed his copy of Susanna's report on the table. It slid halfway to the middle before it stopped. "Seems to me we've got a problem. We've got Susanna going after money for an adult literacy center, a place we all, to the man—and woman—know that we need. But we're going to have a hell of a time getting people to use it."

"I've been an educator for twenty years," Jay Thomas said. "You've got to have the proper environment—"

"You've got to have the proper *attitude*," Lucas said. "And you've got to know that others do, too."

"So why not change it?" B.J. said.

Lou Byers chuckled and shook his head. "You're talking about changing small-town thinking, Bobby Joe. You ought to visit my clinic. I'm having a hell of a time introducing those new bifocals."

Dr. Gurley laughed. "Stick around awhile longer, Lou. You'll make your point." The elderly doctor looked around the table before he spoke again. "Some of you may disagree with me, most of you will probably scoff, but I've lived in this town all my life. I brought three of you into this world. And I know that once this town gets behind something, there's no stopping it. Get these people together, tell them your story and I guarantee you'll get your center staffed and occupied full to the brim."

"You're talking town meeting, Gurley?"

"Why not? We haven't had one in a year."

Bob Barlow poured himself a glass of ice water, then set it down without drinking. "You'll need the VFW hall. I'll make arrangements."

"We've got to make sure that the word gets out," Dr. Gurley went on. "Make sure that it reaches those who need it most. We're talking about nonreaders here. Most of them, if Lucas is right, will give this meeting a pretty wide berth."

B.J. rose from his chair, hoisted his belt and straightened his jacket. "They'll come. They'll *all* come. Know that big red four-by-four sittin' in my window? Supposing I park that baby on the VFW lawn? Big sign—You Got to Be *Present* to Win."

Bob Barlow shook his head. "That's a good idea, Bobby Joe, but there's not enough time to sell tickets to cover the cost of the truck. According to Susanna, we've got to get these proposals in by Monday a week at the latest. Even with overnight mail, we ought to mail them by Thursday. That means the town meeting will have to be Wednesday evening, day after tomorrow."

"Who said anything about covering the cost with tickets? I'm talkin' donation. A *tax-deductible* donation, I might add. A little publicity for Wilamet Chevyland, and I can kiss a few babies, shake a few hands—"

The whole thing was moving much too fast for Susanna, but suddenly she came to attention. "B.J., I told you before. Take a careful look at the list of assurances we have to guarantee to the government. According to the provisions of the Hatch Act—"

"Oh, hell, Susanna, politics can wait for me another year. We're talkin' here about what's best for Wilamet."

"Then we're all agreed," Bob Barlow siad. "B.J. can handle publicity with the *Wilamet News* and the radio. Don, you get Della to help us out at the beauty shop with word of mouth over the weekend. Gurley, get Lucas and Susanna together to plan the program. Jay, Lou and I will review this report in detail so we can sign off on the proposals immediately after the meeting. If this thing comes off the way I think it will, Susanna, you're going to have some hefty figures to add to your data on public support."

"Well, kids, looks like we're off and rolling!" The elderly doctor's enthusiasm hung in the heavy silence that had spread through the emptying conference room, from Lucas's end of the table down to Susanna's.

She glared at Lucas, and he glared back. Then both of them spoke at once.

"You don't need me at the meeting on Wednesday. You've got my report. Besides I have to stay home with Maggie."

"I've got a charter Wednesday night. B.J. can handle the program. I was just a stand-in today—"

Dr. Gurley held up his hands to quiet them both. "Whatever is going on between you two is none of my business...of course, you did cut a heck of a picture on the club dance floor that Saturday night. And Mrs. Gurley would have my hide if she knew I'd let you off without trying to tell you...oh, *hell*! Lucas, Susanna, you're one heck of a team. Get up there on Wednesday and push this thing through. Tell it like it is. Don't make me out to be a liar about Wilamet's worth."

With those words, Dr. Gurley pushed out the door and let it swing closed behind him. Susanna and Lucas continued to stare down the long table at each other.

"You slowed the process considerably."

"I had a good reason."

"You could have shared your findings with me."

"I told you, I thought I was just imagining things, letting my personal experience get in the way."

"*Personal* experience? Lucas, you've only been taking Toby to the center for a couple of weeks."

"I'm not talking about what we're doing with Toby, not directly, anyway."

"Then what *are* you talking about. What makes *you* suddenly such an expert? How do you know what those people you called were feeling? The way you talked, for a minute I almost imagined..."

He had moved from his end of the conference table, and she'd left hers till they stood only inches apart in the middle of the room. Beyond the glass wall, a crowd had gathered, straining to hear their shouted words. Oblivious, Susanna stared into Lucas's eyes.

Then suddenly she knew. The numbered music tapes, the absence of books, Wayne's continual presence whenever there was paperwork, even the hymns in church...

"Susanna, *I'm* one of your statistics. I don't read. I don't write. I'm functionally illiterate, Susanna."

Her mouth went dry as she stared at him. "You... didn't...tell me."

"I wanted to tell you. *I tried.* But there are things I need to explain, things you don't understand—"

Silence and something heavier, weighed in the air between them. Of course there were things she didn't understand, didn't know about Lucas. He hadn't given her the chance! Not that she'd expected to learn anything really significant, certainly not anything that would jar the image of Lucas that she'd carried for so many years. *Illiterate?* Susanna took a deep breath. Okay. Somehow that didn't matter. What did matter, what *really* mattered, was that he hadn't told her.

"I wanted to tell you," Lucas was saying again. "I wanted to tell you first." He was getting angrier by the minute. She wanted an excuse, a reason, a justification, he realized. A quick, pat answer to a question he'd just barely begun to answer himself. Why *does* a thirty-year-old man of normal intelligence just accept the fact that he'll never learn to read?

"Why didn't you tell me?" she flashed.

"I don't know!"

"Why didn't you tell me thirteen years ago when I handed you that note? Why didn't you tell me that first day in the cabin? Why did you let me just go on believing—"

"That I'm just a man? A guy who likes fishing and classical music . . . a man with a weak spot—"

"You're the man I love!"

For just an instant, feeling so deep she felt she could swim in it flooded his eyes. And then it was gone.

"But I'm still just a man, Susanna." He reached out to hold her.

"Don't touch me! You should have told me. You should have told me before—"

"What was I supposed to do, Susanna? Announce it that night on the boat? *You* didn't want to hear it any more than I wanted to tell you. You didn't want to *talk* any more than I did. You wanted one thing and one thing only...to go from the crazy chemistry that's exploded between us since we were kids straight to some magic, risk-free kingdom, with a prince who'd make all your choices for you. You've spent too long away from the basics, Susanna. Basics like this."

He took hold of her arms then, despite her protests, and closed the inches between their bodies, till she could feel the thunder of his heart against her breast. She tried to push him away, but he held her all the harder. Then he claimed her mouth in a kiss so hard and rough and deep that Susanna was caught in a hurricane of tangled, frenzied emotion. Every feeling drained from her body except the passion she felt for him. But as soon as he felt her let go, he ended the kiss and drew back.

Shame rushed in, mixed with anger and hurt. It rose up in Susanna to obscure the truth of what she knew he was saying. She thought of how she'd run from Daryl's lies, and how she'd felt when she finally faced them.

He smiled. A hard, distant, humorless smile. And then he let her go.

He tried to slam the door as he went out, but the heavy glass swung closed on its hinges, hushing the room. Susanna stared after him. Then slowly her vision began to widen.

Beyond the glassed-in wall of the conference room, half of Wilamet stood gaping. Had they seen it *all*? And what had they heard? Susanna turned her back and snatched up her papers from off the table.

What did *she* care, anyway? She was only a summer visitor. She'd be gone with the cicadas. And this time, when she went back to Washington, she'd know better than to try *ever* to return.

Chapter Twelve

Saturday afternoon Susanna waited in the hallway, holding his suit coat as Dr. Gurley descended the stairs.

"Don't baby your sister, Susanna." The elderly doctor rolled down his sleeves. "The best thing Maggie's got going for her is that damn fool Foster stubborn streak that refuses to give in to pain."

"It killed my father."

"Oh, come on now. You don't really believe that, do you?"

"I believe that if he'd rested more, taken it easy when his chest started hurting, maybe given one less speech—"

"Big William Foster with his lip buttoned up? Can't even imagine the sight!" Dr. Gurley laughed gently. Then he slipped one arm around Susanna's shoulders and walked with her toward the door.

"Hasn't your mother ever told you the truth, Susanna? I treated your father for nigh on twenty years. He had a weak heart. I knew he wouldn't last. Your mother knew it. He knew it, too. He went out the way he wanted to go, hard and fast, never still for a moment. Fosters don't give up easily.''

"I never knew he was ill."

"No one did."

"And Mother? If she knew he was sick, why was she always behind his campaigns?"

Dr. Gurley reached for the doorknob, then hesitated and turned back. "You don't know your mother very well, do you, Susanna?"

"Know her? Of course I know her. If anyone's stubborn, it's Mother. She gets these ideas about what she thinks is best for you—"

"And then keeps them to herself, doing her damnedest to support what *you* think you want." The elderly doctor looked at her hard, over the top of his eyeglasses. Susanna stared back in confusion.

"Are you saying that Mother's been happily shipping me off to Washington all these years because she thinks that's what *I* want?"

"*Wasn't* it what you wanted? To pick up where your father left off, to follow his example, instead of maybe, just maybe, following your heart?"

She stood in the hallway, eye to eye with the man who'd brought her into the world, seeing herself as he must see her. Maybe she was the most stubborn one of the lot. Always insisting that everyone fit the role she'd cast them in. Even herself. No wonder she'd never been able to trust her feelings.

"You're saying I'm not like my father, not really." Susanna sighed and turned from the doorway. "Maybe that's why I feel like giving up."

"Maybe that's also why you feel like hanging on. Are you going to be at the meeting Wednesday?"

"I told you before, I've done my share."

Dr. Gurley huffed and shook his head. "What you *told* me, what you and Lucas both *told* me, was that you're just having a lovers' spat. Can't you set that aside for the good of the town?"

Susanna hugged her arms to her chest. "It's not just a quarrel...it doesn't have all that much to do with Lucas and me...it's a whole lot deeper." Susanna stopped, her hand on the doorknob. "I put the report together using the best of my legislative know-how," she went on. "I dug up information that's totally inaccessible to most people, though why on earth the government makes it so difficult... Anyway, I did a *good* job. But it wasn't enough. Not nearly enough."

She stepped onto the porch in the hot afternoon sunshine, Dr. Gurley following. The air was almost too heavy to breathe. Across the porch, a single cicada slowly crawled toward the shade beneath the swing.

"I did what I'm good at, Dr. Gurley. What I'm *not* good at, and what really matters most, is seeing people for what they are. You just got through telling me that I don't even know my own mother. I can't reach out, let them matter as individuals—a woman, a child, a man—each with a *face*, not just a label that puts them in some group."

Dr. Gurley didn't speak for a long moment. Then he fished a big white handkerchief out of his pocket and mopped at his perspiring brow. He shook his head. "Try telling that to the people who love you, Susanna. I think you'd find out that they see you a little differently. Maybe truer than you see yourself."

She let him hug her, then watched him go. "You're right about one thing, though," Susanna called after him. "There's no good reason why I can't come to the meeting on Wednesday. I'll be there."

An hour later, the phone line crackled ominously when Susanna finally reached the remote lodge at Lake Texoma. She was just about ready to hang up when the senator's voice boomed over the line.

"Worst durn luck I've ever had. Haven't caught a fish for three straight days. How're they bitin' on Lake Eufaula?"

"I don't know. I haven't heard."

The senator paused so long, she wasn't sure that he was still there. "Senator Stout? Hello?"

"I'm here, Susanna. And I'm waiting for the rest of the story. What's come up between you and your new young man?"

"Lucas Grant is not my *young man*, senator. Whatever I may have said before was, well... it was a little premature."

"Well, if you don't want to talk about him, then how's your family? How's your sister doin' with that pregnancy? She's holding on, I hope."

"That's what I'm calling about, actually. Maggie's doing just fine. I don't think she really needs me here. I wanted to let you know that I'll be going back to Washington Thursday morning. There's this meeting I have to attend, and then—"

"Got to be present to win, huh?"

"What?"

"A young fellow at the lodge keeps talking about getting home to Wilamet for some big giveaway on Wednesday."

Had word spread that far south? For just a moment, Susanna felt excited. Then she sobered. "Didn't the man say anything about *why* we're giving away the truck?"

"Not as I recollect."

Susanna sighed. "There's going to be a town meeting about the literacy center. The truck giveaway is supposed to be just a draw, not the primary focus."

"Don't give it a thought. Just get up there and tell 'em your story."

"That's what I'm calling about, senator, sort of. It isn't *my* story. I'm going to the meeting, but just to answer questions. You wouldn't believe the work that I did...the case is so convincing, but—"

"But it wasn't quite what they needed, right?"

Susanna bit her lip and held the receiver a little tighter. "I'm just not good at this part of it. As long as the work is, well...*removed*, I'm perfectly capable. I belong in Washington. That's why I'm going back. I thought I'd get a head start on reworking the Elder Care Bill."

"Oh, *damn it*, Susanna. Now you had to go and remind me of the pile of work we've got waitin' for us."

"Sorry. I only thought—"

"Thought you could just walk away from whatever's gone wrong at home and bury yourself in work again? That's not my girl. Susanna, in less than a year, my term is up. I've decided it's going to be my last. I'm not going to run for election again."

"But you said—"

"Now you aren't going to be like all the rest, are you? Holdin' me to all those promises? I said I'd serve Oklahoma till m' dyin' day, but that doesn't mean I have to do it in that confounded city of Washington. The backside of a bass boat is as good a place as any. Come to think of it, sounds like Wilamet could use a little Washington know-how. Ever thought of sticking around there yourself, to help them out?"

"Once. Briefly. But it wouldn't work. I'll see you in September. We'll make good use of your final year."

The line gave one last crackle. Susanna couldn't be sure, but she thought the senator said, "Nuts!" just before he hung up the phone.

* * *

Lucas answered the phone on Saturday afternoon and sat listening to Wayne making his best effort to cheer him up.

"I could drive on out and do those accounts. And you know, I've been thinking that maybe we ought to start publishing a marina newsletter. You know, mail it out to all your past clients? I thought writing about fishing might be good practice when you get started . . . you know . . . started on learning to read."

"I'll think about that, Wayne. It's not a bad idea. For today, for a while, you'd better stick close to home. Maggie needs you now, little brother. I'll be okay."

"See you in church tomorrow?"

"Yeah. Maybe. I don't know. Wayne, there's something else."

"What is it?"

"The meeting in Oklahoma City on Monday? The one with Toby's social worker? Wayne, I'm going up alone."

"But you can't. Lucas, this meeting could make the difference between keeping Toby and losing him. The tutoring is going great. If we just—"

"Wayne, try to understand. If my illiteracy means that I'm not good for Toby, then that's something I'm going to have to face. I'd rather know now, before . . ." *Before I get in any deeper, as deep as I did with Susanna.*

Wayne seemed to understand. "Whatever you say, Lucas. I'll be here if you need me."

Sunday morning Susanna had wanted to beg off going to church, but Maggie would hear nothing of it.

"You know as well as I do, Susanna Foster, that the last thing you ought to do is feed Wilamet's already overstuffed rumor mill by staying away. Everyone is going to be sure you've done something horrid if you don't even show up at church."

"But, Maggie, I *have* done something horrid. What I said to Lucas was—"

"A little too emotional. You overreacted, that's all."

"I was caught by surprise. I kept thinking of Daryl and how I'd let him deceive me. But Lucas is not like Daryl. I was angry that he obviously thought I wouldn't understand. If only he had told me . . ."

Maggie sat down on the edge of the bed and pulled her sister down beside her.

"You know, Susanna, maybe Lucas was right. Maybe you *are* looking for a prince, not necessarily a perfect man, but one without any surprises. Don't you know what loving is really like? I've *still* got secrets from Wayne. One by one, he's finding them out. And there are lots of things *I* never knew about *him*, maybe things he doesn't even know about himself. Nice things, but also things that sometimes drive me wild. If I'd known them all before we were married, then maybe we wouldn't even *be* married. No one would. No one would risk it. Then there'd be no Little Willys or whoever *this* is going to be." Maggie patted her stomach and slid to the edge of the bed. "Now humor us all and get ready for church, will you?"

"Tell me something, Maggie? How did you get so wise?"

"You live. You love. It just sinks in, unless you're totally blind."

Blind? Was that what she'd been? *No,* Susanna thought, she'd just never been able to see the faces. Maybe she never would.

Right up until the very last moment, just before they'd all stood for the opening hymn, Susanna kept hoping that Lucas would come. She'd carefully chosen the seat at the end of the pew, leaving too little room for an extra person, lest someone would think she was expecting him, yet just enough space so that if he came, she could slide over and squeeze him in. But the first hymn started without him, and then it was over. He hadn't come. Susanna sat down. Beside her, Maggie reached for her hand.

Both of them looked straight ahead, listening to the sermon, hearing the words if not the message. They'd be forgiven for that, Susanna was sure. It was an old habit. A habit that had started those first few Sundays after their father's funeral. They'd watch the sunlight pouring through the big, round stained-glass window, casting rainbow reflections on the wall behind the minister's head. They'd think their own thoughts. And now and then she'd squeeze Maggie's hand, or Maggie would squeeze hers, as she was doing now. And things would work out. Didn't they always?

Eleanor was upstairs putting Little Willy down for his nap, and Maggie had insisted on doing the dishes alone. Susanna felt slightly mortified at the disaster her cooking had made of the kitchen. Wayne and she were left in the parlor, sharing the Sunday *Wilamet News*.

When she passed him the comics, Susanna noticed that her brother-in-law still studied the sports page intently, as though he were reading it word for word.

"Wayne?"

"Hmm." He didn't look up.

"Wayne, you might as well quit pretending. I know you couldn't care less about sports. On top of that, you aren't even wearing your glasses." Wayne lowered the paper and looked across at Susanna.

"Do you want to tell me what's on your mind?" she asked him.

Wayne fumbled in his breast pocket and pulled his glasses out of their case. He cleaned them carefully and put them on. When he looked at her, Susanna saw just how miserable he really was.

"You're going back to Washington?"

"Thursday morning, after the meeting."

"I guess I knew you wouldn't stay. Not after you found out. I told him that. Still, he insisted, right from the first, that it wouldn't matter."

Right from the first? Susanna's mind raced over the information. "Then he really did want to tell me?"

"He said you'd understand. I thought for a while you would, especially when I found out that *I've* been wrong, that I haven't really helped my brother very much. I've just been using him, trying to make myself feel needed, important even."

"Oh, Wayne, I don't think Lucas feels—"

"But I guess you don't understand him, either, do you, or you wouldn't be going? Tell me, Susanna, what is it really? Is it just the fact that Wilamet is small potatoes? It isn't true, you know. If you got inside this place, really got to the heart of things, you'd find that out. There are plenty of issues, all of them just as vital as the literacy center, enough to keep you busy for a lifetime."

She wanted to answer. She wanted to tell him that Wilamet wasn't small potatoes at all. It never had been. *She'd* been the one who was trying to feel important, rushing off to Washington, trying to do "something meaningful," trying to make a difference on the big scene, all the while running from the small but, to her, overwhelming demands of intimacy. Demands such as accepting responsibility for hurtful words.

"I'm sorry" was all she could mumble to Wayne. And then she fled to her room.

* * *

On Monday morning, she'd been up an hour when she got the call. Maggie was pouring a second cup of coffee for Eleanor, who was doing her best to keep Little Willy's hands out of the marmalade. Wayne had already left for work.

Maggie paused, Eleanor's cup half-full. "Is something wrong?"

Susanna steadied herself against the counter, her hand still on the receiver of the phone, and looked from Maggie to her mother. "It's Lonetree," she said. "Toby's gone."

Susanna rushed to the hallway to pull on her sneakers, her mother and sister following.

"Gone? Gone where?" Eleanor asked. "I thought he wasn't going to go to Oklahoma City with Lucas this morning. Wayne said one of the guides would be bringing Toby in for his lesson."

"The guide didn't show. Lonetree thinks Toby decided to walk into town."

"But it's *miles* from the lake to Wilamet. That poor boy! I'll call the school and cancel and go with you to search."

"No, Mother. If Toby's able to hitch a ride, he'll show up looking for you. I think it's best if you just go on to work. Call the marina if he shows up."

Susanna turned from her mother to her sister. "Maggie, your keys?"

"Sure. Is there anything else I can do?"

"Call Wayne. Tell him to try to contact Lucas and let him know what's happened. Tell him we're going to try the old farm road."

"Then you don't think you'll find him out on the highway?" Maggie wiped her hands on her apron and reached for her purse to fish out the keys.

"If I'm lucky, yes. But Toby doesn't like to take that route. He hates the noise of the trucks, and he's sometimes afraid that Lucas will head south instead of west to Wilamet."

"Oh, dear!" Eleanor slumped onto the bench beside Susanna. "You don't suppose that Toby's still worried about being sent to the home? There was that episode two years ago when he hid."

Maggie tossed the car keys, but Susanna's hand was shaking so much that she missed them.

"Don't even suggest such a thing, Mother," Maggie said, retrieving the keys. "Toby trusts Lucas now. He knows he won't be sent away."

Does he? Susanna thought of all the times she'd been too busy to offer reassurance. She tried to push the question out of her mind as she hurried out the door to Maggie's old blue Mustang.

She headed up Washington Street at twice the posted speed. Mrs. Petrie was walking her schnauzer, and the little dog went wild at the sight of the careening car. Susanna took a deep breath and slowed to a safer speed.

Her stomach lurched when she reached the ramp to the crowded highway. Trucks sped by, throwing dirt and gravel six feet onto the shoulder. If Toby were hit by a flying stone . . . *No,* she would not allow herself to imagine it.

She tried to watch both the incoming traffic as well as the side of the road. Maybe a kindly motorist had stopped at the sight of Toby's eager, freckled face.

He knew how to hitchhike. One afternoon on the way back to the lake, Lucas had told him a story about how he'd hitched his way to school before the bus route was extended. Toby had asked a great many questions. But Lucas had made sure that Toby understood that hitching was risky. *Like just about everything else in life,* she thought. Susanna tightened her grip on the wheel and stepped down on the gas pedal.

She'd left the highway and covered barely a mile of the dusty road to the lake when she rounded a bend and saw Lonetree. The tall Indian stood in the middle of the road, waving his one good arm over his head. She screeched to a stop.

"Take a left instead of a right when the road divides," he shouted before he'd even closed his door. "We'll go as far as we can in the car."

She reached the divide in less than a minute and made a sharp left, into the trees. A low-growing branch whipped across the window, and the weed-choked road made speeding impossible.

"It's okay," Lonetree said. "We need to go slower. You take the left side, and I'll watch the right. He was wearing that bright red shirt. The one I gave him for Christmas last year. Long sleeved. Too damn hot. But he likes it." Lonetree's voice had begun to waver, and Susanna glanced over at him.

She had to look away. The Indian's cheeks were wet, streaked not just with dusty perspiration but with tears.

"The shirt will make it easy for us to find him, Lonetree." She was glad her voice held more hope than fear.

The road began to narrow until it was simply two thin ruts with a center too high for the Mustang to manage. Susanna pulled to a stop. When the engine died, it seemed very quiet. A cardinal and a pair of jays flushed out of an old oak tree, but when they'd settled, the silence seemed leaden. Then suddenly Susanna knew. The cicadas were gone. Back into the earth. The thought made her suddenly frantic.

"Come on!" she said. "We've got to get going."

"Lucas? Lucas Grant?" The click of the secretary's heels sounded like shots on the hard polished tile of the agency floor. There was no more time to think things over. Right or wrong, he had to go through with it. Honesty had its price. But why the hell did Toby have to pay it? Lucas rose from the bench.

"You have a telephone call, Mr. Grant. Take it here, if you like, then you may go in." He reached for the phone, eyeing the open doorway where Toby's social worker was seated behind the same cluttered desk, wearing her usual pinched, nervous frown. He turned his back and put the phone to his ear.

He listened a moment to Wayne's anxious words, then Lucas felt a cold, hard stab in his gut. "The farm road? Of course it makes sense. I've hiked that road with Toby a hundred times. Wayne, get out there as fast as you can. Tell Susanna and Lonetree to watch out for wells. Pop must have sunk a half a dozen test holes that year before he died."

He was heading out the door, smashing his hat on his head, before it occurred to him that he hadn't canceled the appointment. Should he tell the agency what had happened? What would they do? He sure as hell couldn't see that skinny social worker fighting her way through the weeds and the chiggers, just to look for Toby. Susanna would. Susanna *was*.

He hit the seat of the truck, and was backing it out of the parking lot before he'd even closed the door. He wondered if the truck could do eighty and still make the curves on the highway.

Susanna called out Lonetree's name, just as they had agreed, but this time she got no answer. She checked her watch. Nearly two hours had passed since they'd started their slow, spiraling search along both sides of the old farm road. Her T-shirt was soaked with sweat and dust above where she'd knotted it at her midriff. Her legs, from the tops of her socks to the cuffs of her shorts, were itching like crazy from chiggers.

She cupped her hands around her mouth and called his name again. No answer. From what seemed miles away, she thought she heard the sound of a car horn. But it came from behind her, from back down the road. Toby was up ahead somewhere, tired, hot, probably terrified. Susanna pressed on.

Why hadn't Lonetree answered? They'd agreed to stay within earshot. When his last call had come back faint, she'd reined in her search and moved closer to the road. He should have done the same. What if he hadn't been able to? What if something were wrong? Her heart beat faster.

She thought of the possibilities. A fall? A twisted ankle? A rattlesnake bite? Or maybe he'd wedged his body under one of the ruined farm buildings looking for Toby. With just one arm... Susanna realized that it was the first time all morning that she'd thought of the Indian's handicap. When she reached the road, she crossed to the other side.

Slowly, methodically, she began to walk the area opposite hers, moving in a spiral fashion back the way they had come. She watched for trampled grass, broken twigs, scuffed gravel, anything that would tell her she'd picked up Lonetree's trail. Nothing.

The sun beat down, boiling the air, till the earth seemed to steam with humidity, cooking her in it. She passed through a swarm of mosquitoes so thick she feared she would swallow one, so she shut her mouth and her eyes and blindly pushed on. A low-hanging branch from a pin oak snapped across her face, and Susanna cried out. She tasted blood.

Then faintly, from somewhere up ahead, she heard a sound. Was it just a bird? Or another gray squirrel crashing through the underbrush? She called again. This time she got an answer. Lonetree's far-off guttural string of swearing! She couldn't hear what he said, but she knew he was there, and mad as the dickens. That had to mean that he was okay.

Her heart nearly leaped to her mouth as she hurried toward the sound. "Watch out!" She heard his muffled shout as she drew closer. "The place is full of holes. Watch every damn step you take!"

She came to a crashing halt just in time. In front of her, in the middle of a mass of splintered boards overgrown with weeds, a dark shadow loomed. It was wide enough that had she stepped forward she surely would have fallen in. Susanna's stomach rolled over as she picked her way toward Lonetree.

"What on earth—"

She'd finally reached him, or reached part of him, anyway. Lonetree had kicked off his boots and dug his bare feet into the dirt beside a hole not a foot and a half in diameter. His jeans were red with dust from the cuffs to his belt. Farther than that, she couldn't see. The upper half of his torso, his shoulders and head were halfway into the hole. From far below, she heard Toby's crying.

She dropped to her stomach and flattened her body and squirmed through the dust beside him. A bit of the dirt at the rim of the hole gave way as she reached it.

Lonetree coughed and sputtered. "Be careful!"

"Is he all right?"

"He's fine, but he's heavy as hell. I've got ahold of just one arm. He's afraid to try to climb up."

"Don't let go, Lonetree!" Toby's plaintive voice cried out. "Don't let me fall!"

"Toby?" Susanna tried to steady her voice as she called down the hole. She squinted into the darkness. She could make out a few streaks of Toby's carrot-red hair. "Toby," she called again, "it's me, Susanna. We'll get you out. Just hang on tight."

"If you could anchor my legs, I might be able to lower myself just a little farther—"

"You're halfway down that hole already, Lonetree. I don't think that would work."

"Got any better ideas?"

Susanna looked around them. The ruins of an old barn teetered precariously just twenty feet away. She touched Lonetree's shoulder lightly. The muscle was hot and must be killing him. She'd have to hurry.

"I'll be back," she said, and picked her way toward the barn.

The place was nearly empty, and what was there looked rotten and old, but Susanna found what she was looking for, a length of rope, maybe too short, but it was going to have to do.

She knotted the ends of the rope firmly around her wrists, making a sort of a swing between them.

"You haven't got that kind of strength," Lonetree muttered when she returned. "Once he grabs hold, he'll pull you down there with him. He's got only one foot planted on a rock sticking out of the wall, and it keeps sliding. Besides, you'll never talk him into letting go with his other hand."

"How deep is the hole?" she asked.

"Plenty deep enough," he answered.

"Can you keep holding on?"

"Till hell freezes over if I have to."

"Then let me just lean over with the rope. Toby can grab it and try to keep his balance till you let go of him and grab my ankles, or sit on them, or do anything you have to do to keep me from slipping—"

"Susanna!"

The sound of his voice washed over her, bringing tears of relief to her eyes. She scrambled back from the edge of the hole and sat for a moment looking up at him. "Lucas, hurry, we've got to—"

"I heard. You must be crazy. You're not that strong." He had dropped to the dust and was easing himself toward the well before she had time to answer. Behind him, Wayne was already crouched, ready to hold Lucas's legs.

"Grab my belt," he said as his head disappeared into the hole. Wayne did as he was told, and his face turned red with the effort. Susanna stood by, feeling helpless, hardly daring to breathe.

A moment later, Lonetree's shoulders and then his head shot out of the hole. Then he was beside Wayne, helping to anchor Lucas. Inch by inch, the three of them moved backward, Lucas's calm and soothing tones talking Toby out.

The top of a dusty red head emerged and then a freckled, tear-streaked face. Toby's arms were wrapped around Lucas, who held him for all he was worth.

Wayne and his brother shook hands. Then Lucas turned around looking for Lonetree, but the tall Indian was moving back through the trees, headed for the road. Susanna was running after him. Lucas wanted to follow, but Toby still clung to him.

"You forgot your shoes," Susanna said when she caught up with Lonetree.

The Indian stopped, stood a moment looking down at her, then dropped to a rock, his eyes downcast.

"Lonetree, you saved Toby's life."

He grunted. "Not by a long shot, I just held on. It's a good thing Lucas showed up or we might *all* be at the bottom of that hole. There was water in it. I could hear it. Would have been a hell of a way to go."

Susanna shivered despite the heat of the sun beating down on her back.

Lonetree stood and walked to the road. She followed him. Neither spoke till they'd almost reached the car. When they came in sight of it, the Indian stopped. He flexed his one good arm and reached up and grasped his stump, ripping the sleeve he'd pinned up, till it hung in shreds. His dark eyes burning, he turned to Susanna.

"If I was half a man, I'd have had this fixed years ago," he said. His voice choked for a moment before he went on. "With a hook I'd have had some chance of saving Toby myself. Instead all I could do was hold him and hope. Hope that he wouldn't let go, hope that my good arm wouldn't give out. Hang on."

"That's all any of us do, Lonetree, isn't it? Hold on, till we get some help?" She pushed on by him and walked toward the car. The tears in her eyes were finally spilling over. *She'd* let go. She'd let go of Lucas that day in the bank. Whatever help came for them now would come too late.

By the time the rest of them reached the road, her eyes were dry. Susanna watched Lucas laugh and kid Toby and rough him up enough to let him know that he was okay. Wayne walked easily behind, joking now and then. Things between the brothers would heal, she knew. They caught up with Lonetree and shook his hand. Then Lucas turned toward her.

She'd have headed home, except for the fact that the big silver truck blocked the Mustang, and the heavy brush crowding the sides of the road had made it impossible to turn the car around. Still, as Lucas walked toward her, she stuck the key in the ignition and started the engine. It was running when he reached her.

He stood a long moment looking in, then reached out and traced the length of the scratch on her cheek where the branch had whipped across her face. At his touch, Susanna wanted to turn her cheek to his palm. Instead she drew back.

He dug his hands into his pockets. "Wayne says you'll be leaving Thursday."

"Yes. I promised Dr. Gurley I'd be at the meeting. I'll stick around till then."

"I'll be there, too."

"Toby?"

"He's fine, just hot and scared, like the rest of us."

"Tell him...tell him I love him, Lucas. Tell him I'm glad he's okay."

The tears welled up again, and Susanna made a show of reaching for her seat belt and fastening it. Lucas stood a minute longer, then quietly turned away.

She watched in the rearview mirror as Lucas put an arm around Toby and one around his brother as he headed toward the truck. Lonetree climbed in the bed in the back. The big Indian was the only one who looked back at her as the truck pulled out.

Susanna sat in the car for a moment, waiting for something she couldn't define. She reached out and turned off the key. Around her, in the stillness, a dry wind began to blow, and the leaves of the trees and the moving grass made a rustling sound that reminded her of fall.

Then suddenly she heard it. The whisper-soft sound grew stronger, its pitch a little higher. The cicadas had not all gone underground. The last of them were singing. Singing their summer song.

The VFW hall was packed to overflowing with men, women and children of every size and description. All the seats were taken. People stood in the aisles, flowed out the back door and even sat on the open windowsills.

Overhead the drone of the ceiling fans buoyed up the steady clamor of the crowd. Children squealed, hopped up and down and pleaded with their parents. Teenagers dressed in orange baseball hats and aprons shouted out the flavors of the cold drinks they were pedaling. Now and then a father or mother gave in and signaled one of them over. Susanna was sure she even smelled popcorn.

Wayne had to shout to make himself heard. "They're setting up the old wooden folding chairs down in front of the stage. Come on!" He grabbed Maggie's hand, and she took her mother's. Susanna followed as they snaked their way forward.

"Aren't you supposed to be up on the stage with the rest of the committee?" her mother asked her as Susanna started to sit down.

"Just what I was about to say." Dr. Gurley was suddenly at her elbow pulling her gently forward.

Susanna broke free and stood her ground. "I've brought the report and some of my notes." She lifted her briefcase to show him. "If anyone asks a question, I'll try to answer, but I can do that from down on the floor."

The elderly doctor raised one eyebrow and nodded to the seat behind her. Maybell Richardson had settled into it and was talking, or rather shouting, with animated gestures, to Eleanor.

Susanna groaned and looked up at the stage. A row of metal chairs had been placed in a semicircle just behind the podium. All of them were filled with members of the committee except for two empty seats in the middle and one on the end. Lucas hadn't arrived yet. She'd slip into the seat on the end before he showed up.

She took Dr. Gurley's arm and climbed the steps to the right of the stage. Suddenly the elderly doctor hesitated. Susanna turned. Lucas was coming up the stairs to the left.

She stopped at the edge of the stage, her grip tightening on Dr. Gurley's arm, but the elderly doctor pressed her hand and pulled away. He moved to the podium and tapped the mike. The din in the hall began to soften. Then it hushed.

She looked across the stage at Lucas. The other men wore suits, but he wore his usual dress boots, jeans and chambray work shirt open at the throat, sleeves rolled.

He stood at the edge of the stage, his thumbs hooked into the pockets of his jeans, and shifted uneasily. *Meetings are not my style,* she heard him say as though it were yesterday. He stared across the stage at her.

He saw that she was wearing the simple cinnamon-colored sundress she'd worn that first afternoon at the lake. No suit, no heels, just casual sandals and cool, bare legs. God, she was beautiful. The stage seemed an endless expanse of space with only one purpose—to keep them apart. Lucas looked down at his boots, then ran one hand through his shaggy hair.

As soon as he'd touched his hair in that old self-conscious gesture, her heart went out to him. Susanna moved forward. What did it matter that she was a Washington woman, totally out of place in her own hometown? If Lucas could let go of the privacy he treasured and stand on this stage, then so could she. For the space of a single hour, at least, they could help each other, and help Wilamet.

They were halfway across the stage, heading for the center chairs and each other, when a cheer broke out from the back of the room. Then people applauded. Somebody even whistled. The raucous, ear-splitting sound broke up the crowd, and made Susanna want to cover her ears.

"Atta boy, Lucas!" somebody shouted over the din.

Her knees felt weak, and her cheeks were burning, but Susanna continued across the stage. Clearly the scene she'd played out at the bank on Friday had made the usual rounds. And it was plain to see where Wilamet's sympathies rested.

But when Lucas met her, he reached for her hand. Slowly she lifted her eyes to his face. Instead of the smug smile of victory that she expected to see, his look was serious, in fact almost grim as he turned and looked out to survey the crowd. Everyone hushed. Lucas and Susanna sat down.

He continued to hold her hand while Dr. Gurley tested the microphone one last time. The familiar press of Lucas's callused thumb as it rubbed her palm, and the easy entwining of their fingers, spread warmth from his touch to hers. All her senses began to fill with a feeling of peace. She was *home*.

Dr. Gurley cleared his throat. His look swept slowly around the room.

"You all know that I don't duck any punches," the doctor began. "B.J. here was good enough to offer that four-by-four out front so we could get your attention. But there's a hell of a bigger reason why we're gathered here today. We've come to hear about illiteracy. Lucas, and Susanna here, can explain it all much better than I can. Give them your *full* attention."

The crowd had certainly done that already, Susanna thought. She half wished she could conveniently fall through the floor.

But then she glanced at Lucas. His eyes were fastened intently on hers. She thought of that very first day on the lake when he'd looked at her with those clear, blue eyes. She'd thought then that she'd never seen a gaze so open, so honest. For a moment, there on the stage, the world held only the two of them, and Susanna knew that she still believed.

"Go ahead," she whispered. "I'll back you up. Tell them, Lucas. Tell them about the people, the faces." His eyes held hers a moment longer. Then he stood.

The applause that rippled around the room and rose, then fell, then rose again, was not for the chauvinistic coup they thought he had pulled, she knew, but for Lucas Grant the man, the quiet friend whom more than one Wilamet citizen had turned to personally in times of need.

He stood a moment at the podium, listening to the crowd, then he lowered his gaze, stepped back from the mike and did what she knew he would. Instinctively his hand went up and moved through his hair. And then he turned to look at her. His face was burning with a blush as deep and as crimson red as the one he'd worn all those years ago. Susanna smiled at him, a smile that came from deep inside her where it gathered up all of their memories and spilled them across her face.

Lucas smiled back and turned to the crowd, his broad back straight and proud. His hands, as they grasped the podium, were sure and steady.

"I came here to tell you something today," he said. His deep voice flowed sonorously over the sea of faces, stilling them. "Something about illiteracy. Not what you ought to do about the problem we have in Wilamet. Not what you ought to think of it. Not even about what I learned last month when I was doing the surveys. I came here to tell you about . . . myself. What I came to say is this. *I don't know how to read.*"

In the hushed silence that filled the hall, someone coughed. Then a voice rang out, "I ain't that good at fishin', either, Lucas!"

A ripple of nervous laughter passed over the crowd, and Lucas raised his hand to quiet it. He spoke again.

"My father was a farmer. Some of you knew him, an honest, hard-working, red-dirt *sodbuster*, as we call them here in Oklahoma. He had a spread on a piece of what's now Lake Eufaula. He worked like hell to make that land produce and keep his family together. My mother died on it. So did he. Then the government came along and said that none of that mattered, that they needed the land for a reservoir. You know the rest of that story.

"What you may not know is that my father couldn't read. Nor could his daddy before him. Dad tried to say it didn't matter a hill of beans. The crops would come up or they'd burn to a crisp no matter what was printed in somebody else's book or newspaper. He said that reading didn't matter. But he was only pretending. How do I know? I know because I saw it break his heart when I began to have trouble in school.

"I missed a lot of school when I was a kid. My father protested, but both of us knew that with my mother gone, I was needed on the farm. Anyway, Eleanor Foster tells me I missed out on something called 'phonics.' She says the teachers are partly to blame. I don't buy that. I had them pretty well fooled. I'd learned by watching my father how to keep my secret.

"Then sometime around the middle of junior high school, some people came down from the state office and gave a bunch of us a fancy test. I was labeled reading-disabled, borderline dyslexic. They said something was probably the matter with my brain that made it hard for the left- and right-hand sides to share and process information. It meant that I could memorize nearly every note of Beethoven's Ninth Symphony, but I'd have a hell of a time translating the letters of the alphabet and making them spell out words. A number of things that most people take for granted were going to be simply out of my reach. I'd have to adjust.

"So I did. I dropped out of school and built a marina. I let go of a girl I'd started to love. I let somebody else do my reading for me, someone who cared a hell of a lot. My brother, Wayne, got me through, gets me through to this day, would probably go on doing it the rest of his life . . . if I'd let him.

"But I won't. I won't keep quiet anymore. I've stopped *adjusting*. I think I can learn to read with the method they're using at the center. I'm damn well going to give it a try.

"That's my story. I can't say I'm proud of it. For every one of you out there who can't read, there's a different reason, a different story. Some of you think you're not really illiterate, just better at other things than you are at reading. If you want to know for sure, go home tonight and pick up a can of ordinary household cleanser. Can you read the antidote on the side, fast enough and thoroughly enough to save your kid if you have to? I couldn't. I *can't*. I won't have a kid as long as that's true. And there's a very good chance that I'm going to lose Toby, my foster son, because I can't read. Maybe that's fair.

"I've said more tonight than most of you have heard from me in all of my life. Just one more thing. You don't *have* to give up. You don't have to hide. It's a choice. *Hold on!*"

Like a ripple of wind through a field of wheat, family after family rose to their feet in the hall. Susanna rose with them. The applause crescendoed to a deafening thunder, but as he turned and stepped toward her, she hardly heard it.

His face was scarlet again, but Lucas was smiling. His clear blue eyes held a peacefulness that she'd not seen in them before. Or maybe she was seeing his face, *really* seeing it, for the very first time. She threw her arms around his neck and hugged him as hard as she could.

"I love you," she shouted over the roar of the crowd.

"And I love you!" Lucas picked her up and swung her around. The crowd began to cheer.

Dr. Gurley stepped up to the podium, stood back a minute, then tried again. It took him five minutes to quiet the crowd. "Ladies and gentlemen, boys and girls, if you mean what you seem to be saying, if you *really* mean that you care, then you'll have a chance to prove it in a minute. But first we've asked Susanna Foster to step up here and speak to you about what she's found out about sources of funding to help us get started. Susanna?"

She started to bend down to pull her report from her briefcase, then stopped. What had she written there that would help? Did any of it matter? She straightened and looked out over the sea of expectant faces. Wayne and Maggie and Eleanor, Maybell Richardson, Della Dickers sitting behind them. Was that Della's oldest daughter with a husband and baby already? She'd missed so much. Susanna's throat caught, and she lowered her eyes. She felt she had no right to speak to these people about what they needed.

Lucas touched her arm, and she turned to look into his eyes. And then she knew what to say. She stepped to the podium.

"For the rest of us, for those of us who are sitting here, perhaps feeling glad by now that we *don't* have a reading problem, I have an additional question. It's this. How secure is the future for any of us if it's limited at all for even a few?

"When I first began work on this problem, I went about it all wrong. I was looking for ways we could shift the burden, find money outside Wilamet to support out literacy program. I found some sources of funding, perhaps some of them will be viable. But not right now.

"For now, illiteracy in Wilamet is *our* problem, *our* challenge. That's what having a home is all about. Problems have faces. Faces we know and love."

If she'd had any more to say, she wouldn't have been able to get it past the lump that had closed off her throat. But she'd said enough. The crowd was on its feet again. And once again, their cheers were shut out when she lost herself in Lucas's eyes.

B.J. was grinning, ear to ear, and telling them both that he was proud. Then he stepped to the mike and pulled it close to his mouth.

"Y'all paid good attention, I hope. And you're signin' those sheets that are going around. We got to get busy on this. I don't want anybody votin' for me next year if they can't read *all* my campaign promises."

The crowd broke into affectionate hoots and whistles. B.J. gave up trying to quiet them and raised both his hands in a victory salute.

Susanna smiled. B.J. would do okay. Maybe even get to Washington one day. She might even offer to manage his campaign. Provided she could do it from Wilamet.

Epilogue

Susanna shaded her eyes against the slanting rays of the afternoon sun and looked out the door of the marina. The clear, bright expanse of water seemed limitless, and the smell of spring turning to summer floated in the warming air.

"Toby? Could you come here and take Maggie's baby? I want to go out and watch for the boat."

A moment later, Toby's freckle-faced grin appeared at her side. "I'll bet she wants to look at the minnows," Toby said. "Hey, Ellie, want to come with me?"

The baby laughed and held out her arms, gurgling something in one-and-a-half-year-old baby talk that Toby apparently understood. Susanna sighed, glad for the moment of respite. As the baby passed from her arms to Toby's, the child inside her stirred.

Susanna heard the sound of the boat as soon as she stepped on the pier. Her heart gave its old familiar flutter and hung on the hum of the motor. Lucas was coming home.

An elderly man stood as Lucas brought the boat to shore. "Hello there, Suzy!" he called. He waved his hat over his head. "We're a little late, but don't you fret. We've got one humdinger of a fish for dinner!"

On the other side of the dock, a bent figure straightened, then stood. Lonetree had his own string of boats now, but the stout man's catch would still be a challenge, a chance to better his record. He already had his filet knife out, and was securing it into the clamps of his hook.

Stout's brows were a little whiter and so was his crop of still-thick hair, but the lines of worry had gone from his face and so had the stoop from his shoulders.

"Retirement agrees with you," she said as she bent to kiss his cheek.

"A hell of a lot more than the Elder Care Bill ever did, if I do say so myself. I'm glad it finally passed, but I don't think I'll ever need it. Not as long as I've got my fishing, a fast bass boat and a guide like Lucas."

Susanna smiled and looked toward her husband. He'd just laid out the largemouth bass on Lonetree's cleaning board. The senator left her to watch Lonetree work, and Lucas turned back to Susanna.

"I've brought you something," he said to her.

He took her arms and helped her down into the boat and settled her carefully on one of the cushions. "Close your eyes and hold out your hand," he commanded softly. "Be careful. Don't squeeze too hard. Try to guess what this is, love."

She did as she was told, closing her hand gently around the tiny object. It felt as dry and fragile as a forgotten autumn leaf. And then she knew. She opened her eyes and smiled into his.

"An empty cicada shell! How could it ever have lasted so long? It's been almost two years, Lucas."

"I found it down by the houseboats, stuck to the sheltered side of an oak. I thought I'd give it to Willy, but I wanted you to see it first."

Lucas rose and began to unload the gear, but Susanna sat still for a moment longer. She turned the small brown shell over again in her hand, gently touching the split in its back where the bug had burst forth to go on his bumbling way, singing his song, in search of a mate.

Susanna looked up at her husband. Lucas was whistling. Whistling that theme from the Liszt concerto. The music she'd fallen in love to that first summer. She tried to hum along, but it was as useless today as it had been then. Why couldn't she ever get it just right? Then Susanna remembered. She closed her eyes, letting the sound of Lucas's melody seep into her soul. It had been a cicada summer. And only the males could sing.

* * * * *

COMING NEXT MONTH

CINDERELLA GIRL
Trisha Alexander

They met at a masquerade ball and it seemed to be love at first sight. So why did Victoria leave before Dusty could find out who she was? Dusty was determined to trace her.

A NEW WORLD
Patricia McLinn

Eleanor Thalston refused to be charmed by the twinkling eyes and lilting brogue of the Irish singer she'd hired to improve business at her restaurant. She was far too practical to fall under his spell … wasn't she?

COURAGE TO LOVE
Carole Halston

The proposal was tempting … Rugged widower Jonus Logan made his masculine desire for her plain enough. His beseeching young daughter tugged at every maternal instinct. Did Polly want to love again?

COMING NEXT MONTH

THE SHERIFF TAKES A WIFE
Debbie Macomber

When Christy Manning fell impetuously in love with rugged Montana lawman Cody Franklin, she suddenly had a lot of explaining to do to the folks back in Seattle ... Would Cody wait?

VANQUISH THE NIGHT
Sandy Steen

Tracking down a reclusive Hollywood legend promised to be an incredible coup for Casey's career in journalism ... until Holt Shelton got in her way. How could Casey betray him and the friendly locals who'd taken her to their hearts?

DONOVAN'S CHANCE
Elizabeth Bevarly

Running into Max Donovan cost Rowan a dream vacation; he was wealthy, gorgeous and — now — covered in wine. Rowan couldn't afford another run-in with the rich, another man in her way ... but how could she avoid Max?

4 SILHOUETTE SPECIAL EDITIONS

Stylishly written, these realistic novels combine complex themes and issues with sensitive romantic elements. Enjoy the passion and joy of modern romances.

Now you can enjoy four Special Editions as a free gift from Silhouette, plus the chance to enjoy 6 Brand new titles delivered direct to your door every single month!

Turn the page for details of how to apply and claim extra free gifts!

• YOURS ABSOLUTELY FREE •

AN IRRESISTIBLE OFFER FROM SILHOUETTE

Here's a personal invitation from Silhouette to become a regular reader of Special Editions. And to welcome you, we'd like you to have four books, a cuddly teddy bear and a special Mystery Gift – **absolutely FREE and without obligation.**

Then, each month look forward to receiving 6 more Special Editions delivered to your door, postage and packing FREE! Plus our Newsletter featuring author news, competitions, special offers and lots more.

Its so easy. Send no money now. Simply fill in the coupon below at once and post to -

**SILHOUETTE READER SERVICE, FREEPOST,
PO BOX 236, CROYDON, SURREY CR9 9EL.**

✂

YES! Please rush me my 4 Free Silhouette Special Editions and 2 Free Gifts! Please also reserve me a Reader Service Subscription. If I decide to subscribe I can look forward to receiving 6 brand new Silhouette Special Editions each month for just £9.90. Post and packing is free. If I choose not to subscribe I shall write to you within 10 days - but I am free to keep the books and gifts. I can cancel or suspend my subscription at any time. I am over 18.
Please write in BLOCK CAPITALS.

Mrs/Miss/Ms/Mr _____ EP13SE

Address _____

_____

_____ Postcode _____

(Please don't forget to include your postcode).

Signature _____